Christopher Kerr was brought up in Leigh-on-Sea and was educated at Westcliff High School. He studied law at Brasenose College, Oxford. He is a practising barrister, specialising in criminal law, and lives in London with his wife and two daughters. He wrote this book during the national lockdown in 2020, brought about by the Covid pandemic.

For my wife, Renata, and my daughters, Elizabeth and Hannah.

Christopher Kerr

A Conspiracy of Serpents

AUSTIN MACAULEY PUBLISHERS™
LONDON * CAMBRIDGE * NEW YORK * SHARJAH

This is a work of fiction. Names, characters, businesses, places, events, locales, and incidents are either the products of the author's imagination or used in a fictitious manner. Any resemblance to actual persons, living or dead, or actual events is purely coincidental.

A CIP catalogue record for this title is available from the British Library.

ISBN 9781398465244 (Paperback)
ISBN 9781398465251 (ePub e-book)

www.austinmacauley.com

First Published 2022
Austin Macauley Publishers Ltd®
1 Canada Square
Canary Wharf
London
E14 5AA

Chapter One

St Bartholomew the Great is the oldest parish church in London. It is sandwiched between the butcher's market in Smithfield to the west, and the brutist edifice which is the Barbican to the east.

On a Tuesday morning in late March 2020, the 24th to be precise, a young man, dishevelled and grubby, stood in the Lady Chapel. The early spring sunshine, awash through the stained-glass window, illuminated his face. Tilted up as if to receive the blessing of the Holy Mother, it was lined with sweat and contorted with pain.

His body, sheathed in a soiled and moistened raincoat, leant to the left. With his right arm he crossed himself. His left arm hung lifeless. It had begun to bleed again, and from the sleeve there came a steady dripping of blood, each droplet followed by the next in intervals of seconds. His right hand loosened his collar, and his mouth uttered the words, "Holy Mary, Mother of God, pray for us sinners now, and at the hour of our death, Amen."

No other soul was apparent in the church of St Bartholomew the Great and the sound of a footstep in the vicinity of the south vestry arrested the man's attentions with the force of an electrocution. His body stiffened, and his face twisted with fear. As fast as he was able to, he shuffled back past the north vestry and along the north aisle. He paused to catch his breath in the chapel of the Holy Icon before proceeding towards the west door, the blood now dripping more liberally from his sleeve.

As he passed into the sun-dappled graveyard, he glanced back into the church. He saw nothing but darkness, and heard nothing but birdsong. He proceeded along the path towards the old Tudor Gate. He passed the war memorial and under the arch, and gathered the courage to look back again. There was no one. Maybe he had been mistaken. Perhaps he had shaken off his pursuer after all.

With a groan of pain, he passed into Smithfield. It was as deserted as all the public spaces of London that morning. Leaving a fine trail of blood spots behind him, he limped to the monument to the Marian Martyrs, and sat heavily upon the bench. With his good hand he smoothed the matted hair from his forehead and focused on the inscription. "Within a few feet of this spot John Rogers, John Bradford, John Philpot, and other servants of God, suffered death for the faith of Christ."

With his right hand, he rearranged his left arm on his lap, and then reached into his inside pocket for a phone. But it was too late before he noticed the shadow at his feet. The knife was plunged deep between his shoulder blades from behind, and with nothing more than an exhalation of breath, he slumped from the bench to the foot of the monument. His hand clutched feebly at the bars of the grill, and then went limp. Roscoe was dead.

A large male, wearing a heavy, black overcoat, leaned over the bench. He wore a surgical mask which covered half his face. Through black framed sunglasses he scrutinised the fresh corpse and uttered a guttural sound, something between a snort and a laugh, and then approached the body. He turned it over. Roscoe was bleeding from the mouth, his face contorted into a grimace like the head of a pig in the meat market.

The large male wiped the blood from the blade on the inside of his coat, and then smuggled it back into his pocket. He picked up Roscoe's phone from the ground, and placed it into his other pocket. He then dragged the body into the shaded alcove of the gate house. Propping it up on the debris of the Tudor foundations, he took off his coat and began to work his way methodically through the corpse.

He retrieved a wallet from the trouser pocket, opened it, and took out the contents: students' union membership card, library card, credit card. He grunted and threw the items back into the alcove. He removed some items of paper from Roscoe's inside pocket, unfolding them with podgy, blood-stained, butcher's fingers. Train ticket Oxford to London, 23 March; hotel bill, Paradise Guest House, Paddington. He scrutinised the contents, even analysing the backs of the ticket and the receipt. He grunted once more, and threw the papers on top of the corpse.

Fumbling inside his jacket, he brought out a pocket torch to enhance his search. Then, squatting over the body like a buzzard, he examined every fold of clothing and of flesh. He found nothing but a set of keys. Uttering an oath rarely heard in those hallowed precincts, he threw the keys to the side. Finally, he leered over the body, spat in its face, kicked it in the back, and then made off; slouching back through the Tudor Gate towards the graveyard.

Around the same time that the body of Roscoe was being plundered by his murderer, a short walk to the north east, Peter Bonik cautiously opened his eyes and looked out. It was around 1040. From his window he could see, if he were minded to look, from the western edge of Farringdon Crossrail site all the way up Long Lane to the corner of Aldersgate. The Crossrail site, for ten years a boil on Bonik's back-side, slept like a baby. The road, normally a conduit for traffic from the City to High Holborn, bathed in the early spring sunshine, stood empty. For days now it had been empty. Every day, for a month, it had become progressively emptier. Now, save for the occasional car occupying or leaving the hospital parking spaces, or the odd pedestrian, furtively making his way to the corner shop from the Barbican, it was pretty much deserted. Yesterday the government had imposed a lockdown.

Bonik shut his eyes again and winced. Christ, they had made the most of the last night in the pub. Why the hell had he allowed himself to be persuaded into a lock-in, the night before lockdown, in the Raglan, and finishing off that bottle of vodka? He eased himself out of bed and proceeded, with supreme caution, to the bathroom. His head pounded, his throat was dry and he was shaking. He had to hold his right hand with his left to keep the razor straight.

This, he told himself, *was not the snake flu. It was an uber-hangover.* He stood remorsefully under the shower, and turned it on hot – as hot as he could reasonably stand – and allowed the beer and vodka sweat to wash away from him. Then he turned it on cold – as cold as he could reasonably stand – lifted his face up to the deluge, and drank.

He slung on a bath robe, and went down to the kitchen. Jesus, by the look of it the night hadn't concluded in the pub. His bottle of scotch lay on the floor next to the sofa; beside it a tumbler with the rest of the contents on the carpet. He picked up the bottle and tipped it up. With not a little regret he confirmed that it was empty. He opened the fridge. Good, there was some orange juice. He greedily downed half a pint and put the coffee on.

What was the time? 1055. *Give it another hour,* he told himself, *and then go to the shop. Just one large one – hair of the dog – and he'd be fine*. He poured himself a coffee and put the radio on. The news. There had been no other news for weeks. Snake flu. The global pandemic which had shut down the country, and most of the sentient world.

"Here is an important message from the government," the announcement went. He grimaced, if that wasn't designed to make people turn off, he didn't know what would.

"Stay at home. There are only three reasons to go out: to work if you cannot work at home, to shop for essential supplies, and to take one period of exercise a day."

That was alright. He could combine his trip for essential supplies with his period of exercise. He was restless. He glanced at the clock. 1105. That was late enough. He needed a drink.

Bonik walked out into East Passage. A thick blanket of silence. The noise of construction works and traffic had become so ingrained in his perception of this place, that its absence was almost palpable. A woman came around the corner at the Old Red Cow, and physically recoiled as she saw him. He hoped that this was the result of the Prime Minister's announcement the previous evening, and not his physical appearance, or the smell of his breath.

At the convenience store a small queue had snaked around the corner. He obediently stood in line, a couple of metres behind the person in front; and reflected that such an arrangement, almost entirely self-policed, could only have spontaneously assembled in Britain. Most people were wearing surgical masks which made him feel even more self-conscious. Inside the store they skirted around each other, trying and failing to keep the regulation gap. He bought a bottle of scotch, and returned to his apartment.

He ordered the speaker to play some jazz. Whilst it confirmed the selection, he poured himself a large scotch, and slumped into the sofa. He took a sizeable mouthful, and relished the warmth of the liquid as it went down his neck, almost instantly soothing his nerves, and lightening his mood. The speaker had treated him to a rather good Miles Davis album. He put his feet up and began to relax. He was lifting the tumbler to his mouth for the second time when the phone rang.

"Bonik. It's Carter." It was the Chief Inspector. "Look, I wouldn't normally have bothered you with this but you live in the City, near the Barbican, right?"

Bonik had a feeling this was not going to work out to his advantage but had little choice other than to confirm.

"There's been an incident near St Bart's in West Smithfield, just around the corner from you. A stabbing. A pedestrian came across the body and put in a call. The medics are there and forensics are on their way. Can you get around there and take a look? I wouldn't normally ask but we are short on the ground with this lockdown going on."

Bonik cursed under his breath. "OK. But you know I'm on secondment with the fraud squad. I've been doing nothing but poring over paperwork in the Columbia bond fraud for the last three years. I've not touched a corpse in five."

"I know. As I said, I'm short of bodies – sorry about the pun."

"Alright. I'll get around there straight away."

He took a couple more swigs of scotch, pulled on some presentable clothes, brushed his teeth and treated himself to a generous application of the mouthwash. Then he walked from his apartment along Cloth Fair, the church to his left. As he turned the corner into Smithfield, he saw an ambulance and an unmarked car parked up near the gatehouse. Somebody in a white coat, he guessed forensics, was kneeling down by the war memorial.

He held up his card. "Inspector Bonik. Snow Hill. I've been sent."

Forensics moved to the side. The corpse lay on its back; its posture grotesque. It looked as if it had been propped up against the wall of the gatehouse, and had then fallen back onto the pavement. It was almost naked. A raincoat had been discarded to the side. The jacket was pulled off the shoulders, and the shirt was open to the waist. The trousers and shorts had been pulled down to the knees and the feet were trapped under the opening into the alcove – the head looked up at him, at an angle. The face, drained of blood, eyes wide open, mouth agape, terrified. Bonik looked away, bent over, and retched.

From the corner of his eye, he saw a uniformed officer to his right.

She spoke. "Hello sir, I'm Wendy Graham. I've been sent from Snow Hill. Nobody from CID available, I'm afraid."

He looked up. Christ, she was young enough to be his daughter. Conscious that his breath probably reeked of scotch to the sober, he looked back down and pretended to retch again. She moved away back to the corpse. He straightened himself up, retrieved a mint from his pocket, and put it in his mouth. He joined her at a respectful distance.

"Are you OK, sir?"

“Yes, we must remember to maintain our social distancing now, mustn’t we Constable, even when investigating a murder? Now, who found the body?”

PC Graham pointed to a figure along the path towards the church entrance. He was wearing black trousers, a tweed jacket and a dog collar.

Bonik approached. “Good afternoon, sir. Inspector Bonik. I understand you found the body.”

“That’s correct officer. I’m the Rector of St Bartholomew’s. I was on my way in and stumbled across him. Quite literally, I regret to say.”

“Don’t you live in the church?”

“No, the Rectory is in Amen Court, not far from St Paul’s.”

“And the body, did you move it at all?”

“No, he was exactly as you see Inspector.” The Rector gestured to the corpse, and held a handkerchief to his nose and mouth. He had a rather pained look, a mixture of bewilderment, surprise and disgust. At the same time Bonik got the impression that this was his normal appearance, rather than as a result of recent events – a product of a semi-detached, distaste for the world as he found it.

“What time was this?”

“Getting on for an hour ago.”

Bonik turned to Graham. “Are forensics here?”

“Yes, sir.” She inclined her head to the man in the white coat who had returned to the body and was leaning in to the alcove.

Bonik stood behind him. He was picking up some papers with gloved hands, and placing them into sealed bags. “How long has he been dead?”

Forensics looked up: a thin, white face, devoid of humour, or any trace of humanity by the look of it. The corpse looked more alive.

“I’m Donnelly. Inspector Bonik I suppose. I hear you’re seconded to fraud.” The word *fraud* emerged from the cadaverous opening with thinly disguised contempt. “I can’t imagine how we’re going to manage. People aren’t going to stop murdering each other, just because of the snake flu.”

“Yes, I’m afraid you’re going to have to put up with me. The great detective from homicide has had to shield himself from the pestilence, I’m afraid, along with half the force by the look of it. Could you answer my question please – how long has he been dead?”

“Anything between an hour and an hour and a half, I’d say,” he replied. “Death by a stab wound from behind which penetrated the heart. There’s another stab wound, considerably older I think, to his left arm, but still bleeding profusely. Oh, and there's a trail of blood leading up the pathway from the church."

The words left the opening with a kind of relish, and he gestured to the left.

Bonik glanced towards the Rector. He was still standing at a distance, along the path, the handkerchief held over his mouth.

"Is there any sign of sexual assault, Donnelly? He seems to have been stripped almost naked."

"No sign of it, at least on a preliminary examination. His pockets have been pulled inside out. I'd guess he's been stripped for the purpose of a thorough search."

"Any ID?"

"There are some papers here." Bonik made as if to take them. "Stop," barked Donnelly. "They need to be handled forensically. There may be prints, DNA."

Bonik blushed and realised how out of touch he must have become. "Of course, my apologies. Now where's this trail of blood?"

Donnelly pointed to the ground. He was right. The trail did lead to the church.

"Look, I'll let you tidy up here. You'll leave your details with PC Graham of course." Donnelly nodded. "Constable, I'll catch up with you later."

Bonik turned to the priest. He was wary of priests. Any faith he once had, had evaporated with his early childhood, along with Father Christmas, and belief in the infallibility of his parents.

"Rector, there is a trail of blood which appears to lead from the body back into the churchyard. Have you seen this man before?"

"No. I've never seen him in the congregation, or anywhere else from what I recall."

Bonik followed the trail of blood along the path. To the left a graveyard, the surface raised almost a metre above the surrounding land. The reason – it had been used as a burial pit during the plague of 1665, and also during previous visitations. The sheer mass of the number of corpses had physically raised the ground above its surroundings, still evident 350 years later. Bonik shuddered at the thought. How relevant that grisly morsel of history seemed now.

There was an intermittent and yet clearly evident trail of blood which led up to the west door, the main entrance into the church.

"Can I go in?"

"Of course, it's not locked. We've not been shut down quite yet."

The sun had gone behind some clouds, and it was dark inside. The smell of incense was heavy.

"Have you a torch or something Rector?"

"No, but I can fetch a candle."

The priest removed himself towards the altar at the far end of the church. Bonik peered at the floor, trying to make out the blood. By the time the Rector had returned with a candle, Bonik had made out some droplets leading to the left, behind the choir screen.

"Where does this go?" he said.

The Rector indicated, and Bonik followed him behind the choir into a small chapel with a painting of the Madonna and Child.

"The chapel of the Holy Icon," intoned the Rector. "It's where people like to come for private prayer."

Bonik held the candle to the floor, and saw a higher concentration of blood. "I suspect he had reasons to pray," he said.

The trail of blood continued, intermittently, along the north aisle, past the north vestry, and behind the high altar – into a chapel, considerably larger than the one before. The Rector had followed behind.

"This is the Lady Chapel," he breathed; his voice having become more sanctimonious the deeper they had gone into the church.

Bonik followed the trail of blood to the far end of the Lady Chapel. Here a second and larger pool of blood had been left by the altar, with what appeared to be an impression of footprints. Bonik got down on his knees as the sun came out from behind the cloud and shone through the stained-glass depiction of the Madonna and Child. The light illuminated the ground to the north of the altar, and Bonik saw something lying on the floor. It was a blue, hard-back notebook. He picked it up. It was the size of a wallet and had traces of blood on the cover. He held it up in the light and flicked through it. Most of the pages were empty. There were some notes at the beginning which were smudged, either with blood or water – one or two names by the look of it, and other stuff which meant nothing, as far as he could tell. Much of it was hardly legible. One of the pages had been torn out from the middle. It certainly looked well thumbed. Bonik turned to the cleric.

"Ever seen this before?"

"No, should I have?"

"Not particularly, apart from the fact that it's in your Lady Chapel."

There were footsteps coming from the north aisle, and Donnelly emerged from the shadows, now joined by a colleague.

"Inspector, you really should have waited for us before blundering into a crime scene. You've no idea how much evidence can be lost by the non-forensic handling of material."

"You'll find what you're looking for in the Lady Chapel, Donnelly – a pool of blood. That's where the trail appears to begin. Rector, we'll need your contact details."

"Oh, and I found this." Bonik showed Donnelly the notebook. "I'll want it back as soon as it has been 'forensically handled' by you. PC Graham will have my details."

Donnelly grimaced and took the book by the corner with a gloved hand as if it were a sacred text. Before he could proceed with a lecture about how the evidence may have become corrupted, Bonik muttered under his breath what he could do with himself, and walked out. He couldn't face the scene of the crime again. Halfway down the pathway towards the gatehouse, he turned right through the churchyard. He exited into Cloth Fair and headed back in the direction of the scotch – he needed another drink.

He refreshed his tumbler of scotch, and sat on the sofa. He couldn't get the face of the corpse out of his mind. Maybe his sojourn in fraud had made him soft. He chuckled to himself, and ordered the speaker to play a requiem mass. Lulled by the beauty of the *Christe*, and the soothing warmth of the whisky, he reclined into a gentle doze, and fell asleep to *Et incarnatus est*.

It was the evening of the same day that Bonik's respite was interrupted once more. He had made the welcome discovery that one could still get a curry delivered. He had just sat down in front of the television with a plate of chicken dhansak, pilau rice and an onion bhaji when the phone rang. It was Carter.

"It appears that the deceased is a young man by the name of Daniel Roscoe, second year law student at Oxford, born 6 October 1997. There's nothing identifiable on the notebook apart from his blood and fingerprints. I'd like you to have a good look through the contents though. There are some annotations, codes which don't mean anything to us. I know it's not your department anymore, but maybe you fraud guys can cast some light on it."

Bonik sighed. The days of easy living were over, for a while at least.

Chapter Two

Oxford, 1 May 2019. The city looked unusually lovely that morning, as it should every May Morning. Behind the Great Tower of Magdalen College, the incipient sun had begun to paint the sky in peach, and temper the chill of the night with its growing warmth. Daniel Roscoe and Bill Compton stood on Magdalen Bridge over the River Cherwell. They had stayed up all night to welcome this dawn in the traditional fashion, and had spent most of it in the Turf Tavern. Now they were ready to call it a night. As the sun began to rise above the horizon, the choristers sang the *Hymnus Eucharisticus*, and the bells sounded from the Great Tower. One or two of the revellers began jumping from the bridge into the river.

Roscoe, a little the worse for wear, smoothed the dishevelled hair from his forehead, as was his manner, and consulted his watch.

"I'd better turn in. I have to see my tutor in about six hours," he said.

As the bells rang out, they walked back along the High to Radcliffe Square. As they passed through the Lodge into the Old Quad of Brasenose College, the Morris dancing was just getting underway on the green by St Mary's.

"See you later, Dan." Compton went into staircase four. Roscoe went to his room in the less salubrious part of College, just off New Quad.

Daniel Roscoe had come up to Oxford the previous Michaelmas term in October. He had attended a standard comprehensive school in Sussex, and had won a scholarship to read law. He was the first of his family to go to university, and felt a little out of place. He made few friends in his first term, and kept to himself, spending most of his time in his room, or the College's law library, working his way through his reading lists.

Towards the end of that term, he had met Bill Compton at a tutorial. Bill shared an interest in proper beer, pubs, and talking into the night about politics, philosophy and just about anything after a few pints. And so, Roscoe had spent the Michaelmas term of 2018, and half of the Hilary term of 2019, uneventfully and methodically working his way towards the preliminary examinations in mid-March at the end of Hilary.

He woke up that May Morning to the sound of his alarm at eleven thirty, and groaned. He remembered why he had set the alarm. He had a meeting with Doctor Brockwell at midday. He showered, drank a glass of water and a cup of coffee, and made his way to Brockwell's room in Old Quad.

It was the first time he had seen his tutor since the beginning of that Trinity term. Brockwell, an elderly don in his mid-seventies, opened the door and greeted him with a slightly pained expression. Roscoe guessed why. Brockwell gestured to the sofa in the book-lined study and Roscoe sat.

"Not too early for a sherry, I hope?"

Brockwell poured two small glasses from a decanter, handed one to Roscoe, and then sat behind his oak-panelled desk.

"It's the first chance we've had to talk since Prelims, isn't it? I never had any doubt that you would pass Dan, but it's not the result I was hoping for. I was expecting a distinction, at least a merit. You are one of the most promising students I have had for a good many years, as I've told you. Do you know what went wrong?"

Roscoe knew full well what had gone wrong but he was not yet ready to share it with his tutor, or anyone else for that matter. He had not yet come to terms with it himself. He looked out of the window onto Old Quad, and smiled weakly.

"Whatever it was, Doctor Brockwell; it's gone now. Don't worry, I'll be back to my old form this term."

"Good. Then I'll give you your reading list for First Week. This term we are making a start on the law of contract."

They discussed the plan for the forthcoming term and at the end of it Brockwell shook Roscoe's hand.

"This has been good. It looks like you are back to your old self."

"I think so, sir."

Roscoe thanked him, folded the reading list, and put it into his back pocket. He went out blinking into the bright sunshine of Old Quad and exited the College into Radcliffe Square. He walked briskly along Catte Street into the Broad, avoiding the debris from the May Morning revelries, and turned left to Blackwell's bookshop. It was busy that Wednesday of First Week at the beginning of Trinity term. He went straight to the law department and consulted the list again. Treitel on Contract was the only book he was going to have to buy. He could make do with the College library for the rest.

He passed the coffee shop on the way to the law section and was stopped dead in his tracks. There she was – Vanessa Symonds. She faced away from him but the inclination of her head, the poise of her neck and shoulders, the curve of her back, the suggestion of her breasts; were all unmistakeably, indelibly, branded upon his consciousness.

It was towards the middle of the previous – the Hilary – term that he had properly met her. He had seen her around College, and he had noticed her, but his interest in her was purely – well, academic was one way of putting it. He was still at that stage in his life when he admired attractive women from afar. They were to him as unobtainable as the women in images, in photographs or on screen.

Roscoe was not unattractive. He had dark, rather straight hair, an angular face which, whilst not classically handsome, was interesting to women because of the movement of his mouth when he spoke, and the intelligence in his eyes. His character, whilst reserved, was quietly impressive when observed over time. But his practical ability to deploy those qualities was hampered by a chronic lack of confidence, and a want of experience.

It was in the Fourth Week of that Hilary Term, in February, that he saw her in a debate at the Oxford Union. She was giving a full paper speech at the main debate of the week from the front benches. She was billed in the Union term card as Vanessa Symonds, the Honourable Member from Brasenose College, speaking in favour of the motion: "This House condemns the exploitation of animals for medical research.". Also speaking in favour of the motion was Dame Sheila Thompson, President of the Oxford based animal rights group, the National Association for the Abolition of Cruelty to Animals.

Roscoe's view of student politics was usually one of detached, slightly amused, indifference. But he, in common with most freshers, had been persuaded to part with a hundred pounds in his first term for life membership of 'the world's most prestigious debating society, nursery to prime ministers and other global leaders for one hundred and fifty years'. When he saw that Ms Symonds was to speak, he decided to attend his first debate.

The debating chamber in the Oxford Union is modelled on the House of Commons. At one end of the chamber on a platform sits the President, flanked by the Treasurer and the Librarian. In front of them, at a small table, is the Secretary taking the minutes. The Secretary, Roscoe knew a little – it was Tom Fairford, another Brasenose man. All four officers wear formal dress – white tie for the men, ball gowns for the women. All are elected posts, hotly contested each term, by students with embryonic political ambitions, raving narcissists, and seekers of publicity – Tom Fairford was a mixture of all three.

In front of the Union's officers, the seating for the participants of the debate, like the Chamber of the House of Commons, is divided into benches. Those proposing the motion (the 'government') sit to the right of the officers; those opposing the motion (the 'opposition') to the left. However, unlike in the Commons, there are also cross-benches, towards the rear of the Chamber, for the 'audience' – those not formally invited to participate in the debate – to sit, and keep quiet.

It was amongst this less illustrious company that Daniel Roscoe found himself on a Thursday evening in February 2019. And even in such company he had to peer over the head of another student to see. There on the front bench to the left of the Chamber, as he saw it, was a row of four young men in black tie, the principal speakers for the motion. In the middle was a figure in a crimson ball gown, to which all eyes were drawn, like a moist, ripe morello cherry on the cake, and that figure was Vanessa Symonds.

The motion, of course, was something of a leading question, but she spoke with such conviction in favour of it that he was carried away with the argument. The passion in her voice, the intelligence and conviction in her eyes, the animation of her face as she spoke and the toss of her head as she emphasised her point, captivated him in a way he had not known before.

Afterwards there were drinks in the Members Bar. It was packed. Roscoe queued, eventually managing to buy himself a beer. He couldn't get much further than the end of the bar near the door and felt awkward. He knew no one. Through the crowd of sweat-shirts and denim he could make out the President's party at the far end of the room by the bay windows. And through the black and the white of the President's party he could just make out a flash of crimson. The layout of the Members Bar that evening was the literal representation of his relationship with her – distant, remote, utterly unattainable – and he knew it.

He stood and drank his beer. For a while he made some small talk with another first year student from Queens whom he knew from Criminal Law lectures. And then, after an hour or so, when he was alone once more, he noticed that the room had thinned out. Most people had drifted off, either to bed in ones or twos, or to private parties. He instinctively glanced across towards the bay window, the focal point of his interest since he had entered, although he had no expectation of seeing her. But there she was, no longer surrounded by the President's party, but by two or three Brasenose men he vaguely knew, positioned around her – bees around the honey pot.

Roscoe bought himself another beer, and drank off half of it, continuing to observe the group at the far end of the room. Then, a little emboldened by the alcohol perhaps, he made his way through the thinning crowd of drinkers, and positioned himself at the outer orbit of the group of the three young men who were talking to her – satellites circling the sun.

Before that evening, his view of her had been impressionistic, observed from a distance, or in passing, a fleeting glimpse – too shy to steal a direct look. The brush strokes had suggested her beauty without defining it, the detail filled in by his imagination. Now, he was able to study a portrait of her face, and one in motion. Someone made her laugh to her left. A tilt of her head, an inclination of her chin. A remark from her right, a glance, her eyes now laughing, a suggestion of gold in her hair, lent by the lamplight.

She was maybe a couple of years older than he. Her face, as a snapshot, was not beautiful in any conventional sense; indeed, it was not particularly remarkable. But it was the combination of a myriad of elements in motion, taken as a whole, and so much more than the sum of their parts; the slightly asymmetrical mouth, the way her nose wrinkled when she smiled, the shape of her eyes, and the way they danced as she spoke; the ever so slightly narrowed gap between her nose and her upper lip, the modulation and pitch of her voice, and yes, more prosaically, the way her gown defined the curve of her breasts, the shape of her waist and the upper curves of her behind.

And so there he stood, a minor satellite, wishing desperately that he could think of something interesting to say. As usual he felt awkward and tongue-tied in the company of a woman for whom he felt a powerful and visceral attraction.

But then she looked in his direction, his stomach lurched, she held out her hand, and said, "Tom, where have you been?" And from behind him came Fairford, the Secretary of the Oxford Union for Hilary Term 2019, post-graduate bio-chemist, son of the Chairman of the TCC Chemicals Empire, Old Etonian, and heir to a fortune. He was still in his white tie and tails with his blonde, floppy hair, his easy charm, and good looks. Her face lit up when she saw him. Fairford was taller than he, better looking than he, and in the wrong place at the wrong time; and just for a few minutes, because he could not in his nature harbour a *serious* grudge, Roscoe hated him.

Fairford spoke in a voice, laced with confidence and entitlement. "Sorry old girl, had to see off our guests, Dame Sheila had a train to catch."

Roscoe instinctively stood back. His satellite had been eclipsed. He watched from the corner of his eye, as Fairford wooed her – his hand at the small of her back, the effortless jokes, the easy small talk; so charming, and yet as ephemeral and sincere as the bubbles in the glass of champagne he handed to her.

Roscoe had had enough. He finished his beer and turned to leave, brushing against Fairford's tails as he did so.

Fairford looked around and saw him. "Vanessa, have you met our very own Mr Roscoe, here?"

Her eyes alighted on him for the first time. "I don't believe I have. Did you see the debate?"

She put out her hand. He took it. It was warm and yielding.

"Yes, I did thanks. You were very impressive. You certainly convinced me."

"Dan Roscoe, legal eagle." Fairford slapped his hand on Roscoe's shoulder. "If ever any of the lawyers in College are stuck for ideas for a Sunday night essay crisis, Dan's the man."

Fairford's breath was heady with champagne. He was clearly in full flow, a man to whom everything came so easily – money, conversation and women.

Vanessa Symonds ignored Fairford, and studied Roscoe's face. "So tell me. What convinced you?"

Now she was standing in front of him, and engaged, the words came more easily to him. "As Tom said, I'm a lawyer. Law is fundamentally about justice. It seems to me that basic principles of justice should apply to all sentient creatures, not just humanity. The application of justice should not be dependent on intelligence, otherwise there would be no single principle of justice applying to all people."

He added in one or two references to John Rawls's Theory of Justice, and began to feel a little foolish. She smiled, a broad, golden smile which turned her face into a thing of beauty but he was unsure whether she was smiling with him, or laughing at him. Fairford grunted and moved off to another party further along the bar. That had to be a good sign.

She watched to see where Fairford had gone, and then turned to him again. "But is it just about man-made justice? What about ethics, natural law, morality? Don't you think we are all God's creatures?" she said.

Fairford called from the far end of the bar. "Nessy, time for beddy-byes. Are you coming?"

Roscoe was tongue-tied again. He didn't know what to say. "I've never been able to find God," he said.

"Here." She gave him a slip of paper. "My number. Give me a call sometime. We can meet up for a drink and a chat."

She turned without another word, and walked straight to Fairford. They left together, her arm in his. And Roscoe felt a pang of jealousy he had scarcely known before.

By an effort of will, he managed to restrain himself from sending her a message that same night. He realised that that would be counter-productive, and potentially humiliating. He waited as long as he could bear, and then sent her a message a couple of days later suggesting that they might meet for lunch the next day, or for a drink in the evening. He found himself looking at his phone every five minutes for the first couple of hours; less frequently, and with a sinking feeling in his stomach, thereafter. There was no reply.

Roscoe had some pride but there came a point when his desire to see her got the better of him. Perhaps she was very busy; maybe she had missed his text, maybe she had given him the wrong number. He sent her another text a couple of days later, just asking how she was. It was a couple of hours in the drafting, but designed to appear as casual an enquiry as one could imagine. He even inserted a spelling error to create the illusion that he didn't really care if she read it or not. This time there came a reply the same day: "Hi Dan, I'm fine. How are you?"

He spent more than an hour walking around College, and the Radcliffe Camera, fighting the urge to respond too quickly. Then, after a suitable delay, he replied: "Great. How about that drink?"

Then nothing. Nothing that afternoon. Nothing the next morning. Nothing for the rest of the week. He concluded that she was playing with him. He had encountered it before, in a less acute form. Some women enjoyed having a man on the hook. Every now and again they would give the line a tug, and then, when he came up for air, they would throw him back again. This time Roscoe's pride prevailed, for a while at least. He determined that he would not subject himself to any further humiliation.

But his thoughts were full of her at night, and during the day too. Whenever his mind was free to think, he would think of her, and sometimes when his mind was not free, he would think of her too. In particular, he thought of the time that she must be spending with Fairford, and it tortured him.

He would sometimes wander around College – half hoping to see her, and half dreading it. He feared for his self-respect. But there was no sign of her. He would occasionally see Fairford in the Junior Common Room. Fairford was standing for the Presidency of the Union that term, and was trying to ingratiate himself with the membership in College. But to Fairford, Roscoe was merely a vote, and certainly not a rival. He did not even appear on Fairford's radar in that respect, and there was no mention of, or even a reference to, Vanessa Symonds.

Fourth Week rolled into Fifth Week; Fifth Week into Sixth. Roscoe spent his time industriously enough. He worked his way through the reading lists his tutors gave him, even attending the odd lecture. He completed his essays on time, and they were generally well received. Brockwell, his tutor, was pleased with his progress.

Like any Oxford law student, at the end of Hilary Term of his first year he had to pass Prelims before coming up at the beginning of Trinity. As the days and the weeks passed, he was thinking less of the girl; relaxing with Bill Compton in the Turf a couple of nights a week, and he was hopeful enough of getting a distinction in the exams. Brockwell had told him it was well within reach.

The exams were due to take place on Monday, Tuesday and Wednesday of Eighth Week, just before Easter vacation. Roscoe spent most of the previous week in the law library, and made such good progress on the Friday of Seventh Week that he intended to take the Saturday off; unwind a little and relax before the exams.

He emerged from the library in the late afternoon. And there she was, coming towards him from the Junior Common Room. His stomach lurched, and if he had

had time he would have ducked into a side corridor, or turned around. But she had seen him. There was no going back.

"Hi!" She beamed.

"Oh, hello. I sent you a text."

"Yes, I know. I've just been so busy. I meant to call you, I'm sorry."

There was a pause, a little longer than was comfortable. She studied him, her eyes exploring his face, her smile golden.

"Look the Union's ball, it's tomorrow night," she said. "Do you want to take me?"

He hesitated. "Won't you be going with Tom?"

"Oh, Tom Fairford." She laughed. "We're not joined at the hip, you know. Why don't you pick me up, say at eight? I'm in Frewin Court – staircase seven. Black tie – OK?"

"Alright. Er, do you want to meet up for a drink first?"

She was already on her way into the quad. "Bye – see you tomorrow at eight."

Roscoe felt elated. He walked in her wake, and emerged into the sunset, only to see her heading off towards the Lodge. A myriad of thoughts raced through his mind in succession – some optimistic, some fanciful, some pessimistic, some apocalyptic. And then his thoughts turned to more practical matters as he paced around the quad. *What was he going to wear?* He had to hire a dinner suit. His right hand went instinctively to his fringe. He needed a haircut.

He went back to his room, paced up and down a little more, and then headed out to hire the suit. He had a haircut – spent some time fretting that it was a little too short – and then dropped into the pub to calm his nerves with a beer. She looked even more wonderful in jeans and a T-shirt. He longed to take her out. He imagined her on his arm; the envious looks from men, the looks of vicarious interest from women.

He went back to his rooms. A text from Compton asking if he was on for a pint was ignored. He just wanted to be alone that evening, hugging himself, and savouring his thoughts. Images danced through his mind of what would happen the following night. He would look irresistibly handsome. She would be stunning. They would be the centre of attention at the party. They would be fêted for their sparkling conversation and good looks. Then, at the end of the evening, he would seduce her gently. They would stroll together back to College. She would fall into his arms. They would kiss in Radcliffe Square. He would take her back to his room, and they would make love.

And then there were fantasies of him and Vanessa spending the summer term together, punting on the Cherwell, concerts at the Sheldonian, invitations to all the balls as a couple, cosy evenings together in the Turf, or maybe the Lamb and Flag. His inexperience told his heart and his mind that he was in love with her, and that his unfulfilled hopes of companionship and romance had come true at last. Such thoughts served as a blissful lullaby, and nursed him into a sleep replete with dreams.

The next day he awoke with a keen sense of anticipation, and raw excitement. He spent the day in blissful reverie, the exams quite banished from his thoughts. He began to prepare himself at five. He streamed a recording of *La Boheme* from the Met. He showered and then spent some time deciding whether he would look better clean shaven, or with a day's beard. A counsel of perfection drove him to shave, and then instant regret because of the slight razor burn to his throat.

Nearly half an hour, during the exquisite heartache of the third act of *Boheme*, was spent on his fringe, in a hopeless attempt to strike the right balance between the perfection of the fringe, and the appearance of a man who didn't much care what he looked like. And then of course the dinner suit. In the absence of a full-length mirror, he took photographs from every angle he could reach with his phone before he was satisfied with his appearance.

It was half past seven before he left. He was restless with excitement and without a considerable effort of will, would have left even earlier in order to walk out of view, in the vicinity of her room. He turned into Radcliffe Square, and then along Brasenose Lane. His steps rapid and urgent. It was busy on Turl Street, even more so than a usual Saturday night. A number of couples were emerging from Jesus College in black tie; going to some ball or other for Torpids, or maybe even to the Union's ball. Such was the state of his mind, that he even felt envy towards them, in case he had to share some of her company or attention. It was the onset of a kind of madness which either fulfilment, the long passage of time, or a profound and sudden disappointment, will kill.

He made his way along Ship Street and then into St Aldate's. The pubs were busy now and the streets full of Oxford people, both of the Town and Gown variety; jeans, T-shirts, mini-skirts, party dresses, tuxedos and ball gowns. He turned right into the lane which led past the entrance to the Union and into Frewin Court, the College annex where she lived. What was the time? Quarter to eight.

He couldn't be early, unthinkable. Perhaps ten past? He paced up and down at the far end of the court from her staircase. To be seen would be disastrous. He must appear casual, nonchalant – if she were in, fine, if he missed her, so what? He'd go out in his tuxedo and charm some other girl. Even the fanciful seemed achievable to Roscoe as he monitored the minutes passing by.

Five minutes to eight. OK, he would make his way slowly towards her staircase. He put his hands in his pockets and, in what he hoped looked like a casual saunter, he walked across the court.

And then he heard a laugh; a manufactured laugh, the kind which is expressed towards the beginning of an evening, rather than towards the end, but yet an unmistakeable laugh. And then he saw her. She was coming out of staircase seven, at the other end of the court, wearing the stunning crimson ball gown. Her full shoulders bare, her blonde hair cascading around them, her head tossed back with her laugh, the golden smile, and Tom Fairford on her arm.

Roscoe felt sick. He dodged behind a tree, and watched them as they walked out of the gate and turned left towards the Union building; Vanessa laughing at his jokes, Fairford basking in her attention. He followed after them in a daze on a kind of autopilot. He saw them standing in the queue at the entrance. He stood two metres behind them, transfixed by the living image of his bitter disappointment in motion, being played out cruelly in front of him. She turned her head. She saw him. A flicker of recognition, no more than that, passed across her lovely face.

"Oh, Dan, is it you?"

He said nothing. His throat was too dry to respond in any event.

Fairford looked around. "Well, if it isn't Danny Roscoe, out of his natural habitat. You should be in the library old chap. Isn't it Prelims on Monday?"

She watched his reaction. A small mercy, she didn't laugh.

"Look. Tom turned up. I can probably still get you in if you want."

Roscoe turned and walked away along the lane. As the party hubbub of the Union faded behind him, the Saturday night noise of St Aldates loomed in front of him. He didn't notice it. His insides had just been kicked out.

Chapter Three

And so, the sight of Vanessa Symonds in the coffee shop of Blackwell's bookshop, that Mayday afternoon, was not altogether a welcome one for Daniel Roscoe. He had been reeling for much of the Easter vacation from the humiliation of his rejection which, after night upon night of reflection in the early hours of the morning, it seemed to him to have been deliberately engineered by her and Fairford. Why else would they have been emerging from her room, minutes before he had been due to pick her up?

He stood still in the bookshop, continuing to observe her from behind. She was on her own. No sign of Fairford, or even a girlfriend. Cautiously he moved to the side, and watched her face. She looked different; different from that day at the Oxford Union debate when she had first captured him, and a world away from the confident temptress on the night of the Union ball. She appeared to have taken no care over her appearance. Her hair was un-brushed. The casual way in which she was dressed was qualitatively different from how he had seen her before.

On the evening that she had invited him to the Union ball outside the law library, she had been dressed in a T-shirt and jeans, but they had been expertly chosen, arranged and worn on her body with artifice, so that every curve and nuance was enhanced to its full effect. Now she was casually dressed in a baggy sweat-shirt and some old jeans, in a manner that suggested she cared nothing for her appearance. Her jeans were no longer filled. He could see that much, even though she was seated. She had lost weight.

And she had been crying. Of that there was no doubt. Whenever he had seen her in the past her head was held high, to see and to be seen, confident and proud. Now she sat hunched over her coffee and consumed with her own thoughts. He experienced a feeling of satisfaction that she appeared unhappy, simply because she had not triumphed after his humiliation, and he hated himself for it. She too could feel – what? Disappointment, loss? Who could say. He could not read it in her face. He was still too far to the side and the rear to see anything but a restricted profile. He could not risk her catching sight of him. And yet, even now he wanted to go to her. The impulse was almost irresistible but again his pride was just strong enough to prevent him.

"Fuck her," he hissed, unable to suppress his frustration. He returned to the law section and tried to put her out of his mind.

Now, where was Treitel? He walked along the book shelves – Company Law, Constitutional Law, Contract – Guenter, Poole, Richards. Here it was – *Treitel on the Law of Contract.*

"Dan?"

The sound electrified him. Slowly he turned, and there she was. She had indeed changed. Her bearing, her confidence, her self-possession had gone. The expression in her face was not one recently assumed, or effected for his benefit. There could be no doubt of that. It was an expression which was the result of pressure, or worry, experienced over a sustained period of time. No, it was more than that, it was an expression of *fear*.

For a while he could think of nothing to say. He stood still, the book still open in his hand. She stood six feet away, looking at him. Her face betrayed a need for something he could not easily define – comfort, re-assurance, perhaps even protection.

"Vanessa! How was the Union ball?" He instantly regretted it – an asinine remark, but it was all that came into his head.

"The Union ball – when, what ball?"

"Don't you remember, the Union ball. I *was* a little hurt you know."

Now – a flicker of recognition – a brief, transient return of the light in her eyes. "Oh God. Look, I'm so sorry." She put her hand to her forehead. "I did mean to go to the ball with you – really I did. But Tom, he turned up at the last minute, and there were things going on between us which you know nothing about. Why should you? Look, Dan, I need someone to talk to. I hardly know you at all really but there's something about you – I feel as if I can trust you. I don't know why. Call it intuition. You may not believe it but I don't really have anyone else to talk to right now."

"OK. Would you like another coffee?" He gestured to the table where she had been sitting.

"We can't talk here. Let's go somewhere else."

She walked ahead of him, looking from side to side as she went. They emerged into the Broad.

"Let's go to the Eagle in St Giles. It'll be quiet now. There's a room upstairs we can use."

They walked past Balliol, past the monument to the Marian martyrs, Bishops Ridley and Latimer, and into St Giles. She said nothing, and then she took his hand. They crossed the road to the Eagle and Child, and went inside. The sepulchral gloom and coolness of the old seventeenth-century tavern contrasted sharply with the increasing warmth of the spring sunshine. With the low ceilings and the beams, there was not much to link it to the twenty-first century, save for the silent screen in the corner of the bar, relaying footage of the first test match of the season. Apart from a couple at the far end of the room, and the barman polishing some glasses, they appeared to be alone.

She asked for a vodka and tonic. He, after the excesses of the night before, opted for a pint of bitter. Then, carrying their drinks, she led him upstairs to the Rabbit Room. It was, as she predicted, empty. They sat on either side of a small table, in soft leather armchairs.

"You look as if you know this place well," he said.

"I used to come here quite a lot as an undergraduate. But I've not been here for a while now." She nodded to a plaque on the wall. "Do you know that Tolkien and CS Lewis used to sit here in the nineteen thirties, at this very table."

Roscoe had seen the plaque on a couple of occasions on nights out with Compton, but he had not really noticed it then. It occurred to him that he had not noticed much at all before now.

She took a large mouthful from her drink, and swallowed it in stages; her eyes closed, allowing the alcohol to begin to ease the tension in her mind and in her body. Then she began to talk.

According to the annual report of the National Association for the Abolition of Cruelty to Animals (or NAACA for short), over three and a half million experiments involving animals took place in Great Britain in 2018. Over 1.7 million of these experiments related to the creation or breeding of genetically altered animals. The rest were experiments which took place *upon* animals for the purpose of testing the biological effects of medicinal and cosmetic products.

Over one third of those experiments were considered by the researchers to have caused moderate or severe suffering. One half of all experiments were conducted in universities, and most prominent among these universities was Oxford.

Vanessa Symonds knew these facts because she had joined NAACA in her freshers' week when she had first come up to Oxford as an undergraduate to read biology in the Michaelmas term of 2015. It was because of NAACA that she had decided to stay on at Oxford to read for a DPhil in zoology after taking her undergraduate degree. And it was because of NAACA that, on a wintry January day at the beginning of Hilary term 2019, she found herself outside the Anglo-American Laboratory for Bio-Chemical Research on Mansfield Street. She had been appointed Chairwoman of the University branch of NAACA shortly before Christmas.

Standing to either side of her, and in front, and behind, were one hundred and fifty like-minded students, lecturers, fellows and assorted academics, all protesting about the experimentation which they supposed was taking place behind the coal-black, impenetrable walls of the laboratory. Carrying placards announcing that 'Animal testing is torture' and 'It's not science, it's violence' – they chanted the mantra, over and over, "What do we want? Animal liberation. When do we want it? Now!"

Between the protesters and the grounds of the laboratory was a steel fence, three metres high, topped with barbed wire and spikes. Although the demonstration showed every sign of remaining peaceful, a dozen or more police officers stood in front of the fence, and its gateway, in case of any attempt to force entry. A number of them, conspicuously but not threateningly, held truncheons by their sides as a show of intent should the need arise. Likewise, to their rear, propped up against the fence, but clearly visible to the demonstrators, were a number of inoffensive and redundant riot shields.

Behind the fence was a force which was not conspicuous. It was surreptitious. It was not meant to be seen. It existed in the shadows. It dressed in dark suits. It lurked in cars parked to either side of the building. It peered from the tinted windows of the laboratory, from which one could only see out, and never in. It carried handguns, without authority of law, because the highest authority it knew was its own. Its purpose, whatever the cost, was jealously to guard the secrets of its building, and to exclude any light of enquiry. It relied on Her Majesty's forces of law and order to protect its borders. But if those forces should fail, it lurked and squatted in the shadows, ready to pounce upon and annihilate, dissent.

The police contingent in front of the gates began to part in the middle. The Chief Inspector assigned to the demonstration stepped forward with a megaphone and politely asked the demonstrators to step back. The gates opened, and from the bowels of the Anglo-American Laboratory came a group of people on foot. The more militant wing of the crowd to the left of Vanessa Symonds, namely the assorted academics, appeared to take a dislike to them. There was some scuffling, some barging, some swearing, and even some spitting from the more juvenile elements, and the police moved forward to separate the protagonists. A punch was thrown and one of those who had emerged from the gate was knocked to the ground. The police made an arrest, and the man picked himself up from the ground, brushed some stale snow from his coat, and looked up.

It was Tom Fairford. She recognised him. She had seen him speak at the Union. He was the Secretary. He was a bio-chemist. She had seen him from time to time in the Senior Common Room. They had noticed each other but had hardly spoken. He was tall, blonde haired – good looking but not in the way of a matinée idol. It was a face with a background, an interesting face, a face with an expression of intent which was not necessarily benign. He had public school manners, with a suggestion of cruelty in the way he smiled. In short, she was powerfully attracted to him.

"Hi. It's Tom, isn't it?"

"Yes – Vanessa?"

She nodded. She was flattered that he knew her name.

"I would not have had you down as one of the angry brigade," he said.

"We're not all the same, you know. Sometimes these demonstrations, they attract people who just want a fight."

She saw that he had a cut to his head. "You're hurt. Why don't you let me make amends and clean you up a bit?"

"I'm OK. But I'll walk back to College with you if you are going that way."

"Sure. Do you really work in that place?" She indicated the lab with an expression of distaste.

"You're a zoologist, aren't you?" She nodded. "Look, I'm not involved in any animal experimentation. I mean, I don't know everything that goes on in there but I'm just doing a bit of research for my thesis on enzymes. I've been working there for a couple of weeks. My tutor got me a placement. They're gold dust. The security in this place is like Fort Knox."

They walked back to College together. She persuaded him to come to her rooms in Frewin Court. She cleaned him up. They talked. He was agnostic about animal testing. She was committed. He was attracted to her passion, and her body; she to his confidence, poise, and sense of entitlement. He took her to dinner. That night they slept together.

Their relationship blossomed for a while. And, by the time of the Oxford Union debate in February, she fancied that she might be in love with him. But as that term wore on she knew that it was not to be. He was not the kind to make any sort of commitment. He found her exciting in bed, and in conversation, but he considered her a luxury resource to be consumed. Once satiated he would discard her and move on to the next. The intervals between his calls lengthened, and the time he spent with her after they had slept together shortened.

And as the term wore on, her feelings towards him changed too. She found him less and less exciting, and his conversation limited to his favourite subject, which was himself. As the winter merged into the spring, she realised that her interest in Fairford was now more to do with his role at the Anglo-American laboratory. She wanted to know the truth of what went on in there. She wanted to know if there was any basis in fact for the more colourful conspiracy theories that were emanating from NAACA.

By the time of the Union ball in March, she hadn't seen or heard from Fairford in days. And when she saw Roscoe walking out of the law library that Friday evening at the end of term, she was genuinely pleased to see him. Her invitation was genuine. She liked him. He was clever but not only that, she could see a kind of decency in him; the kind of decency which does not depend upon any animal attraction, but which engenders feelings of security and comfort, especially in times of trouble.

In the Eagle and Child that Mayday, she put it a little more tactfully. After she had recounted the story of the rise and fall of her relationship with Fairford, Roscoe asked her why she had approached him in the bookshop. "You hardly know me," he said.

"I think I can trust you. Call it an instinct. You're also a lawyer, and have nothing to do with this bio-chemical bubble I've been living in for the last few months."

That made him feel good, but then he remembered how he had felt at the end of the previous term. "But why did you do that to me; invite me to the ball and then walk out with Fairford when you saw me coming?"

"That's not how it happened, Dan."

She said that when she had seen him that Friday at the end of Hilary term, her invitation to the ball was genuine. She felt lonely, deserted, and she needed company. She wanted *his* company. But then Fairford had called her on the Saturday afternoon. Most of his circle had gone down for the Easter vacation, and he was at a loose end. When she told him of her plans for that evening, he told her to forget them. He said that *he* would take her to the Union ball; Roscoe would be better off with his books anyway.

She said that she had meant to call him but Fairford had turned up at her rooms early. They had made love, and then drunk champagne together whilst she dressed. She had quite simply, to her shame, forgotten about her invitation, and about him. When she and Fairford had left her room, she was entirely unaware of the time. It was not Fairford's practice to be on time for anything, still less to be early. Either he had timed it deliberately to humiliate Roscoe, or a more charitable interpretation, he had wanted to leave early so as to avoid him – after all, who shows up early for a party?

Roscoe's face burned with indignation but he remained silent and looked into the bottom of his beer glass.

"The tide's gone out for me too." She held up her glass and smiled; her eyes moistened. Then she leaned forward and took his hand. "Look, Dan, I'm sorry. Why don't you get us another drink? I've only just started."

There had been a drinks party at the end of that Hilary term for the University branch of NAACA. It had been a couple of days before the Union ball. Vanessa had drunk too much. With hindsight she had been a little careless. Her head was full of Tom Fairford and towards the end of the night she was talking to Rosie Stubbs, the student liaison officer. She must have mentioned that Fairford was working at the Anglo-American laboratory as a research student. Then, on the morning of the Union ball, she received a call from Dame Sheila Thomspon, the President of NAACA. Thompson asked Vanessa if she were free to meet.

Dame Sheila was a renowned economist, a former financial analyst in the Treasury, now a distinguished academic and a fellow of Christ Church College. And so, that same Saturday of Seventh Week, at around two in the afternoon, Vanessa found herself in Tom Quad, the largest quadrangle in Oxford, of the largest and richest College in the University. Dame Sheila had rooms in staircase eleven, on the east side near to the entrance to the Cathedral.

Her rooms were magnificent. A sumptuous sitting room, looking out onto the quadrangle, richly carpeted in a deep, navy blue, and a splendid bedroom facing onto Christ Church meadow. Vanessa had twice been invited into the bedroom and had politely declined on both occasions.

On this occasion, Thompson was entirely business-like. She sat behind a desk, her elbows resting on the green leather top, smoking a cigarette. She was about forty-five years old. Her hair was prematurely grey and was tied back into a pony tail. She wore distinctive, silver-rimmed, tinted glasses and was conservatively dressed in a grey suit. She spoke in something of a staccato style, with a smoker's voice. On that Saturday afternoon her speech sounded urgent; her sentences punctuated by the way she held and smoked her cigarette. She took a long pull on the cigarette, and began to talk as she exhaled.

"Vanessa, I have been told that you are seeing a young man who has a research placement at the Anglo-American Laboratory. Is this true?"

"Yes, it is."

"I must say that I am a little disappointed. I thought that we had been working closely together this past year, you and I. That is why I made you…", she drew on the cigarette, "Chairwoman of the University branch in December. Why didn't you tell me?"

"I'm sorry, Sheila, I don't understand. He has nothing to do with animal experimentation. He is working on a research project that has to do with enzymes. I know that he would tell me if he were involved in anything else."

"Are you really that close?" She drew deeply on the cigarette again, her penetrating eyes examining Vanessa's face, and then scanning the upper half of her body. "That in itself would make him potentially useful to us. I appreciate that the University branch of NAACA is perhaps more of a social club for students of a like mind, rather than a political organisation and it may be that I should have done more to integrate the branch into national policy. But our interest in this laboratory is not just a protest against animal experimentation, although that is important of course. For some years now NAACA has suspected that the Anglo-American laboratory has been conducting experiments on behalf of the United States government. Indeed, we believe that it is an arm of the government of the United States, and is effectively outside of the jurisdiction of the British authorities."

Sheila Thompson stood up, stubbed out her cigarette in a marble ashtray, and then sat, perched on the corner of the desk.

"For a while we had somebody on the inside of the laboratory. He has gone quiet. We don't know why. But before he went quiet we obtained some valuable intelligence out of him. We know, for example, that the laboratory is operated, financed and directed by the US Central Intelligence Agency. We have the proof. We know that the security guards are all recruited from veterans of the US Military Intelligence Corps. They are all armed, without any lawful authority. We have proof of that too. I have seen the documents."

"Why haven't you gone to the press?" Vanessa said. "Or the Labour Party. There would be an outcry."

"Because we don't yet have proof of the purpose of the experiments. You see, we believe that experiments are being conducted for military purposes, and not for medical reasons. Many people, perfectly reasonable people, are prepared to tolerate animal experimentation if it can be shown to have genuine benefits in terms of human health. But if we could get proof that the purpose of the laboratory is for military research on behalf of the US government, there would be such a scandal that the lab would have to close down. The whole practice of covert animal experimentation in this country would be undermined, perhaps fatally. It's crucial that we get some hard evidence to take to the press. At the moment the press regards us as a bunch of nutcases and conspiracy theorists, and so do most of Her Majesty's Loyal Opposition, I'm afraid.

"And, so do you see Vanessa, that this..." She paused to light another cigarette. "This contact could be exactly what we are looking for. Our previous source had no access to the laboratory itself, only to the administrative offices. From what you tell me this boyfriend of yours will have access to precisely the areas in which we are most interested. Vanessa, will you help us?"

Vanessa then admitted to Roscoe that it was she who had called Fairford later that same Saturday afternoon, rather than the other way around. But she had done it, not because she saw any future in her relationship with Fairford, but because of the promise she had given to Sheila Thompson that morning. She was committed to the cause and this appeared to be the perfect opportunity to gain access to the laboratory.

She told him that it was true that Fairford was at a loose end over the Easter vacation. He was confined to Oxford by his research schedule, and most of his set had decamped to Switzerland for some late season skiing in Klosters. It was true that she did deliberately re-kindle their physical relationship, beginning on that very same Saturday evening; although it was clear to her that their intellectual relationship was at an end.

She then began to plead with Fairford to get her access to the laboratory. She told him that she had to see with her own eyes what was going on. She told him that she could not continue a relationship with anybody involved in such a place unless she was sure his hands were clean. And over the course of a fortnight, taut with sexual tension, she played expertly and remorselessly to instincts which were innate in his character, instincts which linked risk and danger with sexual anticipation.

It was a damp, overcast and oppressive night, a Sunday night, that Fairford finally cracked. The last day in March. Fairford was renting a student house just off the Cowley Road. She had refused his repeated invitations to move in with him for the duration of the Easter vacation and had stayed in College. They had spent that afternoon in Modern Art Oxford, in Pembroke Street. An exhibition of Picasso erotica, chronicling the master's experiences in Barcelona and Paris at the turn of the century, had transferred from the Galerie Nationale de Paris.

That night she had cooked him *coq au vin* for supper. She had invested in three bottles of Bourgogne Rouge Dugat, an excellent burgundy. In the first, she had gently braised the chicken for one hour and forty minutes. The second they had shared whilst she cooked, and the third he had opened, and had begun to consume. They listened to Bach's English Suite No 2. She was beside him on the sofa. It was half past ten.

"So, what do you say, eh?" She playfully flicked his right cheek with her finger.

He leaned back and sighed. "If you really must do this, then I suppose now would be a pretty good time to do it. The security always eases off a bit in the vac once most of the student population has gone down. I drove in to the lab yesterday. The guard barely glanced at my pass."

"Then, let's do it."

It was past midnight by the time he drove her up the Cowley Road into Oxford. He drove a 1955 Bentley S1 Continental Drophead Coupe, gifted to him by his father on his eighteenth birthday. It was his pride and joy with which he had sought to impress numerous women. She too for a time had been sufficiently impressed.

He drove along the High and then turned sharp right into Longwall Street. Here he parked to the side of the road unlit by street lights. He got out of the car, and went to the rear. He fiddled with the façade of the back seat until it came loose. It was just as they had practised. She alighted from the front passenger seat and made her way to the back. With a glance up and down the road, she lowered herself into the rear of the car, and bit by bit inched herself into the cavity. It was a tight fit. He pushed her further into the space, and then replaced the façade, forcing it a little against her back until it clicked into place.

It was like a coffin. There was no light, and no room for manoeuvre. She heard him return to the driver's seat and close the door. She could feel and picture the route as he drove off; the gentle left hand bend into Holywell Street and then the hard right into Mansfield Road, towards the Anglo-American Laboratory for Bio-Chemical Research.

The car came to a halt. She could just make out an intensely bright light through a chink in the coffin. It was the floodlights of the laboratory complex.

A rasping voice, faint but distinct, came from the front of the vehicle. "Pass please? You're a little late tonight Mr Fairford." The accent was undeniably American – probably West Coast – Sheila had got that right at least.

"Late night session, I'm afraid. Burning the candle at both ends."

"Well, go easy with that sir. Can I take a quick look in the back?" She heard heavy footsteps, from the front to the rear. The boot was opened, perhaps a rug lifted, and then closed. Then a sound at the rear driver's side. Some scuffling immediately at her back. Her skin crawled. She held her breath. Her heart thumped in her ears. Thirty seconds, a minute, then the door closed and the heavy footsteps returned to the front.

"OK, Mr Fairford. Have a good night."

Then a whirring sound, a high pitched screech. She guessed the gates were being opened. The car moved forward and she let out her breath. After ten seconds or so, the car slowed and moved in a semi-circular shape. The ambient light appeared to dim and the car drew to a halt. The engine was switched off. Silence.

One minute, two. He had told her to remain absolutely silent. Then the sound of the driver's door opening. The click as it shut. The sound of footsteps on concrete drifting into the middle distance. Then another minute, two and three. Five minutes. She craned her neck up, hoping to hear something. Her shoulder hurt like crazy. The ticking of her watch. Ten minutes. Her heart began to race again, pounding in her ears. Her nose was pressed to the bulwark of the boot. The smell of petrol. Beads of sweat on her forehead. She fancied she could not breathe. She strained to manoeuvre her arm up to her neck to loosen her collar. Then she heard the faintest of footsteps again, approaching. The rear door opened.

Tom whispered. "It's OK."

He eased off the façade which was holding her in and she rolled out. The cold night air hit her face and she breathed again. He helped her out of the car. It was dark. Their breath was snow white against the night. Tom had told her that he had located an apparent blind spot, out of the glare of the floodlights, around the rear of the building, equidistant from the two main entrances and exits. This is where he had manoeuvred the car.

"Follow me," he whispered, "and not a sound."

He took her hand and led her to the rear of the principal laboratory building. With their backs to the wall, they inched around the perimeter; eyes peeled for any guards. It was as he had said. It seemed that the tension of the security cordon was relaxed in the absence of the broad mass of the undergraduate population during the vacation.

As they inched their way to the corner of the building, they saw a guard patrolling the perimeter fence, some thirty metres away. They froze, and instinctively shrank into the shadow of the wall. But the guard's attention was directed to the fence and the danger of any incursion from outside. It was not directed to the laboratory building.

They inched further, unseen, around the corner, and to the secondary entrance which was used by pre-vetted researchers who had been issued with swipe cards. Here they had to move fast. There was a small night light above the entrance. It was not a floodlight, but it was sufficient to alert an observer to their presence. More problematic was a CCTV camera above the door. Maybe it was being monitored, maybe not; but they could not afford to take the risk.

Fairford checked from the edge of the shadows. There was no one in sight.

"OK. Let's go." As he had briefed her, she moved with him, as close as possible to his rear. As he swivelled to face the door, so did she. She was effectively concealed behind his back, as he took the entrance card from his top pocket, and swiped it through the key control. The door lock clicked. He opened it, and they both moved in tandem through the entrance and into the corridor. He closed the door behind him and they both exhaled with relief. They were in.

The lights inside the lab were automatically dimmed at night but they did not need a torch to see their surroundings.

"You're sure there's no CCTV inside?"

"Quite sure." His voice was a barely audible whisper, and he pressed his mouth to her ear. "They are so fucking secretive there's no way they would want any recording of what goes on here. Take it from me. There are no cameras. We have to be careful though. There could be one or two people working here over night."

He led her from the corridor into a large room. It was about twenty metres by ten. It looked like an open plan office. The walls were bare and painted white. On the ceiling, the strips of neon lights were dimmed. The room was filled with rows of wooden benches. On the benches were computer screens. She tapped at a few of the keyboards. Screen savers came up – all password protected. In the corner of the room was a partitioned office. Through a window into this office she could see a single desk, and a filing cabinet. There was no sign of anybody.

"You see, it isn't what you were expecting. There are no cages filled with monkeys smoking cigars, or trying on hand cream."

"Where do you work?"

He pointed to the end of the row. It was next to the wall. She crept over, instinctively walking on her toes. There was a vintage movie poster stuck to the wall next to the desk: 'The Bride of Frankenstein, starring Boris Karloff.'

"Is that supposed to be some kind of joke?"

He shrugged. "If that's the way you people want to paint us, then why not?"

She pulled away from his hand on her arm. "What's your password?"

He tapped at the keyboard and brought up his desktop. A neutral wallpaper. He let her browse through his documents folder. Essays, research papers on enzymes; some of it she understood, some of it was over her head.

"You see, we are not Doctor Frankensteins."

"What is beyond that door?" She nodded to the far wall, parallel to the entrance through which they had come. "This building is huge. This room must be the tip of the iceberg."

She walked over. Set in the wall was a door with the appearance of a safe. It looked like it had been fashioned from steel and had a combination lock. She tapped the wall and the door with her fist. It felt as immovable as a battleship.

"Now I know what you meant by Fort Knox. What is behind here?"

"I haven't a clue. I am a junior research assistant allowed limited access at the request of my tutor. I don't even recall anyone going in there."

"I don't believe you. I know there are animal experiments going on here and I'm certainly not going away empty handed. What would it do for your career if I alerted those guards out there?" She gestured to the entrance.

"You fucking bitch!" He grabbed her throat and she could smell the wine on his breath as he spat the words in her face.

She brought her knee up sharply between his legs. "Fuck!" He doubled up in pain, the breath knocked out of him.

There was a noise at the entrance. He grabbed her and shoved her behind the row of desks.

"Quiet!" he hissed. "Look, I'll get you something, just shut it." He put his hand over her mouth to emphasise the point. She didn't resist.

The entrance door to the room opened. There were footsteps. They could see, from their semi-concealed position, somebody approach the partitioned office. It was a man, middle-aged, glasses, wearing a white lab coat. He removed a key from his pocket and unlocked the door. He went to the filing cabinet. There was the sound of a drawer being opened and then closed. He came out. He left the door unlocked, and approached the vault across the other side of the room. He entered a code on the keypad. There was a solid clunk and the sound of an internal locking mechanism responding. He turned the wheel a quarter turn in a clockwise direction and opened the steel door.

Although it only opened wide enough for the man to enter, she could see that the door was six inches thick. Inside there was a bustle of activity. She could make out a number of people passing in the immediate vicinity of the doorway, and some bright white lights. The door was then closed with a thud, shutting out the noise and the light and the locking mechanism re-activated.

Fairford took his hand from her mouth. "Well I suppose that office is the place to look at then," she said, still whispering.

“I’m not going to stop you. Just keep my name out of it or I’m finished, and so are you.”

“Don’t worry. I’m not interested in you. It’s what’s going on inside that vault that I want to know about.”

She made her way to the office, on her toes, opened the door and went in. He was behind her. It was a small room containing a desk, a computer and a filing cabinet. The desk was empty. The computer locked. She turned her attention to the filing cabinet. It contained hanging files, arranged in some sort of alphabetical order. She began to look through them; conscious that Fairford was to her side, monitoring the vault and the entrance.

The files appeared to contain accounts in the main – balance sheets, lists of income and expenditures, which meant very little to her. They appeared to relate to the years 2012 to 2018. She took out the file for 2018. The last section was alphabetised under the letter ‘V’. She took it out. It appeared to be a research paper – ‘SARS (2003), MERS (2013) and the transference of pathogenic viruses from snakes (2019)’.

Chapter Four

Roscoe sat up. "I've heard of SARS. What's MERS?"

She emptied her glass.

"They are both viruses which cause pneumonia. SARS – severe acute respiratory syndrome. It killed about nine hundred people nearly twenty years ago, a death rate of about thirty percent. MERS is Middle East Respiratory Syndrome, about five years ago. There were more cases – about eight thousand – but a fatality rate of only about ten percent.

"They were both viruses that jumped from animals to the human population, and then spread. What makes them potentially so dangerous is their novelty. If no human has ever had it before, no human has any immunity. All that protects us is the limited rate of infection and the low fatality rate. Since then the scientists have been worried about a similar virus emerging which is both highly infectious and with a high fatality rate – if that happens then you may end up with a global pandemic of terrifying proportions."

"And what's this reference to snakes? 2019 did you say?"

"It seems to be a reference to viruses transferring from snakes to humans. I've never heard of it happening before but any biological organism can host viruses. There's no reason in theory why it could not happen."

"And what about this paper? What did you do with it?"

She held up her glass and smiled weakly. "Another?"

"OK." He began to make his way to the bar, and then turned back. "And the paper, did you say it was in the file for 2018? It looks like a prediction then rather than a statement."

Vanessa went on to tell Roscoe that as soon as she saw the paper, she had decided that she had better bank what she had got and get out of the lab as quickly as possible. Fairford was only interested in getting them both out and not getting caught. It would be the end of his career if they were.

They went out the same way they had come. This time she shielded herself from the CCTV camera in front of him as they exited the door. They skirted around the corner and along the wall back to the car. There were no guards in sight and in the shadow of the wall she was able to secrete herself under the rear seat once again. She heard Fairford acknowledge the guard on the way out.

He parked up at the end of Longwall Street. He removed the façade from the rear seat, but this time he did not help her out. By the time she had made her way around to the front passenger side, the door was locked. He leaned forward and spoke through the half open window.

"OK darling you got what you wanted. You can walk from here."

He wound up the window and drove off without another word. With the paper folded and concealed under her jacket, she made her way along the High to Carfax and back to her rooms in Frewin Court.

Unable to sleep, she took out the research paper from the lab. Tomorrow she would have to surrender it to Sheila Thompson. She retrieved a notebook from her desk and began to read the paper. She was not able to follow all of it but she understood that it was to do with the identification of another pathogenic virus; this time in snakes.

The paper was a discussion of the structure of the virus's proteins. She knew enough to know that it was the structure of the proteins which ultimately determined whether the virus could spread to mammals, such as pigs, and ultimately whether it could jump to humans, and in turn whether it could then be transferred from person to person.

It seemed pretty clear to her that the research going on at the lab was to do with the identification and prevention of another potential pandemic. If this involved experimentation on live animals, was it worth it? She decided that that could wait for the morning. She got into bed and fell into an uneasy sleep.

The next morning, she woke too early – seven thirty. Her heart was pounding. She picked up her phone, found Thompson's number and called it. It went through to voice mail.

"Sheila, I managed to get into the lab last night. I've got something which might interest you. Call me back."

By the time she had made herself a cup of coffee the phone was buzzing.

Sheila Thompson sounded excited. "Vanessa, did you manage to get in?"

"Tom Fairford. He smuggled me in."

"Well what did you get? Did you get into the experimental vault?"

"No, but I've got hold of a paper. It's to do with viruses which transfer from animals to humans. It's pretty technical. I understand some of it but unless you've got some background in bio-chemistry, I think it'll go over your head."

"Don't worry about that. We have people who can follow this stuff and it's not just what's in the paper, it's also to do with the distribution list – who was going to see the paper. Just bring it over right away will you?"

Forty-five minutes later, Vanessa had showered and made her way to Sheila Thompson's rooms. Thompson sat behind the desk, examining the paper. She smoked; the long thin cigarette held up between the middle two fingers of her left hand. Her voice was urgent, insistent and she leaned forward.

"This is to do with viruses like bird flu, swine flu, that sort of thing?"

"Essentially yes. If there's a potential virus which is going to be transferable from animals to humans, then the scientists need to know as much as possible about it because there's no immunity in the human population, unlike with colds and seasonal flu; and so we have to fight it off from scratch. But just because it can jump from an animal to a human, doesn't necessarily mean that it can be passed from person to person. Bird flu couldn't and so it was effectively a dead end. Swine flu could, but it was sufficiently similar to seasonal flu to mean that many people were effectively immune to it and the low rate of infection meant that it wasn't a major problem. But if you get a *novel* virus jumping from an animal to a human and which *can* be transmitted from person to person, then you've potentially got a global pandemic on your hands."

"And so what is the paper about, trying to find a vaccine or what?"

"No, this is not talking about a virus which has started to spread amongst the human population. This is talking about a virus which has been identified in animals – in particular snakes – like SARS and MERS were found in bats – do you remember them?"

She nodded. "I remember SARS certainly."

"What this paper is concerned with is not how to stop the spread of the virus, but how the virus might be able to spread in the first place, first from snake to human – maybe through some other animal like a pig – and then from human to human. It's about what would enable that to happen. Basically its examining the structure of the proteins of the virus. It's the structure of the proteins which enables the virus to attach itself to the cells of another living organism. I assume the lab is researching how that can be prevented. But frankly that's a bit over my head."

"Well, it's certainly over mine." Thompson was deep in thought. After a minute or two of silence, she started to search through an old fashioned telephone index. "Sir John Fawcett". She dialled a number from an antique bakerlite telephone, and sat back in the swivel chair.

"John? It's Sheila. Fine thanks. Can I give you a list of names to check?"

She proceeded to read out the names of the three individuals who were on the circulation list of the paper. Vanessa Symonds had already noted them down before she had left her room. She had appreciated their potential significance when Thompson had first mentioned the distribution list.

"You'll call me back? Thanks, John."

Thompson leaned forward again, grasping her hands together and resting her chin on them. She studied Vanessa. Her intelligent eyes searching behind the face, into the soul.

"Vanessa, you've been with us now for what three, four years?"

She nodded. "The first week I came up. Freshers' fair."

"Yes, and since then you've developed into somebody I've learned to trust implicitly. That's why I made you Chairwoman of the University branch last year. Can I trust you? I mean really trust you with information you simply have to keep to yourself?"

The eyes remained fixed. Vanessa returned her gaze steadily.

"Yes, you most certainly can and I think I've proved it."

"I agree."

Thompson got up from the desk and came around to the other side. She sat in the opposite armchair. She took out the packet of cigarettes and sucked her teeth.

She offered the packet. "Do you?"

Vanessa shook her head.

"A little unfashionable. I know. But then so am I."

She took out a cigarette, fumbled for a silver lighter in her pocket and then lit it. She drew deeply, exhaled and leaned forward.

"For some time now NAACA has not just been about the protection of animals, although of course that remains one of our top priorities. We know that they are experimenting on monkeys, and other sentient animals. They do not seriously dispute it. But it's what these experiments are about which has been troubling us more recently."

She examined Vanessa's expression as if weighing the merits of continuing. She continued slowly, almost lost at first in her own thoughts.

"Before I became an academic, I worked in the Treasury, during the Blair-Brown years. You're probably too young to remember John Fawcett?" Vanessa shrugged. "He was a Parliamentary Private Secretary to one of the Treasury ministers in the late nineties. We became quite close. He went on to become a Foreign Office minister and seemed destined for greater things. Then the Iraq War came along in 2003 and he resigned over disagreements with government policy and its support for the US invasion. Since then he's been on the backbenches, but he's maintained a keen interest in foreign policy. For the last few years he's been a member of the Parliamentary Joint Intelligence Committee. Recently he has become increasingly critical of Britain's relationship with the United States. He's one of these old style internationalists I'm afraid, who have an instinctive distrust of American foreign policy. One summer, a couple of years ago, we had dinner together. He knows that, as well as my academic responsibilities, I am the President of NAACA, and he wanted to tap into whatever information we've been able to obtain about the Anglo – American laboratory. In his role on the committee, he is occasionally privy to classified information. Not the really top secret stuff, you understand. That would only be available to the higher echelons of government. But he did have access to papers dealing with security issues arising from animal rights activists, such as ourselves.

"From what he had seen, it had become obvious to him that the lab had become a front for the US military and not just a civilian medical research facility. He began strongly to suspect that the lab was being used for experiments in biological warfare. That's why I gave him the distribution list. If he can find any connection with the Pentagon or the CIA, then it will corroborate his suspicions."

Vanessa went on to tell Roscoe that by the time she was half way down the High after her meeting with Thompson, she saw that she had had a text from

Fairford. "Call me – urgently. Don't do anything with the paper." When she tried to call back, the number went through to voicemail.

By the time she reached Carfax she had tried calling Fairford three times without success. She knew that Fairford was not one to get easily flustered. He was usually so laid back. There must have been a serious development. She decided that this could not wait. She crossed the road and got on a bus in the direction of Cowley. By the time the bus had reached the Cowley Road, her phone was ringing.

Fairford was urgent. There was a tone in his voice which she had never heard before. She could only describe it as fear.

"Listen, have you told anyone about that paper?" She hesitated. "Vanessa, sit on it. Do nothing. Do you hear me."

The phone went dead, and her repeated attempts to call him back all the way along the Cowley Road came to nothing. She got off the bus just past the Recreation Ground and a short walk to the house.

It was a typical student house in Cowley. Early twentieth century. A basement, with an area, and steps leading from the main road up to the front door. Tom had been living there on his own since the beginning of the vac, his flatmates having gone down for Easter.

As she approached the house, she saw that the street door was ajar. Although it was rarely locked during the day, it was usually on the latch. She went up the steps and into the communal hallway. There was the usual smell of cigarettes and stale carpet. Downstairs and straight ahead was the communal kitchen. Tom's rooms were on the first floor. She went up the stairs.

As soon as she reached the landing she saw that his door had been forced. The wood was splintered and the door apparently opened with a jemmy. Her heart pounding in her chest, she stood at the door. She could hear nothing, apart from the faint sound of the traffic on the Cowley Road and the beat of some music from the house next door. How long since he had called? She looked at her watch – over half an hour.

Cautiously she nudged the door. It opened another few inches. The room looked as if it had been ransacked. Drawers had been opened and discarded, their contents strewn over the floor. The contents of the wardrobe too – shirts, jackets, ties, an overcoat. Somebody had gone to work on the coat and jackets with a knife, their lining had been torn open, their insides ripped out. The sofa had been similarly disembowelled, as had the armchair and the mattress.

The desk had been broken into – the wood splintered with the force of a jemmy – and papers littered the floor. The air was thick with dust. She was alone. Her fear prickled her forehead and a sense of panic was rising in her chest. The music from the house next door had stopped and it was quiet. She took some deep breaths and stood for several minutes, willing herself to become calm and to function.

Had Tom called her from the house, or from elsewhere? If he had called her from the house, then what had happened to him? She remembered the fear in his voice and she retched. She stared helplessly at her phone. He had called her less than forty minutes ago. If he had called from the house, then what had happened had only *just* happened. Her stomach lurched and she instinctively moved away from the window, her back pressed up to the wall.

The window above the desk faced onto the main road. Keeping out of the direct light, she inched forward to the right side of the window until she had a view of the road to the left. The normal traffic flow and a couple of pedestrians about their business. She backed off to the wall again and inched to the left, avoiding the debris on the floor, and careful to remain out of the light. Then she moved forward to the left of the window until she had a view to the right; the bus stop on the nearside, a woman waiting with a pram. She eased further to the left until she had a view of the far side of the road; the bus stop to the city centre, fifty metres to the right. A large man, with glasses, wearing a black overcoat, stood by the stop, lighting a cigarette. There was something about his appearance – the hunch of his shoulders, and something about his lips, sinister and predatory – which increased the beat of her heart, and the prickling of her forehead.

She watched for a minute or two. He was not paying attention to the house. But as she watched, the buses kept arriving and stopping at the bus stop, blocking her view, yet when they drove off, there he was, still waiting. Five minutes passed. Ten. He was still there. And then she saw it. His shoulders arched, his tongue traced the broad flesh of his lips, and he signalled in a way which was almost indistinguishable from a flick of his cigarette butt. Indeed, were it not for her heightened alertness, she would have missed it. He signalled to a car parked up on the nearside of the road, not ten metres from the front door, and then, looking to his left and his right, he began to cross the road.

She moved, quickly, instinctively, an animal urge to get out, to flee as fast as possible from danger. She ran out of Fairford's room and as fast as she could along the corridor to the back of the house. There was a window overlooking the rear garden. It was no more than a couple of metres from the ground. She opened it, her heart thumping in her mouth. She climbed onto the window sill, looked down and jumped.

She landed in some bushes and cursed as her right ankle and knee took the brunt of the impact. She crept around to the side of the bush, took cover and lay still. Silence, apart from the gasping of her breath. She waited, and after a couple of minutes she believed that she heard the window from which she had jumped being shut. She continued to lay still, hardly daring to breathe at all, her heart beating like a demon. She held herself close, into a ball, waiting for discovery, waiting for the blow. A minute, two, turned into five, and then nothing. Slowly her breath came under control and her heart settled into a pounding rhythm and then she began to think.

What on earth had happened to Fairford? It didn't require much analysis to conclude that this was to do with the lab, and, what was more, with what they had done the previous night. It looked as if someone had discovered that the paper was missing, had seen Fairford on the CCTV, and put two and two together. Clearly whoever was behind the operation of the laboratory was prepared to resort to extreme lengths to get the paper back, or at least to suppress its contents. *Did this extend to personal violence, even murder?* She shuddered. It was cold and the light was beginning to fade. She decided to wait until after dark, climb over the back of the wall into the Recreation Ground and then creep, cautiously and furtively back into the city and to safety.

By the time she got back into the High it was after nine. She was exhausted, having made her way back, as far as she could, in the shadows and the half-light, constantly looking over her shoulder like a hunted animal. She debated with herself whether to go back to Frewin Court. It was fairly common knowledge among their friends and acquaintances that she was in a relationship with Fairford. She wasn't the public face of NAACA, but she was heavily involved as the Chairwoman of the University branch, and had recently spoken at the debate in the Union, alongside the national president. *What if someone put two and two together about her too?* There was a youth hostel by the railway station, only £12 a night. She decided she would stay there, and then contact Sheila Thompson in the morning.

The room was little more than a hutch but it was fairly clean. She lay on the bed, and spent most of the night staring at the ceiling, unable to sleep. The single bare light bulb rocked gently at the end of its rope. A damp patch, the colour of cold sweat, seemed to darken as the night progressed through its slow and menacing course.

She finally drifted into a half-waking, half-sleeping state shortly after the hour of three had been struck by the bell of St Ebbe's. She awoke around six thirty, and for a moment lay in the half-light wondering where she was. Then with a sickening realisation she gasped, sat upright, and her heart began to race.

She got up, splashed her face with water from the small basin in the corner of the room, and left the hostel. Then she paced the streets of central Oxford until an hour when she could reasonably call Sheila Thompson. She had barely begun her account of what she had found in the Cowley Road before Thompson interrupted her.

"My rooms have been broken into too. When I arrived this morning from London, the door had been forced and the room ransacked."

"And the paper?"

"They didn't get that. My years in the senior civil service have made me a little sensitive about security. I took the precaution of scanning the paper and destroying the original. But they certainly had a good look for it. They're professionals – they even took the stuffing out of my Chesterfield sofas. They took everything I had to do with NAACA – campaign schedules, minutes, membership lists and contact details. Did you call the police?"

Vanessa's voice was rapid, taut with tension. "No. I thought I ought to speak to you first. I suspected what happened in Cowley Road had to do with the lab, and this confirms it."

"Yes, it has to be. Good. I don't think we want the police involved in this. Not just yet. These people have searched high and low and they haven't found it. With a bit of luck, we won't be bothered by them again. If we call the police, we'll have to tell them about the paper and both our careers will be compromised. I'll tell John Fawcett; if there is anything we need to know he's in a better position than the police to find out."

"I understand why they went after Tom. They know he was in the lab on Sunday night. But what about you?"

"The connection has to be you Vanessa. They know you're with Tom, and the organisation, and so they went after me as the president. If that's right, then the odds are they will have turned over your place too. Look, I've got some tutorials this morning. Why don't you go home, check your room and see what they've taken? Give me a call later, around half twelve. You'd better not come into College. We can meet somewhere for lunch."

As Vanessa climbed her staircase in Frewin Court, she anticipated, indeed expected, that her door frame would be in splinters, and her room ransacked. It was not. It was as she had left it. *How come?* If they could find out the whereabouts of Sheila Thompson, who took precautions to prevent her address becoming public knowledge, it would have been easy work for them to have found out where she lived. For now, she filed it at the back of her mind. She was exhausted from the hostel. She lay down on her bed and drifted into a fitful sleep.

By the time she woke it was past one o'clock. She looked at her phone. There was a text from Sheila.

'Hi Vanessa. Why don't we meet at the Pusey Street café, just off St Giles; say, half past one.'

She splashed her face with water, changed her clothes and went straight out. There had been some kind of accident in St Giles, blue lights were flashing, and the road had been closed off. She had to take a circuitous route along George Street and into St John's. By the time she arrived at the café it was one forty-five. There was no sign of Sheila. The café was quite busy, and she was shown to a table in the corner at the back. She ordered a coffee and listened to the jazz playing in the background. She checked her phone – nothing. At two o'clock she tried calling but the phone was dead.

The sky darkened, and it began to rain. Large droplets began to tap upon the windows, and above on the slate roof. Through the rain drops, flashing blue lights were refracted from the street, and she remembered the accident in St Giles. The couple at the window table were half standing, looking out. Vanessa got up and joined them.

"What happened?"

"Somebody got knocked over. The police were saying it was a hit and run."

Vanessa looked out. An ambulance stood on the far side of the road. A stretcher had been brought into the middle, and what looked like a body was covered with a sheet.

The body was placed onto the stretcher and taken into the ambulance. By the kerbside she saw something else reflecting the blue lights, a pair of glasses, silver frames, tinted lenses.

The body was Sheila Thompson.

Chapter Five

Roscoe listened in silence as she finished her account. She wiped a single tear from her right eye. Another couple had entered the room with their drinks and sat at the adjacent table. Roscoe leaned forward and spoke in a low voice.

"So, are you suggesting she was murdered because of the missing paper? I can understand that they wanted to get it back but why would they resort to killing someone? It could just be a coincidence, couldn't it? She was in a hurry to meet you and she crossed the road without looking." As he said it, he realised it was fanciful.

"As far as the police are concerned it was simply a hit and run. But they don't know about Tom. I'm afraid that it's too much of a coincidence."

"And have you been living back in your room?"

"For the first couple of weeks after Sheila was killed, I stayed at the hostel. Every morning I went back to Frewin expecting to find the worst, but nothing. For the last week I've been sleeping there, or at least trying to sleep. I can only assume that they haven't made the connection with me."

"Have you thought about going to the police?"

"What am I going to say to them?" She was whispering now. "I don't have any proof of anything. Tom's still missing and there's nothing to say that Sheila was anything other than a random hit and run."

"If you know something which might explain her death and the disappearance of Fairford, I think you should."

She glanced at the couple on the adjacent table and finished the last of her drink. He reached out and touched her hand. She allowed him to hold it for a second or two and then withdrew it.

"I'll think about it. Shall we go?"

They went out into the bright Mayday sunshine and walked up St Giles to where Sheila had died less than a month before.

"There's something I want to show you," she said.

She reached out and took his hand and led him into the Gothic building on the corner: Pusey House. He had often seen it in passing, but had never entered, or even considered its purpose.

"Let's go into the Chapel. It's so peaceful."

It was cool inside and the air was heavy with incense. From somewhere the sound of a choir, perhaps rehearsing. Roscoe recognised William Byrd's Mass for Four Voices. They stood in front of the altar. The sun was washing through the stained glass window above, dappling the floor with soft colours and he felt a peace he had not had for some time. She turned to the right to face the icon of the Holy Mother and Child, knelt and crossed herself.

"Holy Mary, Mother of God, pray for us sinners now and at the hour of our death. Amen."

He stood back and watched her as she prayed, on her knees, her face and hair lit by the window, painted in the soft colours from the stained glass palette, and set to the beautiful music which resonated from the choir. To him she seemed as near to perfect as anything in the world. He ached to be with her, not just now, or tomorrow, or sometimes, but always. He ached to be close to her; physically, yes, but not just in the sense of the sexual act. He wanted to hug her, to smell her, to really know everything about her physical embodiment. And he ached to be close to her spiritually too, to spend his *private* time with her – to share his thoughts, his beliefs and his secrets with her. He wanted to share with her the things which he admired, the music, the books and the little bits of art which he loved and no one else could understand why.

And he wanted to explain why he loved them and to hear what she thought, and what she loved and why she loved it. He wanted to immerse himself in everything to do with her and invite her to do the same in him. No degree of proximity for him would be too close. He ached to *merge* with her in every conceivable sense. Roscoe assumed, in short, although he did not know it, that he was in love with her – but perhaps he was deluding himself one more time.

Afterwards they walked in Christ Church Meadow and along the river. Already the college boathouses were open and bustling with activity in preparation for the rowing season. The cocktails were flowing that sunny afternoon and it seemed that many had not stopped since the choir had celebrated the dawn in Magdalen's Great Tower just that very morning. It hardly seemed possible to him that it was the same week, let alone the same day. They stopped at the Brasenose boathouse and sat by the river; their faces tilted up to receive the warm sunshine.

"Are you a Catholic?"

"No. Anglican. Anglo-Catholic I suppose is more accurate." She laughed. The visit to Pusey House had relaxed her. "I'm not particularly devout you know. It's how I was brought up. My father is the Rector of St Bart's in London. Do you know it?"

"I've heard of it."

"I do believe in it though. I don't see there is much sense in anything without it."

"Maybe there isn't any point to anything after all," he said and then regretted it.

She turned to him with a look of almost childlike innocence and disappointment which he could not bear.

"No, I don't mean that. I'm not sure whether I believe in God but I know there must be some sense in… in this." His hand shyly indicated the two of them. He felt awkward and foolish, but she smiled. He smiled. They both laughed and held hands again.

Later, they had a little dinner at a place in Turl Street. Not much was said. There was no need to say much. They both felt comfortable with each other. She felt secure, and he felt a simple and uncomplicated delight at being in her presence. It did not need any explanation. He had no need of anything else. Afterwards, they went back to his rooms in College. They lay on top of his bed, without undressing. She simply wanted to be held. They kissed a little. He held her and she him, and they drifted together into an untroubled sleep.

It was already light when he woke. His waking moment – that first five seconds or so following the resumption of consciousness – was one of untrammelled peace. And nor was that peace interrupted by the following moments of consciousness; that short period when the conscious mind interrogates the waking moment for its reasons, and is sometimes resigned, sometimes reconciled, often disappointed, and sometimes devastated. He knew instinctively the reason for his peace without turning to look at it.

The curtains had not been drawn the previous evening and the early May sunshine streamed through the window. The only sound was that of birdsong. He turned to his side and opened his eyes. But she was not there. She had gone. She had left carefully, her impression still next to him in the bed clothes. He could still smell her hair on the pillow.

The note had been left prominently propped up against the mirror. It was a page torn out of a notebook, written in pencil.

'You were right. I need to go to the police. Tom may be in danger and so may you. Let's meet again when this has blown over. Look after yourself. V.'

She had left the notebook from which the page had been torn, either by accident or design, he did not know which. He shuffled though it, distractedly, his mind elsewhere. Her initials were on the inside cover. Inside a few pages of notes which made no sense to him. He threw it in the drawer of the desk. The note he threw in the bin. His immediate reaction was a pang of jealousy at the mention of Tom Fairford. Then there was the visceral wrench of loss, so powerful it had the physical effect of making him bend. *When would he see her again?*

Over the following few days he could think of nothing else. The shell of pride which had protected him during the previous term and throughout much of the Easter vacation, had been rendered null and void by this second visitation; his self-respect and sense of self-preservation, rendered powerless. He called her repeatedly and sent her numerous texts. There was no reply. He wandered around College and the Radcliffe Camera, the Covered Market and the High, longing to see her, hardly conscious of anyone else. The two focal points of his wanderings were Pusey House and Christchurch Meadow, where the pain of his disappointment was made physical and where he searched for the balm with which to treat it.

After a week, he went to her room in Frewin Court. His heart in his mouth, an iron ball in his stomach. He knocked on the door. As the seconds ticked by – one, two, three, four – without answer, the weight of dread and expectation again gave way to the gnawing pain of loss. There was no sign of her.

He knocked on one of the other doors on her landing which was throbbing with bass. It was answered by a surly undergraduate with a questionable taste in music.

"Do you know Vanessa Symonds in room four?" He pointed.

"Sort of, so what?"

"I've been trying to get hold of her. Have you seen her recently?"

"No, I can't say that I have but I probably wouldn't have taken much notice anyway." His head inclined behind him and Roscoe saw a naked girl, partially covered with a sheet, lying in bed smoking a cigarette.

"Alright. Thanks."

And so the weeks drifted by and Roscoe managed his pain. *What else could he do with it?* For a while he continued actively to look for her and for much longer his mind continued to search for her. He played and replayed, both in his dreams, and his waking moments, the times he had spent with her, and every possible interpretation of what had happened, and what might have happened.

And as he played and replayed events, the pain subtly changed from a sharp cut which made him gasp, to a blow upon a bruise which made him groan. Bit by bit the bruise became less tender, and the blows more infrequent, and he told himself that he was going to have to forget her. His Prelims had been ruined by his contact with her the previous term. He had only just squeaked through, and if he wasn't careful the start to his finals would be going the same way. Brockwell had told him at their last tutorial in Third Week that his essay was simply not good enough, that he had gone from being a star student to something close to a basket case and that if he did not buck up his ideas he was at risk of being sent down at the end of the term.

And eventually he reached a resolution, a conclusion upon which his exhausted mind was at last prepared to settle and rest. He told himself that she was a tease. In his mind, he reconstructed events so as to convince himself that she had been playing with him before Easter, and that she was playing with him again. *Even if there were some truth in her story,* he told himself, *she had used it to entertain herself.*

In his wildest moments, he even imagined she and Tom Fairford partying together and having a good laugh at his expense. In that way, he was able to isolate himself emotionally from the memories. He had no longer lost something beautiful and irretrievable. He had been spared from something damaging and hateful. It had injured him but he would heal and be stronger for the experience. This is what Roscoe told himself, and that was how he was able to get through the term, concentrating on his books, and keeping to himself; terrified of seeing her with Fairford, and feeling the pain of humiliation once again.

And so it was that he went down at the beginning of July in a fairly composed state-of-mind. His work had improved dramatically in the second half of term, and his last essay had impressed his tutor. He went back to his parents' house in

Crawley and spent the first part of the summer working his way through Brockwell's reading list for Michaelmas in the Middle Temple library.

Bill Compton had noticed the *ennuie* of his friend fairly early on in that Trinity term, and had probed just as far as he knew their friendship would permit. They didn't really talk about women. It was one of those male friendships which is confined by some unwritten rule to the male world – the pub, music (in their case classical), an occasional visit to Twickenham for the rugby, and only the odd tangential reference to women, always in jest. There was a kind of recognition that a serious relationship with the other sex, and perhaps marriage, would eventually petrify their friendship – transform it into a statue to be admired and fondly remembered but no longer lived. They wanted to confine this territory to the unspoken margins of their relationship, for the time being at least.

In August they had planned a trip to Central Europe with Tim Purser, Roscoe's old school friend. They spent a few days in Berlin and went to hear the Berlin Philharmonic play Mahler's Ninth. Then they worked their way around Poland, by train and bus. Gdansk, with a couple of days on the beach at Sopot, Warsaw, the lakes, Zakopanie and the mountains, and then Krakow. By the end of it, they had sampled just about every Polish beer and eaten their fill of pierogi, pork knuckle and bigos. They made their way back via Bayreuth (for a little Wagner), Salzburg and the South of France, and returned to England with a strong craving for a curry.

But it had worked for Roscoe. After a while he had hardly thought about the girl at all, except through those haunting closing bars of Mahler's Ninth, when the memories came back to stalk him just a little. Through September he spent his time in the library by day, and a bar by night, where he had got himself a few weeks' work. By the beginning of October, he was ready to return to Oxford, in good spirits and with those memories confined and tamed, if not extinguished.

It was Fourth Week before he saw it. He was not even looking for it. A leaflet, shoved through his door in College. He picked it up, along with the assorted takeaway menus and free newspapers on the mat.

'The National Association for the Abolition of Cruelty to Animals' – the headline took his breath away because of the memories it triggered, ricocheting instantly around his head.

He read on, expecting to see her name. University Chairman, wasn't she? It was the standard Fresher's Fair leaflet – most of it was out of date already. A Fresher's Fair drinks party in Second Week to welcome all new members. A training session on how to conduct peaceful demonstrations in Third Week. A talk from Dame Helen Catchpole, 'the well-known animal rights activist'. He had never heard of her. And then he turned it over and on the reverse was a boxed announcement – 'In memory of Sheila Thompson and Vanessa Symonds. Faithful colleagues and friends. They will always be in our hearts.'

For a while he just stared at the leaflet like an idiot. Then, numbed by shock, he took his laptop and searched: 'Vanessa Symonds'. There wasn't a lot. There were a couple of references to an article she had written for the Oxford Gazette on climate change, and there was a quote she had given to the student newspaper about a NAACA demonstration outside the Anglo-American Laboratory for Bio-Chemical Research in January.

Then below that a headline from the end of last term, 20 June, 2019: "Young student found dead under Magdalen Bridge." He read on. "Graduate zoology student, Vanessa Symonds, Brasenose College, was found dead on Friday in the River Cherwell. Inspector Burden, Thames Valley, said that the police were investigating but that the early signs were that this was a tragic accident. Her father, the Rector of St Bartholomew the Great in the City of London, had been informed."

That was it. The life of Vanessa Symonds. It had not made much of a ripple on the internet. He felt at that moment a terrible sense of loss. It was not just the loss to him. He had already discounted that loss from his life. It was the fact that her life, the life of a person who had attracted, captured and overwhelmed him in such a profound way for a while, had apparently just disappeared from the world with so little impact and recognition.

And in the following few hours that he spent staring into the middle distance, caught in a myriad of thoughts, he faced the fact that she was already dead when he had gone down for the summer vacation, determined to forget her; already dead by the time he, Compton and Purser were touring Central Europe, when she was banished from his mind; already dead after he had returned to Oxford, with her intentionally confined to the penumbra of his thoughts. He faced these facts, and he wept for her and not just for himself.

It would have been possible for Roscoe to have left this subject and to have moved on. The collision of the life of Vanessa Symonds with his life had left no visible craters. It had left a profound impact on his memory and he would surely never forget her. But the pain he felt would diminish and leave no discernible scar.

On a grey morning in late November in that Michaelmas term of 2019, he set off to attend a lecture being given in St John's College by Walter Tibelis on the Socratic concept of justice in Ancient Athens. This was of very questionable relevance to the essay he had been asked to complete that week. Roscoe rarely attended lectures. He preferred to sit in the Law Library absorbing the material himself, rather than having it ministered through the priestly tones of a lecturer. But this one interested him.

He was early for the lecture, and as he walked along St Giles, his thoughts turned once more to Pusey House, as occasionally they did. He had not set foot inside it since those few tortured weeks at the beginning of the previous term. Now he sat in the Chapel of Reconciliation and remembered that May morning and the day that followed. The memories now were a familiar scar, occasionally to be rubbed, as a tender patch of skin will sometimes have to be teased and prodded, but without any significant pain.

As he was leaving, he was approached by a very young man, perhaps a couple of years younger than he. He greeted Roscoe with a smile full of innocence and something akin to pure joy. He held a handful of leaflets.

"Good morning sir. Welcome to this house of sacred learning. May I interest you in our programme of music for the Christmas season?" He proffered one of the leaflets.

Roscoe had been discomfited by this new encounter with his memories, and he now felt a frustration which he had experienced before on his rare encounters with organised religion. He did not take the leaflet and just stared.

The young man looked back with unabated joy, the transient malice in Roscoe's eyes in no way returned, indeed it was neutralised.

"May I help you, sir?" he said.

This was not a perfunctory question. It was a question asked with a real desire to hear the answer and to act accordingly.

"Yes, as a matter of fact you can," Roscoe replied. "I have a question, and I expect you have a ready-made answer but I'll ask it anyway. Why does God allow injustice?"

The young man inclined his head slightly and paused before answering. He paused, not because he needed to think of the answer, for that he already knew.

He paused in order to compose the words in which to communicate a small part of the answer.

"Perhaps because the struggle of humanity against injustice is beautiful."

Another pause. Roscoe said nothing. The words were so simple and yet they took him aback. It was a concept that was wholly novel to him.

"Come with me a moment."

The young man led Roscoe back into the Chapel of Reconciliation to a large painting hanging below the Holy Icon. He had noticed it before, although he had not really looked at it.

The young man walked over to the painting and stood within inches of its canvas. He beckoned to Roscoe.

"Come closer. No, closer. Look at the painting close up."

He pointed at the picture until Roscoe's nose was about two inches from the canvas.

"What do you see?"

"I see some brush strokes, roughly the colour of excrement I would say." Roscoe was still angry, but instantly regretted the words. He stepped back and held up his hand. "I'm sorry. I didn't mean to be disrespectful."

The young man's expression had not changed, save that there was the faintest suggestion of pity to temper the benign smile.

"There is no need to be sorry. You are right. If you are merely describing the colour of the paint, then it is the colour of excrement. Now move back, gradually, slowly. Right back."

Roscoe stepped back. He saw that the paint was in fact a brown pigment used to depict an angry bruise on the knee of a young child, perhaps not a year old. The child had hurt himself and had been crying. Now, he rested his crimson cheek on the breast of his mother and slept, wrapped in golden swaddling clothes. He had been comforted by his mother and slept with a look of profound tranquillity on his beautiful features.

His mother, a young woman of twenty years, dressed in robes of gold and blue, held the child gently in her arms, her cheek resting on the top of the baby's head, with a look of pure maternal love on her face. Together, the mother and child projected an image, it seemed to Roscoe even in his moment of cynicism, which proclaimed nothing but peace and loving kindness to all mankind.

"Does it still remind you of excrement?"

Roscoe's voice was unsteady as he spoke.

"No, it's beautiful."

Roscoe stood there for a minute. Nothing was said. Eventually he asked what the painting was.

"Madonna and Child by Giovanni da Sassoferrato. We are very lucky to have it on loan from the National Gallery, especially over the Christmas season."

After a while, the young man came forward and put his hand on Roscoe's shoulder.

"You see, my friend, you have to stand back. You have to see the whole picture. The detail may be painful to us but without the detail you cannot have the beauty, which is the whole."

But Roscoe could not leave Vanessa Symonds alone because, nagging at the back of his mind, was the brutal truth that her death was unlikely to be an accident. Taken by itself, of course, it could have been. Even her death and that of Sheila Thompson, a matter of a couple of months apart, might have been a coincidence. But put those two events together and add the disappearance of Fairford, apparently in violent circumstances, and the probability of a coincidence grew long indeed.

From time to time Roscoe took out the notebook which Vanessa had left in his room. It was a blue, hard-back notebook, about the size of a wallet. The place from which she had torn the page to write her farewell note was still evident from the middle of the book. Her initials were on the inside cover. There were some notes on the first couple of pages, written in a pale red or pink coloured ink.

He recognised, from what she had told him that day in the Eagle and Child, her note of the names on the distribution list of the research paper – at least he assumed these were the names. And she had scribbled the name of Sir John Fawcett. He also recognised a reference to the transference of pathogenic viruses from snakes. But there was nothing much else that was recognisable. There were some names of places perhaps, and some letters and numbers, but they meant nothing to him.

A few days after his visit to Pusey House, Roscoe resolved that he would have to try to find out more. He found the number of Inspector Burden at Thames Valley police station; Burden was the officer who, according to the newspaper report, had investigated her death. Roscoe made an appointment to see him.

Burden's room at the back end of Oxford police station, little more than a cupboard with a desk, chair and filing cabinet, was grey. The paint was grey, and so was the strip lighting across the ceiling. Burden was grey too. His fraying jacket was grey, and his face had gone grey as the enthusiasm for life had been sucked out of it by the job. The only piece of colour in the room was the raspberry jam in a large slice of Victoria sponge which sat on a grey plate, next to a grey and chipped mug of tea.

He looked at Roscoe across the desk with saucer-shaped eyes, heavily hooded, but which sunk in the middle to form grey bags. His look was devoid of either intelligent enquiry or pity. It was a neutrality borne out of total indifference. He was a man at the fag end of a rather undistinguished career who would rather have been somewhere else and made little attempt to hide it.

Burden teased the piece of cake from the plate with grey fingers, and pushed the end of it, at an angle, through the grey slit in the lower half of his face. He removed the end, more with his lips than his teeth and spoke with the amputated piece of cake in his mouth. His articulation of the words served the double purpose of masticating the cake and communicating his thoughts.

He spoke in a near monotone.

"We have to investigate these cases of course. But most of them are a dead end." He coughed, relieving his mouth of several minor pieces of cake. "Forgive the pun, not intended. The fact is that students get drunk. Sometimes they get drunk and fall over. Sometimes they fall over into rivers and sometimes we find them, er, dead." As soon as the word 'dead' had been articulated by the slit, it was replaced by the other side of the cake.

Roscoe was sitting on a hard back chair, directly opposite Burden's desk. Nobody had offered him a cup of tea or a piece of cake.

"She was a friend of mine. I cared for her. I just wanted to make sure that this case has been investigated thoroughly. She deserved that at least."

"I don't know what she deserved, sir. I didn't know her. What we do know is that her blood alcohol level was three times the limit for driving and she had been taking sedatives. We've got the conclusions of the toxicology report. We also know that she had recently split up with her boyfriend and had been suffering from depression."

"Well, how do you know that? Have you spoken to her boyfriend?"

Burden washed down what was left of his mouthful of cake with a swig from the mug, and eased himself from his chair into an upright position. He brushed some crumbs from the front of his jacket and moved towards the door. He considered that the meeting was drawing towards its natural conclusion.

“We’ve seen a summary of a psychiatric report. It was apparently commissioned by her College a few weeks before her death. I’m sorry for your loss sir.” This was uttered with the sympathy exuded by a washing machine at the end of its cycle. “But this is a suicide plain and simple and that’s the end of the matter.”

“But what about her boyfriend? Have you found him? What does he say?”

“I’m sorry sir but I take my orders from my superintendent. The investigation is closed. There’s nothing more that we can do.”

“Who is your superintendent? I’d just like to know a little more about this? Have you spoken to her father, for instance?”

Burden had now opened the door. “I’m sorry sir. There’s nothing more I can help you with. If you want to make a complaint, you’ll find a leaflet on the procedure at the front desk.”

The latest announcement was finished with a little burp, which Burden politely concealed by averting his face to one side.

Roscoe had considered telling Burden a bit more about what he knew of the disappearance of Fairford and the death of Sheila Thompson. Before the interview his inclination was not to do this. What would it achieve? What he knew amounted to little more than speculation. As soon as he saw Burden, and his apparent lack of sympathy or enthusiasm for anything in particular, his inclination was confirmed.

Roscoe told himself that perhaps all this was a coincidence. Perhaps Sheila Thompson had died in a random traffic accident. Perhaps Vanessa had killed herself. After all, what did he really know about her? He had only known her over a couple of days in total, spoken to her for little more than a few hours. How did he even know that what she had told him about Fairford, and the laboratory, was true. In this way, Roscoe was able to place his suspicions and concerns about this affair into suspension, and resume his life at Oxford. *After all, what else was he to do?*

Towards the end of term however, he did make contact with Vanessa's father. He found the email address on the website of the Church. The Rector called him a few days later.

The voice was the typical voice of a cleric, or at least as Roscoe had always imagined it – with something of the pulpit about it. But after his recent experience at Pusey House he was not so dismissive. The Rector had begun to explain why he had become estranged from his daughter and Roscoe could hear a searing pain in the man's voice, despite his attempts to conceal it.

"Vanessa and I had fallen out you see, Mr Roscoe. You know that she was heavily into animal rights. She disapproved of the official position taken by the Church and we had a rather bad argument last Christmas. We had hardly spoken since. You can imagine the terrible shock when I heard the news. Were you a good friend of hers? If I had known, I would have invited you to the funeral."

"I had not known her for long but we became quite close last spring," said Roscoe. "Then I lost contact with her. I didn't hear about her death until quite recently. Can you tell me, did you know her boyfriend, a man called Thomas Fairford? Were you surprised to hear she had become depressed? I didn't see any evidence of that." There was no answer, just a silence full of pain, Roscoe thought. "Is there anything at all, Rector, which troubles you about the way the police handled this?"

"As I said, we had not spoken for the best part of six months." The voice was laboured and faltering. "You will forgive me, Mr Roscoe, but grief is a very unpredictable emotion. It affects people in very different ways. I felt a terrible guilt for a while because I had made no attempt to contact her for some time, when perhaps she needed me most. You know her mother passed away when she was fourteen, and it is I who should have been available to provide that sort of pastoral – parental, paternal – care. My grief and my guilt after her death drove me to concentrate on my work as a priest to the exclusion of anything else."

There was a pause, and Roscoe sensed the Rector was struggling to control his voice.

"But now you have raised it, yes, there was something which I did find rather odd, and under any other circumstances I would have followed it up more than I did. I received a copy of a police report into the incident. It summarised the conclusions of the psychiatrist, and also the – what do they call it? – toxicologist. I wanted to speak to the psychiatrist to get some sort of insight into what drove her to do this. When I called him – his name was Dr Emile Zeitmann, I think it was, in Harley Street – he simply refused to cooperate.

"First he claimed that he couldn't remember the case, and then when I told him I had a copy of the police report, he said that he would have to locate the file. Then he hung up. Since then he's been impossible to contact. I was in London for a meeting of the General Synod last month, and I took the opportunity to attend the address of his practice. I was brushed off completely in a manner I considered to be most unprofessional. His secretary claimed that he was sick, and would be unable to assist any further with the case."

Chapter Six

On the Saturday morning after Roscoe had spoken to the Reverend John Symonds of St Bartholomew the Great in the City of London, a freight tanker sailed from the Japanese port of Nagasaki on the East China Sea. It was 0720 on 7 December 2019. At 1443 the tanker docked into the Chinese port of Shanghai. Shortly after 1900 hours on the same day, an articulated lorry emerged from the freight tanker's holding area and joined a queue for inspection by the Chinese port authorities.

The driver, a man with Caucasian features calling himself Catesby, and with impeccable manners, presented his papers to the Chinese official when his turn arrived. The official, after examining the papers through spectacles, and then a magnifying glass, snorted his approval, and waved the lorry through into an examination bay.

The driver, dressed in blue overalls, emerged from the cabin. He undid the back of the lorry and watched as the Chinese customs officials entered the trailer and inspected the contents. Then, after a further fifty-five minutes of the People's Bureaucracy, the articulated lorry entered the People's Republic of China.

The lorry made slow progress through the congested centre of the city of Shanghai and then through the western suburbs, along the sprawling mass that is the Yan'an Elevated Road and the Huyu Expressway, past the great Lake Taihu, and onto the Xuanguang Expressway into the Chinese hinterland.

On the outskirts of the city of Tongling, the driver pulled the lorry into a siding. It was shortly after midnight. From the glove box he removed a phone and made an encrypted call to a location over 6,000 kilometres away via a satellite. He spoke in a language which would have been incomprehensible to most people called Catesby. A rough translation would be this.

"All is on track and on schedule. The barrels are loaded. Repeat, the barrels are loaded. Out."

The man calling himself Catesby then allowed himself a couple of hours sleep before setting off onto the Wuda Expressway heading west. At around 0415, he passed the metropolis of Anqing in the Yangtzee Valley, onto the Huanghuang Expressway, and at around 0600 passed the sprawling suburbs of Huangshi. From there the metropolis merged into that of the concentrated mass that is the city of Wuhan into which he arrived shortly after 0730 on 8 December 2019.

The lorry approached the east bank of the Yangtzee river along congested streets teeming with belching vehicles. There were people everywhere, hurrying to and from the markets, scurrying alongside the freight trucks, behind and in front of the vehicles, clutching their shopping baskets and their children. On either side of the road the congested streets were further narrowed by the impressment of street stalls, encroaching on to the thoroughfares heaving with fish and meat and dry goods and wet.

The lorry inched its way through the crowds towards Loading Bay C in the wholesale food market in the district of Wuchang, just east of the river. Catesby backed up the lorry to the bay, the trailer buffeted by the mass of people descending on the market for the morning catch and deliveries. He jumped out of the cab and produced his papers to the man with a clipboard standing by the gate. Two other men in red overalls approached and opened the curtain side of the trailer.

The trailer was stacked with five large, white, plastic boxes, each studded at the top and the sides with air holes. The men unloaded the pallets whilst Catesby signed the papers. He then climbed back into the cab. The curtain was re-attached.

The men in red overalls opened one of the boxes. Inside were two large snakes, with the girth of a man's arm, thick black scales and white underbellies, curled around each other. The sound they emitted, somewhere between a hiss and a chirp, mingled with the sliding sound of their bellies as they slithered around in an obscene spiral.

The men, satisfied as to the load, acknowledged Catesby by raising their hands to their foreheads in a salute. Catesby returned the compliment, uttered a remark in his basic Mandarin and then began to inch his lorry, now divested of its load, back into the sprawling mass of Wuhan.

The men, with the use of a large trolley cart, transported the boxes, one by one, from the loading bay to the middle of the market, where the contents were deposited. In total, nine Japanese keelback snakes, restless from their long journey in confined quarters, writhed around the huge open topped vat.

The atmosphere in this part of the market was viscous with the sound and smells of wildlife. Piglets snuffled the ground with their snouts in a cage. Civet cats prowled a pen lined with straw and eyed the snakes warily, unsure of their status as predators or prey. In the same area of the market, a butcher's counter was redolent with the sound and smell of the abattoir, slabs of red meat of indeterminate origin lined the shop front, glistening and reeking under the eyes and noses of the people of Wuhan.

The man calling himself Catesby pulled over on the outskirts of the city, and reached for his encrypted phone. He made a call to the same location as before, at a distance of over 6,000 kilometres. One point six seconds later the phone rang on a desk, set in a small room, lit by a green desk lamp. A man lay slumped on the desk, his head resting on his right arm. The sound of the phone woke him with a start. He looked at his watch. Ten past five in the morning. It was still dark outside. He answered the phone and said, "Stand by please."

He stood up and turned to a mirror hung on the wall to his right. He adjusted his collar and tie and checked his shirt cuffs. He took a comb from the top pocket of his jacket and tidied the fringe of his hair. He picked up the phone, opened the door to the room and proceeded along a corridor. No sound came from his steps on the thickly carpeted floor. At the end of the corridor was a door. Outside the door stood a guard. As he approached the door, the guard pressed a button to the side. After ten seconds or so, a light to the side of the door turned green.

"You may enter," said the guard.

The man entered the room. The room was lit by a bedside light. In the bed lay the Director. He wore blue pyjamas and had propped himself up against some pillows.

He took the phone from the man and said, "This is the Director."

He listened and his face, still creased from his sleeping position, broadened into a grin.

"Excellent. The gunpowder is lit. Well done Mr, er, Catesby." He chuckled to himself and handed the phone back to the man who proceeded to leave the room. The Director switched out the bedside light and went back to sleep.

On 31 December 2019, the Wuhan Municipal Health Commission reported to the World Health Organisation that a cluster of cases of pneumonia had resulted in the identification of a novel coronavirus. On 12 January 2020, the Peoples' Republic of China published the genetic sequence of the virus. The short term genetic nomenclature was Acl19266*int*6+red31[*sus*B77]. On 14 January 2020, the World Health Organisation reported some limited human to human transmission of the virus and that there was a risk of a wider outbreak.

By 17 January 2020, three cases of the virus had been discovered outside China; two in Thailand and one in Japan. On 30 January 2020, the Director-General of the World Health Organisation declared the outbreak a Public Health Emergency of International Concern. On 11 March 2020, concerned by the alarming levels of spread and severity, the World Health Organisation characterised the outbreak of the virus as a worldwide pandemic. The most probable source of the virus was identified as an indeterminate population of snakes in a wet market in the district of Wuchang in the city of Wuhan. It was designated 'Serpensvid 19' from *serpens,* the latin for snake. By then the popular press in the United Kingdom had characterised the virus as snake flu.

Chapter Seven

Daniel Roscoe, determined to exorcise the memory of Vanessa Symonds, spent most of his time during that Hilary Term of 2020 in the Stallybrass Law Library, at the far end of Old Quad in Brasenose College, Oxford. On Fridays he would allow himself a night out with Bill Compton. They would sit in the Lamb and Flag, or sometimes the Wheatsheaf, talking more often than not about the Six Nations. Bill had suggested early that term that the Eagle and Child served a decent pint and it might be worth a visit. Roscoe declined but would not give a reason when pressed to do so.

Their conversation would occasionally veer into politics but it was biased towards *party* politics. They debated the result of the general election back in December and Brexit but their conversation did not extend to the insidious pandemic which leered and spread like a creeping shadow across the face of the globe. It had not registered in their consciousness. To them, and to most of the people in the UK, it still seemed distant, innocuous and irrelevant, until it was too late.

After the excesses of Friday night, Roscoe would conclude the weekend by having Saturday dinner in Hall. He would then wander along to the Junior Common Room for movie night, usually something a little cultish. Tonight it was a film someone had unearthed in the video shop near the railway station. Roscoe slumped into a stuffed armchair at the back of the TV room to wait for the film, and picked up a copy of one of the tabloids. 'Boris's Battle Plan for Snake Flu Pandemic', screamed the headline.

His eyes lazily scanned the page, without taking it in particularly and then the lights were turned off. He remembered seeing the film years before with his father, late one Saturday night in a horror double bill on BBC 2. A young man, traumatised in childhood, becomes obsessed with filming the reactions of people experiencing fear. His obsession grows, and he begins to *induce* the fear in his subjects, fascinated with filming their creeping sense of panic, an act which ultimately climaxes in their death at his hands. For reasons of which he was not conscious, after twenty minutes or so, Roscoe's attention returned from the film to the newspaper. He retrieved it from the window sill and took it out into the sitting room where the light was better.

He stood under the light and read. "Britons could be forced to put their lives on hold for three months under 'battle plan' for snake flu that would see troops on the streets, police ignoring minor crime and patients turfed out of hospitals amid warnings that one in five workers could go sick."

His thoughts immediately turned to the paper Vanessa had taken from the Anglo-American Laboratory for Bio-Chemical Research. He dropped the newspaper, hurried along the corridor to the law library and turned on one of the computers. He searched for snake flu. He read about the early days of the outbreak in January and realised that, although he must have been aware at some level of these stories, they had not registered in his conscious mind; so ready had he been to isolate himself from the rest of the world that term.

He read that a professor of public health at Cambridge University had predicted in 2017 that a virus might jump species from an animal in China, and spread quickly to become a human pandemic. It had since been hypothesised that the virus had originated in the wet markets in Wuhan in an animal, most probably a snake, and had spread to a human, perhaps via another mammal such as a pig. In the more sensational tabloid press, there was even speculation that the virus had been created by the Chinese as a biological weapon to sabotage the economy of the United States.

Roscoe read that the 'battle plan' referred to in the newspaper was speculation about the government's plans for a lockdown, and that international efforts were being coordinated to find a vaccine, not least at Oxford University. He read that the genome of the virus had been identified. And then he read, towards the more academic end of his research, this: Acl19266*int*6+red31[*sus*B77]. It was the short term genetic designation of the virus. The letters and numbers swam before his eyes. He was tired. He had had a couple of beers whilst watching the movie. But this symbol, if that is what is was, arrested his attention like a beacon because he had seen something like it in the notebook left by Vanessa Symonds in his room.

He took a piece of paper, found a pen, and scribbled down the symbol. He simulated the italics by slanting his hand to the right. He shut down the search engine, turned off the computer and made his way back to his room in Old Quad.

Where had he left the notebook? He opened the drawer of his desk. He had shoved it under a pile of bills, correspondence and assorted papers. He thumbed through the pages, and there it was – on the second page – Acl19266int6+red31[susB77]. It was the same as the note he had made, save that she had underlined the letters which were italicised.

Roscoe took a deep breath and sat down. How could it be that the unique genetic designation, or nomenclature, of a virus, first identified by anyone in the world in January 2020, appeared in a note made by Vanessa Symonds in the spring of 2019? One thing seemed to be clear. The virus could not have originated in a wet market in Wuhan; at least not in December 2019. Roscoe swallowed hard as he began to appreciate the implications of the notebook. What was it that she had told him about the paper she had taken from the lab? Something to do with the transference of viruses from snakes. But the paper wasn't just a discussion of a theory. The paper contained the genetic code of the virus which was the cause of the pandemic.

Roscoe's heart began to pound, and the sweat prickled on his forehead. He realised that the business of the Anglo-American Laboratory for Bio-Chemical Research was not to prevent the spread of such a virus, but the exact opposite – its creation and propagation. He was in possession of information which was, to say the least, explosive. But how could he prove it? Vanessa was dead. Thompson was dead. Fairford had vanished – probably dead too. He flicked through the few pages of the notebook which had any content. The names of the people on the circulation list were on the first page. Wait – there was another name. Of course, Sir John Fawcett – the Member of Parliament Sheila Thompson had called when Vanessa had first shown her the paper.

There was quite a lot about Fawcett on Wikipedia. His background would not have marked him out as a socialist. He was born into a wealthy family in 1965. His mother was the daughter of a former US ambassador. She had married into a minor branch of the English aristocracy. His father was a first cousin of the Earl of Chelmsford. He was educated at Winchester, then Balliol College Oxford in the mid-1980s where he became President of the Oxford Union and Chairman of the Labour Club. After Oxford he had proceeded to study international politics at Harvard, participating in an academic exchange with the Moscow State Institute of International Relations. He went on to serve as an intern in Bill Clinton's campaign for the Presidency in 1992. Returning to the UK in 1993, he became active in the Labour Party. After the death of John Smith in 1994, he attached himself to Tony Blair and worked as a volunteer in Blair's campaign to become leader.

After Blair succeeded Smith as leader of the Labour Party, Fawcett's rise was meteoric. He became an advisor to Blair on US affairs, and Bill Clinton in particular, playing an important role in forging a strong personal bond between the two whilst Blair was still in opposition. In 1996, he was awarded the safe seat of Canonbury and Islington in North London upon the retirement of the sitting MP and was returned with a majority of 32,543 in the 1997 general election. In 1998, Blair had made him a Parliamentary Private Secretary in the Treasury, and in the first major re-shuffle two years later, he was promoted to Financial Secretary to the Treasury. After Blair was returned to power in 2001, Fawcett was made Minister of State in the Foreign Office, with special responsibility for US and North American affairs.

Then, in the build up to the Iraq War in 2003, Fawcett's career took a different turn. He became increasingly critical of US foreign policy in the Middle East. At first his opposition was voiced in coded terms whilst still keeping within the official government line. However, when the decision was made to go to war, Fawcett broke publicly with Blair and resigned. He became increasingly vocal in his criticism and with the occasional appearance on Question Time and the Sunday breakfast shows, he developed a public profile of dissent towards the mainstream New Labour position on the United States. This made him the darling of the hard left, and a confidant of many of the radical leftist protest groups; one of which was the National Association for the Abolition of Cruelty to Animals.

With age, a bout of ill health, and the election of the Conservative-Liberal coalition government in 2010, Fawcett became less vocal. Like many on the hard left, he appeared to be motivated more by an antipathy towards those on the right of his own party, than towards those on the other side of the House. He knuckled down to the duties of a constituency MP, and during the coalition government appeared to become a fairly unremarkable, time-serving back-bencher. After the election of a majority Conservative government in 2015, he put himself forward for the Parliamentary Joint Intelligence Committee, and to the surprise of many received the approval, not just of the Labour leadership, but also of the government. Since then he had become something of an elder statesman in the public imagination.

Roscoe called Fawcett's parliamentary office the next morning, without much expectation of making any progress on a Sunday. To his surprise, a receptionist answered.

"I'd like to speak to Sir John Fawcett please."

"His next constituency surgery is on Saturday, sir. Shall I make an appointment for you?" She sounded as if she were reading from a cue card.

"No, I'm not one of his constituents. I need to speak to him about something else. It's important."

"He's a busy man sir, as you can imagine. Can I ask what it's about?"

"Can you just tell him that it's about Sheila Thompson."

"Sheila Thom… Is that with a 'p'?"

"Yes. Tell him it's urgent."

"I'll leave a message with him sir, but as I said, he's a busy man. Can I suggest you send an email? The address is on the website."

This was spoken in the sing song style of somebody repeating the same mantra dozens of times a day. Roscoe had little confidence that the message would get through. He wrote an email, simply saying that it was to do with Sheila Thompson. He made no mention of her death and no mention of the research paper, or the individuals named upon it.

Roscoe had little appetite for work that day. He found himself looking at his phone every few minutes. It was shortly after lunch that his phone began to vibrate in his pocket. It was an unknown number, a call he would not usually take. He took this one.

"Hello. Is that Mr Roscoe? John Fawcett here. I've just seen your email. We need to talk. Not over the phone. Can you meet me at my Parliamentary office in Westminster? Shall we say five o'clock tomorrow afternoon?"

He sounded abrupt and authoritative but at the same time there was an urgency in his voice which was a little unsettling. Roscoe was taken aback. He hadn't expected to hear from Fawcett in person so quickly.

"Yes. I think I can manage that."

"I will email you the details of where to go. I will meet you. Do not tell anyone else about the meeting. Understood?" The last words were spoken slowly, deliberately and with an emphasis calculated to impress.

"OK."

Fawcett hung up.

Chapter Eight

Monday had dawned damp and overcast, befitting his mood, and had continued in the same vein for the rest of the day. Roscoe moved through the drizzle, the collar of his raincoat turned up, as he walked past Worcester College and along Park End Street towards the railway station. He was already soaked. He had noticed, really for the first time, that a number of people on the streets, maybe as many as one in ten, were wearing face masks; either of the surgical variety, or by way of a cloth wrapped around their mouths and noses.

For most of the previous day, Roscoe had immersed himself in the news about the pandemic on the internet and on the radio and television. He had to catch up with what he had missed. It seemed as if, along with much of the country, he had been sleep-walking for the last three months and had finally woken up. Now, there was a growing panic about the spread of the virus, and increasing speculation that the government was about to announce a national lockdown.

He glanced at his watch. He could catch the 1340 to London. That would get him into Paddington not long after two thirty. He wanted to leave himself plenty of time before the meeting with Fawcett to check out Dr Emile Zeitmann, the psychiatrist mentioned in the police report into Vanessa's death. He remembered what the Rector had said about how difficult it had been to get hold of Zeitmann. What was that all about? It was the opinion of Zeitmann which had led the police to the conclusion of suicide. There was no doubt that Zeitmann existed. He had a website and he apparently had a practice in Harley Street. Roscoe intended to pay it a visit on his way to Westminster.

He was comfortably in time to get the 1340. He usually enjoyed the commute by train back and forth to his home town; Oxford to Paddington, then Victoria to Crawley. He would sit back, relax into the anonymity of the traveller, and read a book. Now the atmosphere was subtly different. Everyone eyed each other with suspicion and there were invisible barriers constructed by each individual or family unit to keep out the infection. He went to sit down in a group of six seats but was met with such hostile looks from the couple by the window, that he looked elsewhere. He found a twin seat, facing backwards.

Roscoe's nerves had got the better of him, and for the first ten minutes he just shut his eyes and tried to breathe steadily. If what Vanessa had told him was right, at least Fawcett knew something about the research paper. But what had happened to the paper? The original, it seemed, no longer existed. Sheila Thompson had destroyed it. Had she sent the scanned copy to Fawcett? The crucial question was who else apart from him, Roscoe, knew that the paper – which could not have been written any later than the beginning of April last year – contained the genetic notation for snake flu? That was the dynamite which he and, to his knowledge, he alone was holding.

The train pulled into the station at High Wycombe. And as he thought the problem through, his fingers played with the spine of the notebook in the pocket of his raincoat. He looked at it again. The notebook was not new. On the inside cover it said 'Oxford University Press 2016'. But that was no clue as to when Vanessa had made the notes. She had dated her notes at the top of each page – April 2019 – a precision which was a product no doubt of her scientific background. But that was no guarantee that the genetic code had not been noted down at a later time. Could the ink be dated? He very much doubted it. No, the only proof he had that the virus existed, eight months before it was first detected as a novel coronavirus in Wuhan, was locked in his memories.

He alighted from the train at platform three at Paddington. The station was much quieter than usual, more like a Sunday than the beginning of the afternoon rush hour. He had decided whilst still on the train that he was not going to take the notebook into the meeting with Fawcett. It was too valuable a commodity. He rented a secure locker at the left luggage office and left the notebook inside. He came out onto Praed Street and consulted his phone. It was a ten minute walk to Harley Street, and Dr Zeitmann's practice address. The rain was more steady now, soaking the bottoms of his jeans and dripping down his neck. He made his way along the Marylebone Road and then right into Harley Street. It was about a third of the way down on the right, that a red brick, Georgian terrace house stood that should, according to the website, be the premises of the practice of Dr Emile Zeitmann, FRCPsych.

Roscoe approached the street door. There were three brass plaques – each roughly six inches by four – to the side of the entrance, bearing the names of the practitioners within: Thomas Megantik MRCPsych, Shafak Rahman MClinPsychol, and Sarah Golding MFDS. Above all three names it was apparent that there had once been a fourth plaque. A rectangular shape of differently shaded plaster, having been shielded from the sun – roughly six inches by four – appeared where the fourth plaque had once been fixed. The raw plugs for the screws which had held it in place, were still there.

Roscoe peered through the window. It looked like there was a reception desk. He pushed on the door and it opened. Behind the desk was a small, elderly lady who looked up from her book with a smile.

"Hello. Can I help you?"

Roscoe shook his coat, and dripped onto the mat. "Yes, I was wondering, is this where Dr Emile Zeitmann is? Is this his practice?"

The smile of the old lady dropped, and her face assumed a careworn expression at the mention of the name of Zeitmann.

"Well." She put down her book. "It used to be. He hasn't been here now since, well around, last summer I would say."

"Do you know where he is?"

"I have no idea, I'm afraid. It was all a bit sudden in the end. And it was such a shame. He *was* a lovely man – that's before he had his troubles of course, and so were Tom, and that nice Mr Shafak. Now it's just me and Dr Golding."

"Sarah Golding?" Roscoe indicated backwards to the plaques.

"That's right. Dr Golding's a dental surgeon and the others were psychiatrists; partners, you see. They've all gone now."

"What happened? Can you tell me?"

"Well, I'm only the receptionist you see, sir. But it started with Dr Zeitmann's drinking. Then, from what I heard, they got into trouble with money and paying the rent, and then the next thing I know is that they've all moved out. They occupied this floor and the first floor and Dr Golding's down in the basement. Their rooms were all cleared out over a weekend. Well, that must have been about September, October time I would say. I don't know much more than that, to be honest with you."

"Was Dr Golding their partner?"

"No, but she shared the lease. So I understand anyway."

"Is Dr Golding here now?"

“She should be in around now, yes.” She glanced at the clock on the wall – it was just before three o’clock – and then she consulted a register. “Dr Golding has an appointment at three twenty.”

Roscoe walked down the steps from the pavement to the basement. He knocked on the door. A young woman opened it.

“Dr Golding?”

“No, I’m her assistant. This is Dr Golding.” She indicated to a middle aged woman in a white coat who was preparing some apparatus by a dentist’s chair.

Roscoe took a step inside. “Do you have a few minutes Dr Golding. I wanted to ask you about Emile Zeitmann.”

“Not you too. I thought we had finally seen the back of all that. What do you want to know?”

“Around the summer of last year he wrote a report about a friend of mine. She was found dead in the River Cherwell in Oxford a few days later. I understand that the report concluded that she was depressed. I know that her father has been chasing Dr Zeitmann to find out more about what happened but Zeitmann was apparently very elusive and then went missing. I just want to try and find out the truth of what happened to her. She meant something to me.”

Golding looked into his eyes for a second or two. “Yes, I can see that she did.” She looked to her assistant. “Jenny, will you leave us for a few minutes? I won’t be long.” The assistant went into a room at the back.

Dr Golding looked at her watch. “Look, I’d like to help, as far as I can, but I don’t have long. I have an appointment in fifteen minutes. Sit down for a moment.” There were two chairs by her desk.

“Zeitmann, he was a good man. His son died of cancer, er, two years ago now. Something like that. It knocked him for six. He began to drink. Then when his wife left him he took to the bottle in a fairly major way, I understand. He began to gamble. Got into debt, and then around Christmas – when was it – November 2018, I think it must have been – there was a big scandal. It turned out he had been helping himself to the funds of the business. The other partners called in the police. The regulators were involved. The practice was nearly closed. But they were allowed to continue for a few months until Zeitmann’s alcoholism and his gambling simply engulfed them. Then they were shut down.” She looked up. “The premises are still empty.”

“I see that Zeitmann’s name plate has been removed from the wall but the names of the other partners are still up there. Do you know why that is?”

She shook her head. “Nothing to do with me.”

“And what happened to Zeitmann? Do you know?”

“Oh yes. I heard from his ex-wife. He killed himself last summer. He was found by the police hanging from the ceiling by the light cable. Shocking business, yes?”

By the time he had emerged into the street, the drizzle had stopped, and the sun was glimpsing through the clouds. What time was it? Still only three fifteen. He decided to walk and clear his head. There was a definite direction of travel in all of this, and he didn’t like it a bit. Anyone who had had any connection, direct or indirect, with the research paper from the lab appeared to have ended up dead, or had at least disappeared.

An investigation into the death of Vanessa Symonds had concluded that it was suicide. That in itself was a questionable coincidence. But now it seemed that the credibility of the psychiatrist whose report was the very basis of that conclusion was completely undermined. Had Zeitmann been pressurised, or even blackmailed, into writing the report? If so, did that mean that the police were somehow compromised as well?

He stopped and stood still for a few moments. The implications of all of this were hard to contemplate. Could it be his imagination was just getting the better of him? He walked on down Portland Place and into Regents Street. By the time he got to St James’s Park it was still before four o’clock. He sat on a bench and contemplated the imminent meeting with Sir John Fawcett. The only people who, to his knowledge, knew about the circumstances in which the research paper had been taken were himself, Vanessa, Fairford, Sheila Thompson and Sir John Fawcett. *Could he trust Fawcett?* At least he appeared to be on the same side from what he had read about him. He resolved though to be careful, and to try to find out what Fawcett knew first.

Sir John Fawcett reclined in a captain’s chair behind a large partner’s desk, with a red leather top and contemplated Roscoe, his hands clasped under his chin, his index fingers forming an inquisitive point underneath. His feet were propped up on a foot stool beside the desk. He was a distinguished looking man, in his mid-fifties, with an officer's moustache, hair greying at the temples and a voice clipped by the establishment he feigned to despise. He wore a grey, pin-striped, Savile Row suit. The sun now shone through a window which looked out onto the Palace of Westminster and glittered on the gold tie pin, set with a single ruby, which he wore on his Old Wykehamist tie.

"Would you like a cup of tea?" Fawcett pressed a switch. "A pot of tea, Ms Driver, please."

He penetrated Roscoe with his gaze, a faint smile playing around his mouth. "Well, what do you know about Sheila Thompson?"

"Can I ask what you know about Sheila Thompson? You wouldn't have asked me here if she wasn't pretty important." Roscoe felt uncomfortable. This man exuded an air of authority which seemed to defy any challenge.

Fawcett took his feet off the foot stool and re-arranged his elbows on the desk.

"Sheila was an old friend of mine. We got to know each other when I was a junior minister in the Treasury in the late nineties – before you were born, I suspect, Mr Roscoe. Her death was a considerable shock. When I knew that you had something to say about her, I was naturally curious. What is it that you wish to say, exactly?"

Roscoe was encouraged. Vanessa's account was true so far. He had to go a step further. "Do you think there was anything suspicious about her death?"

"What do you mean, suspicious. It was a road accident – a hit and run."

"We both know that she told you about a research paper which had been stolen from the Anglo-American Laboratory on Bio-Chemical Research. She asked you to look into the distribution list."

Fawcett's face darkened. He sat up. "How do you know about that?"

Roscoe began to sweat. He realised that his voice was trembling as he spoke. "A friend of mine told me. It was she who took the paper. I believe that she was killed and that there is a cover up to portray her death as suicide. I came to you because I can't think who else to turn to. I hope and pray that you are on the same side."

Fawcett leant forward on the desk, his eyes narrowing.

There was a knock on the door, and it was opened without reply. "Tea, Sir John. Shall I serve?"

"No, just leave it on the desk please. Thanks."

He waited until the door had shut, and sat back again. His face relaxed.

"I was working with Sheila Thompson on animal rights issues when you were still in nappies. Yes, you may rest assured that we are on the same side. What do you know about the research paper?"

Roscoe paused. He returned Fawcett's gaze. The smile had returned but it was a smile which was confined to the mouth. The rest of the face remained unamused, suspicious, even hostile. There was something in this man's eyes which he didn't like and his instinct was to hold back.

"My friend believed that work was going at the lab on behalf of the US government. I believe that the paper proved that, and that is why she took it to Sheila Thompson."

"What is the name of your friend?"

Roscoe hesitated, but what harm could it do – she was dead, and everything Fawcett had said so far corroborated her story. He must be on side.

"She was called Vanessa Symonds, a postgraduate at Brasenose."

"Did she tell you what the paper contained?"

"No, just that it was a research paper produced by the lab and that the distribution list would prove that the lab was controlled by the American government. She hoped that if they could prove that, then there would be overwhelming pressure from the public to close it down."

Fawcett relaxed, although the tension in his eyes remained. "Let's have some tea." He stood and poured from a silver pot. "Milk, sugar?"

Roscoe took his tea and Fawcett returned behind the desk. "Your friend was right of course. The distribution list confirmed it. It included key figures in the Pentagon and the CIA."

"Why haven't you done anything about it? This was nearly a year ago?"

"Listen. These things take time. If you run to the press with something like this, it could blow up in your face. Things move behind the scenes. I passed on the information to the relevant people but I have not been privy to every development since. I understand that you are concerned about your friend. I have contacts, as you can imagine. I will see what else I can find out and I will be in touch. I have your number. But you must understand that there is nothing you can do and you are involved in things which are way above your head. Look, if I promise to meet you again, let's say this time next week, will you give me your word that you will mention this to no one, not a soul?"

Roscoe felt he had little choice but to agree. *What else could he do?*

A slight figure in an over-sized raincoat, Daniel Roscoe left the building of the Parliamentary offices and looked up at the face of Big Ben. It was six forty. He turned left towards Westminster tube station. A larger male stood by the cigarette kiosk, examining a copy of the Standard. As soon as Roscoe had passed he looked up, his eyes following the raincoat through thick, black framed spectacles. He shoved the paper into a waste bin and followed. He watched as Roscoe stood at the ticket machine and then, keeping a distance of several metres, he joined the escalator descending to the Circle Line. Momentarily losing sight of Roscoe, he shoved the occasional smaller pedestrian to the side with his elbows in order to speed his progress. Then, on reaching the platform for the westbound service via Paddington, he saw Roscoe waiting, his hands in his pockets, for the next train.

The male looked up to the indicator. The next train was due in two minutes. With his eyes fixed on the space between Roscoe's shoulders, the male inched his way along the wall until he was directly in line with Roscoe and the edge of the platform. He waited until he could hear the approach of the train, licked his lips, and then moved forwards, his eyes never leaving a point just below the middle of Roscoe's shoulder blades.

The hot air began to billow in from the tunnel. The approaching whine of the train grew more urgent, until it reached the crescendo of a piercing scream, and the man advanced upon his target, when a young woman, pushing a pram, passed between him and Roscoe's back. The male cursed and stepped back just as the train screeched into view.

The train drew to a halt at the platform and Roscoe boarded, followed by the young woman with the pram. The large male got into the same carriage. It was emptier than usual but still standing-room only. The male stood by the door, leaning against the partition furthest from Roscoe. Roscoe stood in the aisle, holding on to one of the overhead straps. Roscoe faced towards the front of the train. The male faced in the same direction. This time his eyes were fixed on a point just below Roscoe's left shoulder. In his pocket his fingers caressed the handle of a knife; his thumb working its way along the thick end of a steel blade, three inches in length.

The train stopped at St James's Park. One person got on. The male moved to the other side of the doors, closest to Roscoe. This time he did not slouch against the partition. He held on to the handle with his left hand and in his right he continued to finger the knife, all the while his eyes fixed on Roscoe's shoulder blade.

The train pulled into Victoria and a dozen people boarded from the main line railway station. The male took the opportunity to make room, by moving along the aisle towards Roscoe. Now four people stood between him and Roscoe. At each station he inched closer by pressing into his obstacles, each person in turn making way for him, fearful of infection.

As the train arrived into Paddington, the male was directly behind Roscoe and slightly to his left. He removed the knife from his pocket and with a grunt he plunged it towards Roscoe's heart. At the same moment, Roscoe let go of the strap in order to disembark and the full force of the blade went into the anterior muscle of his left arm. He screamed, turned, saw the murderous eyes and forced his way, with the disembarking stream of people, off the train onto the platform. His eyes swimming with the searing pain in his left arm, he looked around as the train pulled off, but could see no sign of his assailant.

He looked down. His left arm hung limp at his side and blood dripped from his sleeve.

An old lady had turned to look at him. "Are you alright, dear?"

Roscoe ignored her with a polite smile and a nod, and turned in the other direction. He shuffled to the exit at the end of the platform and made his way slowly up a flight of stairs and then towards the gates leading to the mainline station. He winced as he grasped his arm, attempting to stem the flow of blood. He had to get to the left luggage office. He had to retrieve the notebook. The railway station was emptier than usual and keeping himself to the perimeter of the concourse, he was able to avoid the attention of all but a handful of commuters.

He sat on a bench towards the far end of the concourse, behind a burger bar, within the shadow of the left luggage office and caught his breath. He was out of sight here, away from view, unless somebody came deliberately looking for him. He managed to ease the left sleeve of his raincoat from his arm. With his right hand he took a handkerchief from his pocket and with his teeth he was able to fashion a crude bandage around the wound. It hurt like hell. He had to think. *What was he going to do?* Either what had happened was an extraordinary coincidence or perhaps even Fawcett, contrary to what he had said, was not on the same side. The idea of going to the police was not an attractive one, given what he had found out about Zeitmann, and the credibility of the police report; nor did he want to risk dragging his parents into this awful mess.

Suspicious of anybody within the immediate vicinity and holding his left arm to disguise his wound, he recovered the notebook from the left luggage office. He needed to find somewhere to clean himself up a bit and recover. There were some cheap places just over the other side of Praed Street. He withdrew a hundred pounds in cash before leaving the station. He would find himself a room for the night with access to a bath, or at least a wash basin, where they wouldn't ask too many questions of somebody bleeding from a stab wound.

Feeling increasingly weak, and in a state of shock, he eventually settled on a grubby looking place nearby, just off Sussex Gardens. In his state, there wasn't a great deal of choice. The door was ajar, revealing a threadbare carpet, slung along the length of a dismal passage. A single bare light bulb hung from a cable in the middle of the corridor, serving merely to emphasise the gloom of the encroaching dusk. Behind the counter, at the end of the passage, sat a woman, a cigarette dangling from her mouth.

"What can I do for you?"

Roscoe stepped through the door, the air thick with cigarette smoke, and cheap perfume, and approached the counter. "A room and a bath – just for tonight please."

Her eyes, heavily painted with mascara, were drawn to his left arm. He looked down. There was a patch of blood on his sleeve which had seeped through his handkerchief, and she must have seen how awkwardly he was holding his arm. "Been in the wars, haven't you? We don't want no trouble. This is a respectable place."

"No trouble. I promise. I've cut myself. How much for the night?"

The woman hesitated, her eyes examining his face, and his upper body, calculating the balance of power.

"Seventy, in advance." She had doubled the price.

He handed over three twenties and a ten. She examined the notes, put them in her pocket, and gave him a key which she had retrieved from behind the counter.

"First floor, second on the right. Bathroom on the top floor."

"Have you got anything to drink?"

She ferreted under the counter and produced a half bottle of vodka. "That's another ten." He handed it over, took the bottle and the key, and went upstairs.

The room was tiny. A bed, a wardrobe, and an evil smell of body odour and foul linen. He gingerly removed his coat and shirt and examined the wound. It didn't look good but the flow of blood was beginning to slow and congeal. At least it didn't look like it had hit anything vital.

He sat on the bed. It sagged in the middle with the sound of decrepit springs, and gave off a ripe odour, the accumulated filth of several former occupants. He unfolded the handkerchief to find a clean patch and soaked it with some of the vodka. After some considerable hesitation, he padded the wound with the handkerchief and yelped with the searing pain. He then tied the handkerchief again, as best he could, around the wound. He took a swig from the bottle and retched at the taste of raw alcohol. It was most certainly not the finest of vodkas but at least it was calming his nerves and dulling the pain. He took a few more generous swigs, and using his raincoat as a pillow and trying to keep his nose and mouth as far away from the bedclothes as he could, he drifted into a kind of sleep, troubled and fitful.

He awoke several times during the night in a cold sweat, reliving the moment when he was stabbed and unable to erase the image of the bloodshot eyes of his assailant, leering at him through thick, black spectacles.

Roscoe awoke, for the last time, shortly before five thirty. The night, far from resting him, had soiled him, both in mind and body. His heart was pounding in his ears, as he tried to work out what to do. His arm ached like hell. He found the bathroom on the top floor. It was in keeping with the rest of the establishment and he was reluctant to lower himself into the bathtub. The water was cold but at least it was clean and he was able to wash himself down with his hands. He used the reverse of his handkerchief, and what remained of the vodka, to clean and bind his wound. It had stopped bleeding for the time being.

He consulted his phone – only ten percent of the battery left. It looked like the lockdown was on. The prime minister had announced it the previous evening, at around the same time that Roscoe had been stabbed.

"Stay home. Protect the NHS. Save Lives."

As Roscoe left the boarding house at around seven o'clock that morning, the landlady gave him a look of pure malice. But at least the weather had lifted. He emerged into sunlight, under a bright blue sky, to find a surreal urban landscape.

The streets were empty both of cars and pedestrians and he could hear birdsong. That was better.

You see, my friend, you have to stand back. You have to see the whole picture...

Slowly, painfully, he shuffled down to the Bayswater Road and then east. His destination, St Bartholomew the Great, in the City of London.

Chapter Nine

Inspector Peter Bonik sat on his roof terrace and contemplated the sky. It was blue; not grey blue, or green blue, or blue with a haze or a shimmer, or a hint of imperfection. It was a deep, beautiful blue. A sky like that in the middle of the City was a rare thing. To his right, a hundred feet below, was Long Lane. Behind him was the Barbican and Aldersgate. To his left was St Paul's, somewhere behind the buildings on Middle Street and Cloth Fair. And there in front of him he could just see the steeple of the Church of St Bartholomew the Great. Just beyond that was where he had first seen the body of Daniel Roscoe just over one month before. And above him was this glorious sky.

He took another mouthful of the South African sauvignon blanc, chilled, £4.99 from the corner shop. The air smelled and tasted a little like wine, didn't it? There had hardly been any traffic to soil and sully it since the lockdown. It tasted pure. If not like wine, then spring water from the mountains. He sat back in the deck chair, put his feet up on the skylight and relaxed for the first time in weeks. It was his day off. There was something to be said for this lockdown. The peace and quiet for one thing. There was the occasional boom-boom from a passing car, and the odd clank from the Farringdon Crossrail site – otherwise near silence. You could even hear the seagulls from the river in the morning, and the birdsong from the churchyard in the evening.

And then he felt guilty. He remembered that almost 27,000 had already died. The numbers were beginning to come down but even now six or seven hundred were being added to the count almost every day. Who was it who said something about tragedy and pain being necessary to make humanity more perfect; that pain was the anvil upon which God sculpted humanity to make it arc towards a Christ-like ideal? C S Lewis probably. At this time in his life Bonik was a sceptic but he had an enquiring mind. He read and he occasionally, just occasionally, dipped his big toe into faith.

And there was something in it, wasn't there? Didn't people always say that the war had brought out the best in the British? That's what his nan had always said. And what was it the Queen had said?

"Everyone will be able to take pride in how they responded to this challenge. And those who come after us will say that the Britons of this generation were as strong as any. That the attributes of self-discipline, of quiet good-humoured resolve and of fellow feeling characterised this country."

There was something in that. Some people were noticing their neighbours for the first time in years.

Everyone had been forced to stay at home. That was the first thing. Whether in families, or on their own, everyone had been forced to reflect, whether they wanted to or not. Young or old, weak or strong, clever or not so clever. People were forced to find new ways to keep alive their careers or their relationships and their sanity. The rupture from the normal, from the routine, the boredom or the vacuum, had become the midwives to creativity and invention.

Experimentation in social interaction on the internet had brought companionship to people who otherwise would have spent most of their time in isolation: virtual pub quizzes, open houses, dinner parties – virtual environments in which the shy or socially inadequate could spread their wings. But this was not a way of living which would be going away with the virus. This was surely an innovation which would be here to stay.

Social media platforms had progressed just a little along the path from frivolity to social responsibility. Comedy had flourished. The arts had flourished. Free broadcasts of plays from the National Theatre, and opera from Covent Garden, had drawn audiences the likes of which they would never have seen from the fee paying public. Free concerts from the London Philharmonic had brought new audiences to classical music, drawn by the novelty, but surprised by sounds they had never really noticed before. Free Shakespeare from the Globe. The impenetrable language of Elizabethan England brought to life for thousands by performance on the internet. Museums – from the British Museum to the Rijksmuseum – had thrown open their collections to people who otherwise would not have ventured from their sofas.

There were signs of a surge in creativity as big as any other period in history, comparable to that resulting from a major war, but this time it was a war in which everybody was on the same side. Some had written novels, some diaries, reflections or just musings. The large majority would never be published but, by expressing and externalising their feelings, people had liberated themselves in a medium they had never experienced before, emotionally and intellectually, in ways they had not known before. And advances, of course, in science and medicine. The signs that great leaps forward were possible because of the necessity of invention and unprecedented international collaboration.

People had begun to paint – not just on walls and skirting boards, but on paper, or cardboard or canvas. And people had begun to read again. And people had begun to cook again. And people had begun to think and reflect again. Even better, people had begun to encourage their children to write or paint, and read and cook, and to think and reflect again.

And they had begun to exercise more. First they had begun to exercise without going out, just for the hell of it, by watching You Tube. Then they had left their houses, when the regulations permitted, and instead of slumping into their cars, they went for a walk, and they took a good look for the first time in a while at their immediate locality. And either they admired the beauty, or they took note and were determined to do something about it in better times.

And when they did so they were able to breathe clean air. At this point Bonik's eyes returned to the blue. Because of course, there was the environment. Global pollution had dramatically decreased. The skies had cleared. The stars had become visible at night in places where they had no right to be seen. The air had become clean in places where it had been dirty for decades. Asthma had reduced. Children were breathing clean air in the cities.

So many people had woken up to the reality that they could work perfectly easily at home. They did not need to get into their belching cars. They did not need to ride their vomiting buses, or pack into their sweating tubes. And they were healthier for it – both in their bodies and in their minds. People had learned that they did not need to fly half way around the world to do business. People had learned that they did not need to fly half way around the world to find fulfilment either. They had learned that you could find it in your own country. You could find it in your own town or city or neighbourhood. You could find it in your own home, either alone, or with your family.

And people had become much more engaged in public affairs because for the first time many of them realised that public affairs meant *their* affairs. They watched the press conferences. They noticed the politicians. They could recognise them. They could even name them and they could reach a judgment as to whether they agreed or disagreed with them, not on the basis of their voice, or their looks, or their dress sense, but on the basis of the content of what they said.

And, Bonik mused – his musings now affected by the wine just a little – much of this revolution had been enabled by the most fundamental revision of the role of the state since 1945 – and probably more fundamental still. Would it not become the new consensus that all people formed a collective for the common good. Everyone would be expected to contribute how they could; whether through paid work and taxation, or whether through voluntary effort and goodwill. In turn, the collective benevolence of the state would envelop you in culture, in sustenance, and in security. There was even talk of a universal basic income for all – people would not work to live; they would live to work in ways they chose. And the peoples of the world would come together, and they would demand an end to war, and there would be a worldwide ceasefire, and universal peace.

At this point Bonik had wandered further in his musings, from the sublime to the fantastic, and he drifted into a pleasant little doze with a smile on his face.

Bonik had started with the blood-stained notebook he had found in the Lady Chapel; that is, once he had retrieved it from forensics, a few days after the murder. It was one of those hardback notebooks, pages a little yellow. It didn't look new. There were some notes on the first few pages written in a distinctive pinkish-red ink. Some initials – VS April 2019. Some names. It looked like Sir John Farrer, maybe, and a telephone number. The name didn't ring a bell – nothing on the internet – but that might be interesting. Then, a list of names: Brad Perkins, Tom Chevening, Spiro Giddens, maybe. The last two were smudged, it looked like water staining.

On the second page there was a sequence of letters and numbers. Like Carter had said, it looked like a code. It didn't make any sense to him whatsoever. There were some notes which he couldn't make much sense of either. He squinted to make out the handwriting; 'the transference of... something... viruses from snakes.' Well, that was topical anyway. Was Roscoe a medic? The Chief Inspector hadn't said. Roscoe was certainly an Oxford man according to Carter. Maybe he was involved in this research that was going on to find a vaccine.

There were some notes at the back of the book too. They were in a different hand, and there was more blood staining on the paper. It was even more difficult to make out. But there was a phone number and a name – John Symonds. Bonik did a quick search on his phone. When he saw the result he sat up – John Symonds, Rector of St Bartholomew the Great. It looked as if Roscoe's presence in the church was planned and that the Rector must know a little more than was immediately apparent. He dialled the number.

"Rector? It's Inspector Bonik, City of London Police. Can we meet? It's about the dead body we found outside your Church on Tuesday. Yes, not easy to forget. We need to talk. Can I pop around this afternoon?"

There was a pause. "Must you?" The distaste for anything corporeal was visceral. "The Church is closed down. New orders from the Archbishop. Can't we do this over the phone?"

"It's a little sensitive, I'm afraid. I think we need to meet."

"Oh, very well. Come to the Rectory. It's in Amen Court. Do you know it? Lodgings for Anglican clerics. It's off Warwick Lane by St Pauls. I'll meet you there in the gardens. Shall we say tomorrow morning?"

"I'll see you there in half an hour."

PC Wendy Graham had responded to his call and by the time Bonik arrived at the entrance to Amen Court, she was waiting by the arched entrance into the courtyard. As he approached, she backed off, as if there were some kind of invisible barrier between them. Bonik remembered. Living alone and spending most of his time in front of a computer, it was easy to forget.

"Sorry, social distancing. How that's going to operate in police work, Christ alone knows. Let's hope we don't have to arrest anyone. Anyway, thanks for responding at short notice."

She smiled. "So, it turns out the priest knew him all along."

"Well, there's clearly a connection there. Leave me to do the talking. Now, how do we get into this place?"

There was a bell rope to the side of a wooden door under a red brick arch. Bonik guessed it was nineteenth century, although it looked like it was modelled on the middle ages. He pulled the rope. There was a low chiming sound. After about a minute the Rector opened the door, revealing a garden court-yard. There was a square of what looked like terraced alms-houses and a lawn with a large oak tree and flower beds in the middle. The Rector's habitual look of faint disgust was hidden underneath a surgical mask. He stood well back and invited them in with a wave of his hand.

"I really should be self-isolating you know. I'm seventy one this year. Will you please use the hand sanitiser? It's on the table there."

After cleansing their hands to the Rector's satisfaction, they walked into the courtyard.

"Would you mind awfully standing by the wall over there and I'll sit on the bench. I'd remind you please not to touch anything." He looked them up and down as if the infection could be seen like soiled overalls, or dog poo.

The Rector sat on a park bench at the far end of the lawn, under the oak tree. Bonik and Graham went to a brick wall which ran along the edge of the courtyard.

"Now, be careful to stay two metres apart, both of you." He indicated by parting his hands.

Bonik's patience was wearing thin. "Rector – it is Rector John Symonds, isn't it?"

"That's right."

"We have to ask you some questions about the murder in Smithfield on Tuesday."

"Pardon. Can you speak up? My hearing isn't what it was, I fear." The Rector put his hand behind his ear.

Bonik's patience snapped. He walked forward until he was roughly two metres from the cleric, who had shrunk back into his seat.

"Two metres, OK." He took a step back. "Even better, three metres. You must understand sir that this is a murder enquiry. It's about the young man who was found dead in Smithfield on Tuesday. He had been inside your Church, remember? We found a notebook and what must have been his blood in the prayer room."

"It was the Lady Chapel actually."

"Never mind what it's called. You told us you didn't know this man. Is that right?"

"I told you, I've never seen him before."

"Can you explain, sir, why he would have your name and telephone number written down in a notebook?"

Symonds looked baffled. “No. Not at all. Do you know who he was?”

“Yes, Daniel Roscoe, second year law student at Oxford.”

The Rector’s expression briefly lost its composure. He let out a deep sigh and ran his fingers through his hair.

“Oh dear. If only you had said. Yes, I did know him. I’m very sorry to hear that it was he. Daniel Roscoe, my goodness.” He paused for a few seconds, thinking through events in his mind.

“I wasn’t lying to you, Inspector. I never met him. I had no idea the body was Daniel Roscoe. I had no reason to connect it to him, you see.”

Bonik looked back at PC Graham and nodded. She took out a notebook and a pen from her pocket. “Can you tell us how you knew him? Look, do you mind if we sit here?” He indicated a bench at a right angle to the bench upon which the Rector sat.

Clearly the news of Roscoe’s death had thawed the Rector a little. “No, of course not. Please do.” He indicated, and inched further along his bench. “He knew my daughter, Vanessa. She died Inspector. My goodness, it must be getting on for a year now. It seems like it was yesterday. She was a student at the same college as Daniel, Brasenose. She was found dead by the police in the River Cherwell, early last summer. The police concluded that she had killed herself, and we… well, we hadn’t spoken for months.”

He bowed his head. Graham was about to ask a question. Bonik raised his hand to stop her. After a minute or two the Rector raised his head again. His eyes were red and he had been crying.

“Daniel Roscoe called me. It must have been, what, November time, I suppose. I don’t know how close he was to Vanessa but he was certainly affected by her death because he had been to see the police about it. He couldn’t understand why she would want to kill herself. The police told him, as they had told me, that she had become depressed, she had recently split up with some boy, and she had been drinking, so they said. I didn’t know about any boyfriend, Inspector, but as I said I hadn’t spoken to her for some time. But it didn’t sound like my daughter.

“You see, I had received a copy of the police report into the case, after many times of asking. It referred to a psychiatrist’s assessment which suggested that she was suffering from clinical depression at the time of her death. I tried to contact the psychiatrist, er Dr Brightman – no, Zeitmann – I think it was, in Harley Street, but he claimed not to remember the case. Then I was told that he went sick. I've tried a number of times since then but with no more success, I'm afraid to say."

"Did you say Zeitmann?"

"Yes, I think it was Zeitmann – Dr Emile Zeitmann. I'm pretty sure."

Bonik retrieved the notebook from his pocket and turned to the back. "Yes, I thought so. Did you mention this to Mr Roscoe?"

"Yes, I did. Why?"

"Because there's a record of Zeitmann's address and telephone number in his notebook. Rector, did you say your daughter's name was Vanessa?" Bonik remembered the initials 'VS' at the front of the book. "Could you just take a look at this." Bonik reached out and dropped the notebook on the near end of the Rector's bench.

He picked it up and opened it. "This is her hand. This is my daughter's writing."

"Would you mind just taking a look through the notes on the first couple of pages and tell me if any of it makes any sense to you Rector? What about the names?"

The Rector looked through the notes with an expression which was a mixture of grief and bewilderment. Then he pointed at the page. "Well, I've heard of Sir John Fawcett of course. But why Vanessa would have made a note of his name and telephone number, I have no idea; unless it was to do with her animal rights work, of course. That's the sort of thing that John Fawcett used to get involved with. But the rest of it means nothing to me."

Bonik stood up. "Did you say Sir John Fawcett?"

"That's what it says. The rest of it – no idea. You know she was a bio-chemist. Not my line of country at all, I'm afraid." He thumbed his way to the back. "But these notes at the back are made by somebody else by the look of it."

"Yes, we think those are Roscoe's notes. It's a different handwriting and in quite a different ink. Listen, could we have the police report you were talking about?"

"Yes, of course. Bear with me a moment." The Rector disappeared into one of the terraced houses and emerged a couple of minutes later holding a brown envelope.

"Thank you, sir. That was helpful. We'll be in touch if we need to ask you any further questions." Bonik gestured to Graham and they walked to the door. The Rector called after them.

"Inspector. Just one other thing. Dan has called me a couple of times since Vanessa's death. I think he just wanted to know if I had found out anything more from the police. You see, he had become convinced that there was more to her death than at first appeared and that the police were covering something up."

"Graham, does the name Sir John Fawcett mean anything to you?"

"No sir."

"How old are you anyway, sorry for asking?"

"Twenty four."

She *was* young enough to be his daughter then. "Yes, I suppose he was a little bit before your time."

It was just before lunch-time the following day. Bonik had been sitting at his desk, puzzling over the notebook; Graham was sitting opposite him; the two metres distance measured out, on the orders of the Superintendent, with some masking tape.

"John Fawcett was one of the rising stars of Tony Blair's government after New Labour came to power in 1997. Even I know that. Ring any bells?" She shook her head.

"I suppose you've heard of Tony Blair, have you?"

She nodded. Bonik wasn't convinced.

"When I was at school, Graham, you were supposed to have at least some awareness of events before your eighteenth birthday."

"Sorry, guv."

Bonik consulted the computer.

"Yes, here we are. Treasury, Foreign Office, resigned 2003 over the Iraq War. Since then he's been a sort of left wing firebrand, in with all that Stop the War brigade, animal rights, you know." Graham still looked blank. "But why on earth would Roscoe have his telephone number in this notebook?"

Bonik picked up the phone. "Well, there's only one way to find out I suppose." He dialled the number written in the notebook next to the name of Sir John Fawcett. It went to divert.

"Hello, I wonder if I could speak please to Sir John Fawcett. I'm Inspector Peter Bonik. I'm with the City of London police."

"I'm afraid Sir John isn't in his Parliamentary office today. You may know that Parliament is in recess for the foreseeable future because of the pandemic."

"Understood. But how can I get hold of him please. It's important."

"He's at Boreham House. His country seat in Essex. Can I ask what it's about please?"

"Yes, it's about a murder of a young man in the City of London. I have reason to believe that Sir John knew him, and he may be able to help us with our enquiries."

There was a pause, and a subtle difference in tone; from the neutral indifference of an automaton, to active engagement. "I see. May I have your name and contact details please, er, Inspector… Very well. I'll pass on your message directly."

"Many thanks. I look forward to hearing from him."

Bonik put down the phone. "Graham, I'd like you to check out this Dr Zeitmann." He turned to the back of the notebook. "Dr Emile Zeitmann, Harley Street, London W1. Better give them a call first. I doubt there'll be any psychiatric clinics open for business at the moment. Hardly the time to sit down for some cosy *tête a tête* with a shrink, is it? I'm going to see what I can find out from Roscoe's university. *Brasenose* College wasn't it – what kind of a name is that anyway?"

He found the telephone number on the website of the College. The phone was answered by someone who sounded as if they were eating a sandwich, and resented the interruption.

"Brasenose College, Oxford. Porter's Lodge."

"Good afternoon. Inspector Bonik. City of London Police. I'm making enquiries about a post-graduate student of yours called Vanessa Symonds. She was found dead in the Cherwell last summer. We have reason to believe that her death is connected with a murder we are investigating. Can you put me through to someone who would have known something about her? Maybe her tutor?"

"I'm just the porter sir. I don't know nothing about no murders, or students in the Cherwell in the summer. There's not much call for that sort of thing around here. I don't know who to suggest. I'm afraid there aren't many people about these days. Just me and the missis. You've chosen a bad time. Most of the guvnors have gone home for this here lockdown, you see. Let me see what I can do. What was the name of the student in the Cherwell again?"

Bonik left his contact details, not at all confident that the porter had bothered to take a note of them. He took up the police report into Vanessa Symonds's death once again. It was unusually brief in his experience; a couple of double-sided pages of A4, stapled together. The officer in charge was an Inspector Burden, of the Thames Valley Constabulary.

There was a brief description of the circumstances in which the body had been found – face down in the Cherwell, partially concealed by some river flora and dead for over eight hours by the time she had been discovered by a passing cyclist. It was believed that she had some history of clinical depression, and that she had recently split up with her boyfriend, a postgraduate bio-chemistry student called Thomas Fairford. The report quoted from a psychiatric assessment, apparently commissioned by her College and conducted by Dr Emile Zeitmann, 42b Harley Street, London W1. A short report which appeared to be signed by Zeitmann was attached. According to this she had been diagnosed as suffering from clinical depression and prescribed anti-depressants in early March 2019.

The report went on to quote from a post-mortem examination. There was no note of the pathologist's name. Death had been a result of blunt trauma to the head as a result of a fall into shallow waters, coupled with drowning. An analysis of the deceased's blood indicated an alcohol concentration of 214 milligrams of alcohol per 100 millilitres of blood. That was high – two and a half times over the legal limit for driving. There was no printout of the post-mortem, just the summary in the conclusions of the police report. Bonik considered that even somebody as laconic and detached as Rector John Symonds had a right to be dissatisfied with that explanation for his daughter's death. No wonder he had not let it rest.

It was later that afternoon that Bonik, with a degree of surprise, heard again from the College porter who had managed to contact Vanessa Symonds's moral tutor, an elderly don called Dr Amelia Dann. The term 'moral tutor', so she explained, was a slightly misleading expression. It was not an organised attempt to impose sobriety and chastity upon the student population. Each student, when they joined the College, was allocated a member of the teaching staff to whom they could go if they had any problems such as financial worries or mental health issues. She had been allocated to Vanessa Symonds.

The voice was elderly. "Yes, inspector. Of course I remember Vanessa. Such a bright, committed young woman with such a promising future ahead of her – a terrible tragedy. It was really quite a shock."

"Had she spoken to you, Dr Dann, about being depressed in the weeks or months before her death?"

"No. In fact she had never spoken to me in my role as her *moral* tutor. The only interaction I had with her was as her tutor in theoretical biology when she was an undergraduate. I think I had only seen her maybe once, at a College drinks party, in the six months or so before she died. But she never gave me any reason to think she was distressed in any way. She was always such a well-balanced, delightful girl. A pleasure to teach in fact."

"Dr Dann, if the College had commissioned a psychiatric report into Vanessa, say a few weeks or so before she died, would you have known about it?"

"Absolutely, of course. As her moral tutor, the impetus to commission such a report would have come from me. It is unthinkable that any other authority in College would have commissioned it without notifying me, and equally unthinkable that it would not have been shared with me. Are you saying that there was such a report?"

"Apparently, yes. Look, is it possible for you to check in the College records to see if any such report was commissioned? It was undertaken by a psychiatrist called Dr Emile Zeitmann of Harley Street."

"Can you spell that? Things are taking a little longer at the moment, I'm afraid, because of the lockdown. You're fortunate because I'm one of the few people still living in College but I'll see what I can do and get back to you."

Graham poked her head around the door a couple of hours later. "I've done some digging on Zeitmann. Shall I come in?"

"Take a seat."

She took out her notebook. "From what I can make out Zeitmann had one or two issues, to put it mildly. He had something of a breakdown after the death of his son. He started drinking and gambling and the practice got heavily into debt. The Royal College of Psychiatry, the regulatory body, took over the practice at the end of 2018. It seems that Zeitmann was allowed to continue to practice for a while but he was in a pretty bad way. He ended up killing himself – found swinging from the ceiling last summer."

Bonik put his hands on his head and sighed. “Christ, what the hell is going on here?”

The phone rang. “Hello, Bonik here. Dr Dann, thanks for getting back to me. Have you managed to find out anything?”

“No, I haven’t and that’s the point. I’ve been through all the papers in the Principal’s office, including Vanessa’s personal file. I’ve also searched all of the relevant College databases. There was no psychiatric report commissioned by this College; nor is there any trace of any correspondence of any kind with somebody called Emile Zeitmann. This is really most troubling, Inspector. What could possibly be behind it?”

“I don’t know yet. But I intend to find out. Thanks for your help, Doctor. I’m most grateful. Yes, of course. I’ll be in touch.”

He put the phone down. “Look, Wendy, I’m going up to Oxford tomorrow. I’m going to check in with Thames Valley police and try to get to the bottom of this report. There’s clearly something very odd about this psychiatric assessment. I want you to stay here and see if you can find out who did the toxicology work on the blood sample. Presumably it’s the forensics department which services Thames Valley. This report just doesn’t add up. Maybe Roscoe was on to something after all. But why on earth somebody would want to cover up the circumstances of the death of a clergyman’s daughter, Christ alone knows. Oh yes. Before you go.” Bonik fished in his inside jacket pocket. “Roscoe’s notebook. You’d better put this back into the exhibits safe. It may turn out to be important.”

Graham nodded. She took the notebook, placed it in a clear plastic bag and applied a seal, the blood of Daniel Roscoe was still clearly visible on the cover.

The next morning dawned bright and clear; the latest in a succession of such mornings which had bejewelled the lockdown. Bonik drove up the M40 to Oxford. There was no traffic to impede his progress. The sky was blue, not an aeroplane in sight and Louis Armstrong’s trumpet sounded loud and clear from the radio.

Graham had drawn a blank on the toxicology report. She had called both the laboratories which were known to work for Thames Valley police and had described in as much detail as she could the nature of the case. Neither laboratory had any record of a blood test under the name of Vanessa Symonds, or any test carried out for Inspector Burden around that time. Bonik had decided to drop in on Burden unannounced. He didn't want to give him a chance to prepare any answers.

The little man at the reception desk at Oxford police station spoke from behind a glass screen. "Inspector Burden?" He flicked through a loose leaf file. "He's on long-term sick according to this."

"I need to speak to him urgently about a murder investigation. Peter Bonik, City of London Police." Bonik put his warrant card under the counter.

The man inspected it. "I can put you through to his supervising officer if you want."

Bonik decided to take a risk. "No, I need to speak to Inspector Burden. It's a matter which concerns him personally. I'm happy to see him at home if you give me his address."

"I can't do that sir. The best I can do is to give you his number."

Bonik sat in his car and dialled the number. A voice, monotonous with lethargy, eventually answered.

"David Burden? My name's Peter Bonik. I'm with the City of London Police. I want to talk to you about the death of a young woman called Vanessa Symonds in Oxford last summer. I have reason to believe that her death is connected with the murder of a young man called Daniel Roscoe in London on 24 March. Do you remember the Symonds case?"

There was a pause. "I remember it very well. Why should I have forgotten the case? That's why I've been on gardening leave for the last three months."

"I need to speak to you about it. I'm happy to come around to your home address, if that is convenient."

"Convenient. Why would it be convenient? I don't suppose my convenience has anything to do with it. But come if you must."

The house was in Wolvercote, just north of Oxford; a new build in concrete, set back from the road by a concrete driveway. The only items within the confines of the Burden residence, which did not have the appearance of concrete, were a yellowing weed growing from a piece of grouting in the drive and the brown curtains, drawn to shut out the light.

The door was opened by a small woman Bonik assumed was Burden's wife.

"You must be the Inspector he's been talking about. You know we're not really supposed to be letting anyone in now with all this social distancing, and David does have asthma."

"I can stay out here if you prefer. We can talk on the drive."

A thin voice came from within. "Show him in Susan. I'm not going to be locked in by a bit of flu; such a lot of nonsense."

Bonik was led into a sitting-dining room. It had the smell of a room which had been much lived in and had been deprived of fresh air for some considerable time. The television was on – one of those mindless daytime quiz shows. A man in carpet slippers and a grey cardigan shuffled towards it and turned the sound down. Bonik assumed he must be around fifty but he looked closer to seventy. He shuffled backwards to the armchair from which he had come, his eyes remained fixed on the television.

"Take a seat if you want." Bonik remained standing. "Vanessa Symonds. I remember it well. I also remember Daniel Roscoe. He was murdered you say?"

"Stabbed. His body was found near the Church of St Bartholomew the Great. You knew that her father was the Rector?"

"Yes, he kept pestering me for further details of her death."

"Only natural I suppose."

"I wouldn't know about that. Don't have kids. I didn't have further details of her death anyway. You see, although I was nominally the officer in charge of the case, I was told not to waste any more time on it. I produced a short report for the records and then was told by my Super to close the case."

Mrs Burden entered with a tray. On it was a mug of tea and a sandwich made from white, processed bread. She placed the tray on her husband's lap. It had clearly not occurred to either of them that he, Bonik, might have wanted a drink; not that tea would have been his first choice.

"Do you know who commissioned the psychiatric report?" said Bonik. "It certainly wasn't Brasenose College. I checked."

"That's what I was told. I sent a report upstairs – bare facts of the case; girl, Vanessa Symonds, found drowned in the Cherwell, suspected accident/suicide."

Burden took a bite out of the sandwich, wrestling with what appeared to be a slice of pale pink ham inside. He spoke as he ate, mouth open, fragments of sandwich distributed outwards. Bonik moved back to stand out of range.

"I made some enquiries – found out she had been knocking around with some boy called Tom Fairford and he had gone missing. Vanished without trace.

Couple of weeks later I was sent a summary of the psychiatric and the results of the blood test and was told to complete the police report. That's what I did. It looked to me like a suicide – depressed, booze, lost her boyfriend; it bore all the signs. She topped herself, pure and simple." The final word was stifled by the remainder of the ham sandwich, which was shoved in the mouth to coincide with the last syllable.

"Didn't you ask any more questions. Did you just leave it there?"

"I was only doing what I was told," Burden said, indignantly. "Then I start getting calls from her father. He had contacted the psychiatrist who had told him he couldn't remember the case. Then the shrink goes missing. The father wouldn't leave me alone, some priest or other. Then this Dan Roscoe turns up and starts asking questions. So I did some digging, see. It turned out that the psychiatrist was dodgy – that's what it looked like to me anyway. He had a drink problem and was in debt. I made some enquiries with the Royal College of Psychiatrists. It turned out that he had a bit of a history. He had been found out doctoring reports for clients in return for extra cash."

He paused as if that were a sufficient explanation, flushing down the remnants of the sandwich with a loud swig from the mug of tea.

Bonik looked at him, expecting a follow up once the tea had gone down, but Burden's eyes returned to the television.

"Well, what did you do about it?"

Burden sighed, visibly irritated at the interruption. "Look, I didn't just leave it at that, did I? I queried it. I sent a memo upstairs. And then I was told in no uncertain terms to drop it. Above my pay grade. Who was I to question that? I was assigned to the Banbury strangler case. You'll remember that. It was in all the papers. Then about three months ago I was put on gardening leave, as they say, told to go on long-term sick. Full pay, pension. Who was I to argue with that? That's all I know Inspector. I don't think I can help you any further."

Burden placed the tray on the floor, eased himself out of the armchair, and shuffled towards the television. Half way there, he turned back.

"Do you think the priest, her father, suspected this Roscoe of killing her and took his revenge?"

"No, I don't think that's very likely. Alright. You've been helpful, up to a point. Thanks very much."

"Not at all. Can you see yourself out?" He continued his shuffle to the TV.

As Bonik walked to the front door, the TV was turned up again; the banal whine following him to his car.

It was now clear to Bonik that there must have been a cover up surrounding the death of Vanessa Symonds. Why it had happened was anybody's guess, but he intended to submit a full report of his suspicions to the Divisional Chief Superintendent as soon as possible. He arrived back at Snow Hill later that afternoon. PC Wendy Graham was waiting for him.

She read from a notebook. "You've had a message from The Right Honourable Sir John Fawcett, MP. He said could you call him as soon as you got back to the station?"

"OK. I wonder if he is 'Right Honourable'? Most of these MPs are anything but, if you ask me. Can you put the kettle on – I'm parched." Bonik picked up the phone and dialled the number. Sir John answered after the second ring.

The voice was clipped and urgent. "Inspector Bonik? What's all this about a murder and what has it to do with me?"

"Young man called Daniel Roscoe, sir. We found his body in Smithfield on Tuesday the 24th. No doubt it was murder. He had been stabbed in the back. The thing is, we found a notebook belonging to him close to the scene. It had your name and telephone number in it. Did you know him, sir?"

There was a pause. Fawcett's tone changed. He spoke slowly and deliberately as if each word were being vetted before it was allowed out.

"Yes, Inspector. I recognise the name. Student up at Oxford. He came to see me about the death of a girlfriend. She was heavily involved in the animal rights movement, campaigning against the use of experimentation in laboratory testing. That sort of thing. Roscoe seemed to have become fixated with some wild conspiracy theory that she had been killed by people involved at the Anglo-American Laboratory for Bio-Chemical Research in Oxford and that there had been some sort of cover up about her death.

"There have been all sorts of theories flying around that the laboratory is an arm of the US government which is being used to manufacture biological weapons; long before the current health emergency. I can only presume that he came to see me because of the public stance I've taken over the years towards American foreign policy, and because of my position on the Joint Intelligence

Committee. This snake flu pandemic probably sent him over the edge, poor chap."

"When was this sir?"

"It was er, it would have been on Monday the twenty-third. He called me. Wanted to come and see me. I humoured him for a while and then managed to fob him off with some story about how I would look into it and get back to him. He sounded a little deranged to me. So he was killed the next day, you say? Have you any idea who did it?"

"Not yet sir, no. Our enquiries are at an early stage."

"Well, I'm sorry to hear it but I really don't know that I can be of any further assistance Inspector. I have no knowledge of this young man apart from our brief meeting in the Parliamentary Buildings."

"We may need to take a formal statement from you, sir at a later stage. In the meantime, if you recall anything else of significance, you know where to reach me."

And so Bonik wrote his report, submitted it to the Divisional Chief Superintendent and his investigation hit a dead end. And it came to pass that at the back end of April, having done not very much for a few weeks, he spent that glorious afternoon on his roof terrace, sipping a chilled South African sauvignon blanc.

But Bonik's day dream of the worldwide ceasefire and universal peace to be declared from that roof terrace was sharply interrupted by his phone. He awoke abruptly, tipping the rest of the sauvignon blanc – now distinctly tepid – over his shorts and marvelling at the rooftop view which confronted him.

"Fuck, where am I?"

He came to his senses and retrieved the phone from the floor. It was Chief Inspector Carter.

"Bonik. There's both good news and bad news on the Roscoe case. The good news is that there's been an arrest – a fellow Oxford student by the name of Thomas Fairford. The bad news is that you're off the case – not my decision. It came from upstairs. I expect you'll be glad to get back to City Fraud, won't you?"

Chapter Ten

Goldford Row, London WC1, lies between High Holborn to the south and Theobalds Road to the north, at one of the more prosperous ends of the capital's legal district. Flanked by rows of Georgian terraces, sumptuously refurbished in chrome and silver and gold, it feels, smells and tastes of money, lucre and fees. Fees, one should add, more of the private variety than those prised with difficulty from the hands of the legal aid authorities.

On a bright September morning in 2020, Monica Whitlow, of the firm of Shallow, Mallow and Marsh, ascended the pristine steps which led to the Chambers of Sir Archibald Whittering QC at No 3 Goldford Row. She pressed the intercom and asked for admission, pleading a conference with Mr Rock Tattinger QC and his junior, Mr Tarquin Quinell-Smith.

Tattinger, a man of 40 years, with a distinguished hint of grey at the temples, sat back in his leather upholstery, releasing a pleasant whiff of expensive *eau* from his Savile Row suit. Adjusting his cuffs to display a modest margin of rich Indian cotton, he bade Ms Whitlow take a seat at the other end of the mahogany table.

"You know Tarquin, of course, Monica."

"Yes, we've worked together," Tarquin declared, unable to control the urge to hear his own voice first. "The Sotheby's fraud. You must remember it Rock."

"Of course, splendid success." By which remark, he meant the brief fee. "Now, what about young Mr Fairford?"

Monica began with the heart of the matter. "I've just told your senior clerk that Sir Joseph, his father, has now agreed your fees."

A faint but distinct smile of self-satisfaction crept across Tattinger's mouth. It was with considerable difficulty and only in the interests of good taste, that he managed to mitigate it to a benign look of mild indifference.

"Tarquin and I have been examining the brief, and exploring ways in which we might be able to undermine the prosecution case. I'm afraid to say that there are some aspects of the evidence which are not necessarily to Mr Fairford's advantage."

"Yes, you could say that."

"In particular, the text messages. From what I gather, there is evidence of threats being issued by young Tom to this Roscoe chap only a matter of days before the murder. This one, for example, is not entirely helpful to our defence." Tattinger tapped on his keyboard.

"Here it is: '22 March 2020: Roscoe you are a fucking thief. She killed herself because of you. Now I'll fucking kill you'. A little crude but to the point, I think you will agree. And that's just the most direct of them I fear. And the prosecution doesn't appear to have even gone down the path of getting cell site evidence yet. That could really sink us if it places Fairford in the vicinity."

Monica turned up an expert report. "It can only place him in the vicinity if he made a call or sent a text around the time of the murder. The cell sites do not pick up the phone if its inactive. According to this the phone was switched off on 23 March, the day before the murder and then disabled."

"Mm, a double-edged sword, I fear. Although there's no direct evidence to put him in the locality, it's a bit of an unfortunate coincidence that his phone goes down the day before the murder."

Tarquin, a young man who had reached the age of thirty-three, seemingly effortlessly, his self-regard growing with each succeeding year, eased his posterior into a more upright position to Tattinger's left. The broad smile he had worn since hearing about his fees had only partially subsided. "Is Tom still saying nothing?"

"He's said nothing to the police and so far is refusing to give us any instructions," said Monica. "Every time we try to put any of the evidence to him for an explanation, he clams up and claims to have no memory of what happened. He won't even speak to his father. He looks emaciated and utterly terrified. Personally, I've never seen a client who looks so traumatised. It's as if he's had some sort of breakdown. You will have seen that we've instructed a psychiatrist and a psychologist to assess him to see whether he's fit to plead."

"The mystery is how someone with his background could have ended up in that state," said Tarquin, whose own background included (in no particular order) Harrow, Cambridge and being born to the first daughter of a baronet.

"Eton, Oxford, heir to a fortune and, according to his father and his college, not a trace of any trouble at the time of his disappearance. Maybe he went to the wrong school." Tarquin found this joke rather amusing and turned to Tattinger expecting confirmation of the same, before remembering that his Learned Leader was a grammar school boy; in Tarquin's book, his one serious shortcoming.

Tattinger, unmoved, turned up a witness statement from the evidence bundle on his laptop.

"According to his father, Fairford went missing around Easter of last year. His housemates say that when they returned after the vacation there was simply no trace of him. His possessions had gone. No sign of any break in. It was as if he had never existed. The police drew a blank and filed it as a missing person case. Sir Joseph then instructs the top private detective agency in the country, quite probably the world. They have no more success than the police. And then nobody hears a word until Fairford turns up a year later, down and out, in this hostel for the homeless in Rochester Row, about a month after Roscoe's murder."

Tarquin peered at the statement over his Learned Leader's shoulder. "Do we know how the police traced him to the hostel?"

"There's a statement from the arresting officer," said Tattinger, "but nothing I've seen to explain why the police were there."

"We've only had the preliminary disclosure so far," said Monica. "The Plea and Trial Preparation Hearing is on the 14th of this month, and so we should get the full bundle sometime in late November. Everything's been delayed by the pandemic."

Tarquin sat back, spread his legs and took the cue to return to his favourite subject. "When are we going to get jury trials up and running again? That's what I want to know. Damn silly bit of flu. Justice delayed is justice denied after all."

Justice, or rather the pursuit of it on behalf of the very rich, was also the source of his extremely generous income, although this of course was mere coincidence.

Tattinger, mildly irritated by Tarquin's interruption, held up his hand to silence him, still examining the statements.

"I'm not so troubled by the DNA evidence though," he said, tapping his keyboard. "There's a match with Fairford, as I understand it, from the samples taken from the inside of Roscoe's raincoat. But that could just about be explained by innocent association. There's evidence which connects Fairford with Roscoe through this girl, Vanessa Symonds and there's evidence that they met at least once. They were in the same college after all. They might very well have had some physical contact with one another, at some stage at least. Fairford's DNA could still have been on the coat many months later if it hadn't been cleaned. But what is going to be much more difficult to explain to a jury is the combination of the DNA with these text messages. Could that really just be coincidence? One of the first things we're going to have to do is get an expert to analyse Fairford's phone. Has Roscoe's phone been looked at?"

"From what I've seen so far, it doesn't look as if he had one on him," said Monica. "There's no mention of a phone on the exhibits list."

"That's unusual. We don't appear to have statements from the officers who found the body, do we Tarquin?"

Tarquin's analysis of the papers so far had been strictly of the preliminary variety. In short, he hadn't read them. He took his paper copy and flicked through the pages. After a silence only just on the right side of embarrassing, he announced with his usual authority, "No, only from the scenes of crime officer, chap called Donnelly."

"Well, we'll just have to wait to see what we get in November. In the meantime, we need to get Fairford looked at as soon as possible. Without instructions, all we can do is try and find holes in the prosecution's case. Frankly, from what I've seen so far, unless he talks I don't fancy his chances."

The Middle Temple is a collection of buildings, some modern and some dating back to the sixteenth century, lying to the south of Fleet Street and flanked by the Victoria Embankment. After the Knights Templar had fallen foul of the Pope and met particularly unpleasant ends tied to wooden stakes, the lawyers moved in. Most of the lawyers who had not fallen foul of impecuniosity or inertia or both, had since moved out – to more illustrious premises further north.

One of the lawyers who had succumbed to extreme inertia and occasional impecuniosity, was Jack Tapsell, barrister at law, member of the Honourable Society of the Middle Temple, and tenant (practising barrister and member of Chambers) at 2 Sumping Court, one of the less salubrious sets of Chambers which still languished in that Honourable Estate. Tapsell's career had peaked over thirty years before, the day he had graduated from Pembroke College Oxford with a first class degree in jurisprudence. It had gone downhill ever since.

Tapsell at least looked like a criminal barrister. He was almost fifty-five, slightly overweight, but in a homely rather than a morbid way. He tried, except in the hottest of weather, to keep up standards. He wore a three piece, dark grey, woollen suit bought off the peg at John Lewis, but from one of the more respectable outfitters. His facial expression at rest was one of chronic disappointment, as if he had left something of value somewhere but had forgotten what it was.

He had made his way into Chambers that day for want of anything better to do. The lift was out of order again. Hardly a surprise. It hadn't been serviced in 25 years. He climbed the stairs, a pained expression on his face, to a particularly undistinguished door, upon which the paint had begun to peel. The Chambers of Dominic Blackford QC, proclaimed the sign, a man five years Tapsell's junior who had long since overtaken his modest little career.

Tapsell forced the door with his shoulder, the lock had slipped again, and wiped his feet on the mat. Joe, the junior clerk, having just made himself a mug of tea, ignored him. Tapsell felt almost embarrassed to go in the clerks' room. The last time they had found him a decent brief was Operation Pellew in 2014, since then it had been a diet of bog standard crap. The senior clerk caught his eye and lifted his right hand in a half-hearted salute.

"Morning, sir." Tapsell waved.

He made himself a cup of instant coffee in the cupboard which doubled as a kitchen and plonked himself down at one corner of the communal desk in the communal room, in which all members of Chambers who wanted to keep their outgoings to a bare minimum, confined themselves. A lone pupil sat at the other end of the table and immediately tried to look busy, obviously harbouring under the illusion that Tapsell wielded any influence in Chambers whatsoever. She looked about twelve.

After an appropriate interval and effecting an air of care-free efficiency and confidence, she pretended to have just noticed him.

"Good morning, Jack. Let me know if you've got any work you want me to do, won't you." He was amazed she knew his name. She'd obviously been learning the Chambers website off by heart in order to scrape up every last vote when it came to tenancy applications. She had finally got to him.

"No, thanks. Jane, isn't it? No, it's a bit quiet at the moment actually." He had long since given up any attempt at impressing junior members of Chambers, or senior ones either for that matter. He stared into the middle distance, nibbled on a chocolate digestive and then started reading the comments pages in the *Times*.

At lunchtime, nothing much having happened in the intervening couple of hours, he went for a stroll along the Strand and returned with an economy cheese and pickle sandwich from the corner shop. Jane was still sitting at the table, looking industrious and still hoping to attract the attention of any member of Chambers who should stray into the room.

She looked up as he entered. "Jack, George was after you – about 20 minutes ago." She pushed the phone towards him. He sat down in a state of some wonderment. The last time the senior clerk had called him was 8 October 2015 – to wish him a happy fiftieth birthday.

He dialled. George answered with his usual greeting to the public, the tone sounding more like a threat than a welcome. "2 Sumping Court!"

"George, it's Jack Tapsell. Jane said you wanted me."

"Oh yeah. I've picked up a nice little murder for you, sir. Crown Prosecution Service Complex Casework called, asking for you special. A real turn up for the books."

Tapsell choked on a bit of pickle. "A murder – where, when?"

"Southwark, sir. Plea and Trial Preparation Hearing on the 14th of this month. You know that TCC Chemicals? It turns out the defendant's the son of the Chairman, Sir Joseph Fairford. Should be quite a high profile job."

Tapsell was still in a state of confusion and wonder. "They asked for me especially, did you say?"

"I know. I wondered about that too but they were quite specific. Said you were the right man for the job."

Tapsell was moved by his clerk's confidence. "OK, well that's a good development. Have we got access to the papers yet? Good. Can you get Joe to print them off for me – you know I can't be dealing with all this digital case stuff."

Tapsell put down the phone with a mixture of excitement and trepidation. He had never done a murder before.

"Well, Jane. It looks like I might have something you can help me with after all."

It was late afternoon and the communal room was beginning to fill with barristers returning from court, sniffing around for another brief and trying to scrape a living out of the carcass which is the publicly funded criminal justice system. Their esteemed head of Chambers, Dominic Blackford, poked his head around the door. "Jack, can I have a word?"

Blackford's room overlooked the Middle Temple rose garden, where, according to legend and Shakespeare, the Wars of the Roses were ignited. The room was a little cramped but at least Blackford had his own room and desk. Behind the desk he had hung a large, gold framed photograph of himself, four feet by three, no less, wearing a full-bottomed wig, taken on the day he took silk, a couple of years previously. Tapsell hadn't seen it for a year or two and winced at the sight – revulsion at the sheer vulgarity of the gesture, coupled with just a little bit of jealousy.

"Jack, I hear you've got a murder!"

"That's right. Prosecution brief. Did George tell you about it?"

"Yes, it sounds as if it might make a few headlines. Have you decided on a leader yet?"

So that's what it was about. Blackford was angling for a brief as his leader.

"The CPS don't want a silk. It looks like a pretty straight forward case from what I've seen so far, a simple stabbing. I'm doing it on my own, or maybe with a junior, if they'll give me one."

"Well, I'm pleased for you Jack. Last time you had a leading brief was that Pellew case, wasn't it? I've always thought the CPS treated you appallingly over that. Hung out to dry from what I remember."

Yeah, that's not what you said at the time, you bastard, Tapsell thought. Operation Pellew was an old bruise he preferred not to prod. As Blackford opined further, Tapsell felt like throwing himself out of the window into the rose bushes. "If the police don't tell you what they've got, then you can hardly disclose it, can you?" he smirked. "Telephone evidence wasn't it?"

"You know very well Dom. You were part of the Chambers enquiry from what I recall. There were text messages showing that the drugs courier was an innocent dupe. Messages which the police decided to sit on. I knew nothing about them until the day before the Court of Appeal hearing."

"But the Court of Appeal said, let me see if I can remember, you should have been more alert about the potential for digital evidence and should have pressed the police for it. 'No grip of your disclosure obligations', I think the phrase was. Is that right?"

Blackford wore an oily grin which Tapsell had an almost irresistible urge to punch. "You've got it in one. The CPS pinned the blame on me."

"But why didn't you challenge it?"

"You may recall that I was going through a nightmare of a divorce at the time."

"But the puzzle is, why are the CPS trusting you with a murder now?"

"Oh thanks. That's most encouraging."

Blackford chortled. "No, I didn't mean it like that. I'm pleased for you Jack. I just think you should ask for a leader, that's all – to cover your back if nothing else."

"I didn't realise you needed the work Dom. I thought you were pretty busy with all that Customs work which has mysteriously migrated from my practice to yours over the last few years."

"Come on Jack. You can't blame me for that. HMRC couldn't trust you with any sensitive case after Pellew. You know how paranoid they are about disclosure. They had to send the work somewhere and I offered to do it at junior rates."

"Yes, I was very pleased for you Dom. Now, if you don't mind I'd like to get back to reading the papers. I don't need a leader. I've been at this game since you were still in the sixth form. Besides which, I want the opportunity to try to resurrect my practice."

Tapsell turned to go back into the common room, and then paused. "By the way, who's the new pupil – Jane isn't it?"

Blackford's smirk broadened. "Yes, a first from Newcastle and a merit in the Bar exams. Damn attractive too – I think I might be on to something there."

Tapsell's loathing reached a new high. "Christ Dom. You're old enough to be her father. Why on earth would she be interested in an oily, narcissistic bastard like you, apart from the obvious of course – she's desperate for a tenancy in Chambers like any pupil. But there are rules about that, as you well know."

Blackford put up his hands and laughed. "Only joking Jack, calm down."

"I'll stick with her brains thanks. She's bright. First from Newcastle, eh – Chambers is looking up. I think I'll try and get her a noting brief."

"Good luck Jack."

After another couple of hours listening to his colleagues swapping anecdotes about life at the Bar, Tapsell began to lose the will to live. He took the tube to Edgware Road, picked up a kebab and a bottle of red wine and got back to his flat just after eight. It was a small ground floor apartment in Maida Avenue. He had had to sell the house in Brighton after the divorce but it was pleasant enough facing onto the Regent's Canal.

He poured himself a glass of wine, opened the polystyrene box that contained his dinner and unfolded the notes Jane had prepared which summarised the evidence in the case of The Queen v Thomas Fairford.

The body of Daniel Roscoe had been found in Smithfield in the entrance to the church of St Bartholomew the Great on 24 March 2020, at around eleven thirty in the morning. That was the day after the announcement of the lockdown. Smithfield would have been unusually quiet, if not deserted. There was a statement from the scenes of crime officer, Michael Donnelly, describing the condition of the body. It seems that Roscoe had been stabbed twice on two separate occasions. That was unusual. Once in the upper arm causing a wound which had bled freely, but which appeared to have been inflicted at least twelve hours before death. The second was a deep incision into the upper back, between the shoulder blades, penetrating the left lung and the anterior wall of the heart, causing almost instantaneous death.

There were no statements yet from the officers who were first on the scene, just a statement from a Detective Chief Inspector who had taken over the investigation of the case in the summer, summarising what had been found by the officers. That was unusual. There was also a statement from the Rector of St Bartholomew the Great who had found the body. He had literally stumbled upon it on his way to the Church from the Rectory.

It appeared from the blood trails that the body had been moved, most probably by the murderer, from the martyrs' monument into the portico under the Tudor gatehouse and had then partially fallen back onto the pavement leading into the churchyard. Tapsell chuckled ruefully to himself. He knew it well. He had been married there nearly thirty years before. The corpse fallen back onto the pavement could well be an appropriate symbol of the marriage which had followed.

Roscoe had clearly been inside the church. There was a trail of his blood leading from the Lady Chapel, besides which it turned out that he was a friend of the Rector's daughter at Oxford. It looked as if Roscoe must have been looking for the Rector. Well, he certainly found him. And this was interesting. The Rector's daughter, Vanessa, had died in the early summer of 2019. The coroner in that case had concurred with the conclusions of the police and recorded a verdict of accidental death or suicide. Roscoe suspected that there was a cover up to do with her death and had been calling the Rector to find out what he knew about it.

Tapsell looked up for a moment and forked a piece of shish, generously coated with minted yoghurt and chilli sauce, into his mouth. *Why would there be a cover up?* He remembered that the deceased's father was Sir Joseph Fairford, a powerful industrial magnate and donor to the Conservative Party. Was it being suggested that his son had killed Vanessa Symonds too? Why else would there be any suspicion of a cover up? This case suddenly looked a little more complicated than it first appeared.

There were statements from a couple of students and dons. William Compton, a friend of Roscoe's in College, confirmed that Fairford and Vanessa Symonds had been an item for some time. He knew that Daniel Roscoe had been seeing her too but he wasn't able to give much detail of the extent of their relationship. He did not think that they were sleeping together but Roscoe had spoken of an occasion when Vanessa had stood him up and gone out with Fairford instead. He was pretty cut up about that. There was clearly a foundation for some bad feeling between them. But then shortly after that, Fairford vanished. The College knew nothing of his whereabouts, neither did his housemates nor his father.

There were victim impact statements from Mr and Mrs Roscoe, Daniel's parents, expressing their devastating loss at the tragic death of their son but they were unable to cast any light on the circumstances of his death, or why anyone would want to kill him. It seemed that Roscoe, like many students, liked to keep a wall intact between his home life and his new existence as a semi-independent adult.

There were two statements from the officers who had arrested Fairford. This was in late April at the height of the pandemic. They had been called to St Mungo's hostel in Rochester Row because of a disturbance. A young man had arrived at the hostel, unannounced, in a state of extreme distress, refusing to abide by the social distancing rules and apparently under the influence of alcohol and possibly drugs.

He was arrested under the provisions of the Emergency Powers (Serpensvid 19 Pandemic) Act 2020, detained and sampled. Routine testing revealed a match between Fairford's DNA profile and a profile on the database under the file of Daniel Roscoe. There was a full match with a sample of genetic material recovered from Roscoe's raincoat. In fact, there was a probability of a billion to one on that Fairford had had close contact with Roscoe at some point before his death.

Fairford's blood was found to contain traces of class A drugs. A medical examination revealed that he was clinically addicted to crack cocaine and heroin. Scarring on his body suggested that he had self-harmed. In short, he was in one hell of a mess. How he had come to be in that state was anybody's guess. When the police tried to interview him, he said nothing. Indeed, he appeared almost *incapable* of saying anything.

He was found in possession of a phone, so he must have had access to some income. More importantly were text messages which had been sent in the days before the murder. Database records confirmed that they had been sent to a number registered to Daniel Roscoe. The general tenor of them was that Fairford blamed Roscoe for Vanessa Symonds's death. He appeared to believe that Roscoe was responsible for them splitting up, and that Vanessa, in a state of increasing despair, took her own life.

No direct evidence. Nobody saw him do it. The papers were silent on whether there was any CCTV but presumably if there were then it would have been served. But all in all it was a pretty strong circumstantial case – motive, DNA, texts. Eye witness evidence can be unreliable. It depends on eye-sight, lighting, perspective, accuracy and the honesty of the witness. But the motive, the DNA and the texts were objective, mutually re-enforcing evidence.

What was that old case again where the judge compared circumstantial evidence to the strands of a rope? He couldn't recall the name but he remembered the analogy. One strand can snap but three strands bound together can form a rope of unbreakable strength; strong enough to hang a murderer anyway, if they still hanged people.

What was a little odd is that no phone had been recovered from Roscoe's body to confirm the receipt of the messages? But there was no doubt they had been sent from Fairford's phone and no doubt that they had been sent to Roscoe's number. No phone. Odd in this day and age. What *had* been found on the corpse?

He fished out the provisional schedule of unused material, wiping a bit of chilli sauce off the page.

"To be completed by counsel," it said.

Tapsell groaned. He removed himself to an armchair, refilled his glass and turned on the TV. The unused material schedule could wait until tomorrow.

"Jane, are you on your feet yet?"

(By which he meant, in barristers' jargon, whether she had had her first court case yet.) It was a few days later, and it was just the two of them in the common room.

"No, not until January."

"Looking forward to it?" She nodded with the enthusiasm of youth and inexperience. "Good. I think the magistrates' courts are just about getting back to normal now so there should be plenty of work. Anyway, thanks very much for the notes on the Fairford case. Very helpful. I've got a conference at the CPS this afternoon, if you're interested in coming along."

"Yes, I'd like to very much. It's an interesting case."

"Do you think it's a strong case?"

Her face immediately took on the look of a pupil under examination, a mixture of adrenaline and controlled panic. He reminded himself that every moment like this was crucial to the life of a pupil. The impression made on any single member of Chambers at this stage could be the difference between getting a tenancy, in other words a permanent place, in Chambers and rejection. He was suddenly, in her eyes at least, in a position of power over her, and he didn't like it a bit. Clearly she thought that he wielded some influence. A few months in Chambers would disillusion her on that score.

"In some ways it is a strong case and in some ways it isn't," she said, hedging her bets – the classic opening of the ambitious pupil. "On the one hand, of course, there are no eye witnesses. It's purely circumstantial. But on the other hand, good circumstantial evidence can be the best evidence of all. There's that old Court of Appeal case, *R v Donovan* (1930), which says that circumstantial evidence is like the strands of a rope. One strand might be weak but several strands put together can form a very strong bond."

Donovan – of course that was the case.

Tapsell's enquiry had been the result of a genuine desire to discuss the case, to bounce it off another mind. But now it felt like he was subjecting her to some sort of *viva voce* examination. He remembered at a distance of thirty years what life was like in pupillage. Much less competitive in those days. A white male, with a good Oxbridge degree, who could put two sentences together, could walk into a pupillage after a cup of tea with his prospective pupil master. Bad old days. Now it was more of a level playing field but that meant that it was intensely competitive to get a pupillage in the first place and virtually a fight to the death to get a tenancy. She was competing with two other pupils for a single place in Chambers.

Tapsell tried his best to put her at her ease. He didn't want to judge her, or appear to be judging her.

"You know a lot more about circumstantial evidence than I do," he said. Not very effective but he couldn't think of anything else to say.

She didn't miss a beat. "Here you have the evidence that there was a background of some animosity between Fairford and Roscoe. You have the text messages and you have the DNA evidence. Each one taken in isolation can be explained. Even the messages on their own are not enough. But when you put all three together you have a pretty strong rope."

She reminded him a little of his daughter, her eyes dancing with enthusiasm when she spoke. He wondered, as she continued, how long that enthusiasm would last. It was probably about ten years in his case, before the daily diet of blood, sweat and tears, and professional disappointment, finally got the better of him. Since then it had just been a way of earning a living. Thank God Lucy had decided to go into medicine, rather than follow in his footsteps.

"When I was a pupil, case conferences used to be in Chambers. In fact, there was a rule that no barrister could even take a seat in a solicitor's office. Something about touting for work I think. It was frowned upon in those days. Nowadays its positively encouraged. We're expected to wine and dine and generally hawk ourselves around to get a decent brief."

She looked confused. God he was showing his age.

"Conference is at two-thirty, CPS headquarters. Time for some lunch?"

As they were working their way through the elaborate security cordon in order to get in, Tapsell wondered why the case was being briefed out of CPS HQ Complex Casework, rather than the ordinary case work unit which serviced central London crime. After all, apart from the fact that Sir Joseph Fairford's son was the defendant, there was nothing special about this case. It was about as simple a murder as you could get. Why else would they have instructed him?

The CPS lawyer, O'Brien, didn't look a lot older than the pupil. A pale, thin young man who said very little but took copious notes. Beside him throughout the conference sat the officer in charge of the case, a man introduced as DCI McKendrick. He was dressed in an immaculate suit – not a common occurrence amongst police officers – and looked as if he worked out at the gym, another notable anomaly. He remained mostly silent, speaking in sepulchral tones, just to answer direct questions. He looked as if he would only break sweat in the most extreme circumstances and didn't seem to feel the need to blink. The eyes manoeuvred in their sockets like the guns of a battleship and the resulting stare was somewhat disconcerting.

Tapsell began by outlining the strengths of the case, even deploying the rope analogy. McKendrick was unmoved.

"There are some areas which need attention though," he continued. "What about CCTV? Is there any?"

McKendrick's eyes manoeuvred from O'Brien's notebook to a point just above the bridge of Tapsell's nose. "No."

"OK, enquiries were made I presume with the City of London authorities. There must be cameras in Smithfield."

"This will all be dealt with in the disclosure schedule sir."

Tapsell was about to press him further but the guns held their aim relentlessly and he thought better of it.

"Alright, we can return to that at a later time. I haven't seen any record of what was on Roscoe's person. Did he have a phone?"

"There was nothing of significance sir."

"No phone, no wallet, keys, etc."

"Only a wallet with a student identity card, a little bit of cash, and a set of keys to his room in the College. Nothing else sir."

A pause. This was unbearable. Tapsell began to wish he was back at Southend Crown Court on a diet of offensive weapons and bladed articles.

"Is there any record of that, a search log?"

"It'll be dealt with in the disclosure schedule, sir."

O'Brien's head was down scribbling in his notebook; presumably the words 'disclosure schedule' figured quite prominently.

"Have you made any enquiries into the death of the Rector's daughter, Vanessa Symonds? It appears from the Rector's statement that Roscoe told him that he thought there had been a cover up surrounding her death."

"I'm making enquiries of Thames Valley about that."

"And… are your enquiries casting any further light on the matter?"

The guns were immobile, primed and aimed right between his eyes. "Not yet."

It was said in the same tone that he might have said 'keep your nose out of things which are not your business.'

"Yes, and I suppose it will all be dealt with in the disclosure schedule." McKendrick nodded.

"Officer, you came into this case quite late, didn't you?"

"Yes, I was assigned to the case after Fairford was arrested."

"What happened to the original investigating officer? I haven't even seen a statement from him, or indeed her – I don't even know who it was."

"It'll be dealt with on the disclosure schedule, sir. *He* won't be making a statement. His evidence wouldn't add anything anyway. The Rector discovered the body and you've got the statement of the Scenes of Crime Officer."

"But why can't *he* make a statement?"

"He's working undercover, sir. Unconnected case and highly sensitive. We don't want any chance of his identity being compromised."

"And you, DCI McKendrick, are you at Snow Hill?"

"No sir, Special Branch."

Chapter Eleven

The disclosure schedule turned up a couple of days before the first hearing. As usual it was in two parts. The first part, marked 'non-sensitive', was the document which was served on the defence. Its purpose was to list the items which had been generated by the investigation but which did not form part of the evidence in the case. The defence were entitled to know about the existence of the items and either they would be served with the schedule, or they would be deemed irrelevant and withheld. The defence could then make an application to the court for the withheld items to be served as well.

The schedule contained the usual items. There were a few statements dealing with the routine handling of exhibits. There was the crime report and the investigation log, redacted to remove things like names, addresses, telephone numbers. Nothing surprising about that and these items were attached to the schedule.

Item six referred to 'police file into the death of Vanessa Symonds'. The defence already knew about the existence of such a file because the Rector had referred to her death in his witness statement. A note had been made by O'Brien that this 'neither undermined the prosecution case, nor assisted the defence' – the usual jargon meaning that there was no need to disclose it – 'Clearly Not Disclosable' was the conclusion scrawled on the right hand side.

That was reasonable enough, Tapsell told himself. Vanessa Symonds was the link between Fairford and Roscoe. But the police had concluded the death was suicide with no suspicious circumstances, and so, on the face of it, there was no need to disclose the file. The fact that Roscoe thought there had been a cover up was pure speculation and it was no part of the prosecution's case, after all, that Fairford had killed Vanessa Symonds.

Item seven was simply a note on the schedule which said, "Enquiries made of City of London Corporation for relevant CCTV footage covering 24 March 2020 in Smithfield EC1 – there is no CCTV relevant to this case."

There was no accompanying statement or notebook entry to explain this. Tapsell put his defence hat on for a moment. It raised a number of questions. Was there *ever* any CCTV footage of that area on 24 March? Surely there were cameras in such an open area of central London. Were they working at the time? When had the police made the enquiries? Had they been made too late, after any relevant footage would have been erased from the system by the passage of time – usually 28 days. That arsehole Tattinger would want chapter and verse about that.

The second part of the disclosure schedule was in a brown envelope marked 'Sensitive. For Counsel Only.' As usual, it was hardly a top security operation. The envelope was stuck down with a piece of sticky tape. Tapsell opened it. This time the document was printed on pink coloured paper and was marked throughout as 'sensitive'. Nothing unusual about that. He had seen many such documents dealing with matters such as the existence of informants, covert recording devices in vehicles, and the like – the sort of thing one would get in undercover police operations. But what could be sensitive in a case like this – on the face of it a bog standard stabbing?

There was one item on the schedule: "Matters concerning the original investigating officers in the case." There was then an explanatory note attached to the schedule which was signed off in the name of DCI Michael McKendrick, Intelligence Liaison Division, Special Branch. It said this.

"A Detective Inspector was the first officer on the scene. He was on short term temporary secondment from City Fraud. He has since returned to other duties. He is currently working on a sensitive undercover operation which has no connection whatsoever with the investigation into the murder of Daniel Roscoe. No evidence has been taken from him in order to preserve his identity. I can certify that I have familiarised myself with the early stages of the case and all aspects of the investigation, before I was assigned to the case, and am entirely satisfied that there is no material capable of undermining the prosecution, or assisting the defence."

The CPS lawyer O'Brien had then noted in the margin of the schedule that there was no need for any disclosure arising from the 'early stages' of the investigation; although it was possible that there would need to be an application to the trial Judge to prevent any questioning surrounding its circumstances.

"Does that often happen?" Jane was sitting beside him.

"No, it doesn't. I've never seen anything like it before. They are effectively seeking to prevent any enquiry about the police investigation before McKendrick became involved after Fairford's arrest. It could cover a multitude of sins – the search of the body, the enquiry into whether there was any footage, the death of Vanessa Symonds. I don't see how we are going to get away with that. We are up against a very smart silk from 3 Goldford Row, Rock Tattinger. Have you heard of him?"

"Is he that guy who represented Countess Penelope of Greece in the libel case last year?"

"That's right. He's also appeared for one or two film stars in his time, not to mention the odd disgraced politician. We used to be in Chambers together. It must be getting on for twenty years ago now. In fact, he was very nearly my pupil before he went on to greater things. Jane, I'm sure it's not going to happen to you, but it is one of the more depressing aspects of a mediocre career at the Bar when you begin to see your pupils sailing past you into silk and glory whilst you are still chugging along in first or second gear."

She thought he had made a joke and laughed. A very healthy attitude. He laughed too.

"Yes, Rock Tattinger QC, counsel to royalty and the stars and the fees to match. At a thousand quid an hour, I should think he is going to enjoy every minute of taking this schedule apart. I doubt the judge is going to wear it either. It'll be the Honorary Recorder of Southwark, old Peter Greenberg, I should think. Spent his life at the Bar defending like a rottweiler, from what I recall."

"I don't think it is Judge Greenberg actually, Jack. I was looking at the list for next week. It's a High Court Judge – Mr Justice Guggenheim."

Tapsell took the list. "What's a High Court Judge doing sitting on a case like this? There's something about this I just don't get. On paper we've got a routine murder case. In practice its being handled by CPS HQ Complex Casework, allocated to a guy from some fancy Special Branch division and tried by a High Court Judge. Can I borrow your laptop for a minute? Yes, here we go. Sir Patrick Guggenheim QC, senior Treasury Counsel 2012–2016 – basically that means counsel to the government – then appointed Special Advisor to Her Majesty's Government for National Security and Terrorism, and made up straight to the High Court Bench in June this year. A pretty meteoric career by the look of it. I think Rock Tattinger would have preferred old Peter Greenberg somehow."

Her Majesty's Crown Court, sitting at Southwark, squats on the south bank of the River Thames between a pub called the Butcher's Hook and Cleaver, and a building known as the Testicle – otherwise called City Hall, the seat of the elected Mayor of London.

Every day from Monday to Friday, whether the weather be fair or foul, a queue of people form at the entrance to the aforementioned house of correction at around nine in the morning. A conger line of characters, stretching from the revolving doors down to the sandwich shop around the corner, form, and bake or soak according to the season, and at best idle impatiently, waiting to pass through the airport style security.

Assorted, and random, offerings from the ranks of the elderly and the unemployed, brandishing their jury summonses; thieves and robbers; the indignant innocent; the indignant guilty; the relatives of the indignant innocent and the indignant guilty; the curious and morbid waiting to take their places in the public gallery; and then just the plain old barristers, some older than others, congregate, waiting their turn to be searched, frisked and verbally assaulted by the guards. Thanks to the benevolence and largesse of Her Majesty's Courts Service, the average waiting time had recently been reduced to half an hour.

Jack Tapsell, the residue of his dignity having been diminished yet further by the experience, emerged from security blinking into the lobby of the Court. *Oh wonderful, the lift was out of order again!* His trolley bag rendered thus redundant, he lifted it with a grunt and exercised his aching back by carrying it up two flights of stairs to the robing room on the second floor. Jane was already there, probably having read the advice in the Pupil's Court Guide to arrive early. Tapsell allowed his breath to return before bidding her a good morning and slumped into one of the less uncomfortable chairs.

A sigh of unfolding fabric of the finest hue and the whiff of an expensive scent, heralded a presence behind him.

"Ah Jack. How good to see you after all this time."

Tapsell turned around. Yes, it was Tattinger. The same oily voice. The same easy charm. The same coiffured hair, greying a little around the temples but in an irritatingly distinguished way. The suit, more expensive, but the cut – Tapsell noted with some satisfaction – had the merest hint of vulgarity; an irrefutable sign that money mattered to Tattinger just a little too much than it should to a proper gentleman.

"Have you met my junior, Tarquin Quinell-Smith?"

"No, I don't believe I have."

"I hope you've seen our application for disclosure?" Tarquin's voice matched his face. The tone was one of rich self-satisfaction, tempered with an underlying tone of sarcasm. The sub-text was – of course you've seen it; you've been up half the night trying to rebut it. The face was a perfect conduit for the voice. It was fixed into what appeared to be a permanent grin of smugness, the product of private fees and the sure expectation of further private fees to come. Tapsell wanted to punch it. It was only good manners which restrained him.

Tapsell introduced himself to Roscoe's parents before going into court. It was so long since he had dealt with a serious case of violence, let alone homicide, that he had forgotten the pressure of knowing that so many of the hopes and fears of bereaved families, seeking some sort of comfort in resolution, depended on the efforts of prosecuting counsel. He saw the grief permanently etched into the faces of Mr and Mrs Roscoe and he felt the weight of responsibility descend upon his shoulders.

Mr Justice Guggenheim sat impassively in Court Six like a sphinx. Tapsell sat to the left of counsel's row, Jane beside him. McKendrick and O'Brien sat behind. Tattinger and Tarquin sat on the right, closest to the jury box – empty of course; this was only a preliminary hearing. A man he supposed to be Sir Joseph Fairford was seated behind, next to Tattinger's instructing solicitor. For all the man's wealth and power, he too bore the haunted look of a bereaved parent, as if his son were as dead as Roscoe.

His Lordship stirred for the first time. "Yes, is the defendant to be produced?"

Tapsell looked behind him. The door to the cells was opened behind the glass screen and a pale, gaunt figure was ushered to a seat in the dock by two security guards. So this was Fairford. He looked anything but the Old Etonian and Oxford graduate and anything but the privileged son of an industrial magnate. He looked a physical and mental wreck. His face appeared as if it had been emaciated with drugs or drink, or both. His sunken eyes darted around the courtroom with a look – there was no mistaking it – of fear.

"Yes, Mr Tapsell."

"My Lord. I appear for the prosecution in this case. My Learned Friend Mr Rock Tattinger of Queen's Counsel appears for the defendant, together with my Learned Friend, Mr Tarquin Quinell-Smith."

“Mr Tattinger. How good to see you again,” intoned His Lordship. “Is your client ready to enter his pleas to the indictment?”

Tattinger unfolded himself and his silk robes, emitting a waft of an expensive bouquet in Tapsell’s direction. “My Lord may have seen that we have served psychiatric and psychological reports which establish that Mr Fairford is not fit to plead. In short he has suffered a complete mental collapse. The precise cause is not known but it has undoubtedly been exacerbated by a chronic abuse of alcohol and illicit drugs. As I understand it the Crown do not seek to contest this finding.”

“That’s correct, My Lord,” said Tapsell. “The defendant has been completely unresponsive to every attempt to obtain an explanation for the evidence served by the prosecution. He has been examined by the police surgeon and we do not seek to go behind the experts instructed by the defence. We accept that he is not fit to plead to the indictment.”

“Thank you. In that case, in due course, we shall have to proceed with a trial of the facts to determine if a jury can be sure whether or not Mr Fairford committed the act of killing Daniel Roscoe. I understand that a trial date in March of next year is suitable to both parties?” (His Lordship’s clerk nodded). “In the meantime, Mr Tattinger, I understand you have an application?”

“My Lord I do. I trust my Lord has had an opportunity to look at it.”

“I have Mr Tattinger and characteristically well drafted, if I might say so.”

“Yes, well I have my junior to thank for that, at least in part.”

His Lordship bestowed his most benign smile upon Tarquin and the latter bowed his head in a display of *faux* modesty. This mutual round of self-congratulation was not the best start to the hearing, thought Tapsell.

“My Lord, the position taken by the Crown with regard to disclosure, in our respectful submission, falls far below what is required. There are essentially two complaints. First, my Lord may have had an opportunity to read the statement of John Symonds, the Rector of St Bartholomew the Great. He is the person who discovered the body and called the police. It’s at page I/20 in the digital bundle, my Lord.”

His Lordship’s eyes did not need to stray to the papers. “I’ve read it,” he said.

“My Lord will have seen from that statement that the deceased in this case, Mr Roscoe, made contact with the Rector on no less than four occasions in the weeks leading up to his death. It is clear from this statement that Mr Roscoe wanted to talk to him about the death of his daughter Vanessa, in Oxford, in the early summer of last year. The Rector says in his statement that Mr Roscoe had formed the view that there had been a cover up concerning the circumstances of his daughter's death and that her death had been neither accidental nor suicide, contrary to the conclusions of the coroner."

"The Rector doesn't say why Mr Roscoe had formed that view, though, does he Mr Tattinger, and unfortunately Mr Roscoe is no longer here to tell us exactly why he concluded there were grounds to go behind the findings of Her Majesty's Coroner."

"No. But my Lord will also have seen the statement of Mr William Compton, a friend to the deceased. It is clear from this evidence and also elsewhere, that my client Mr Fairford was in a relationship with Vanessa Symonds at or around the same time as her involvement with Mr Roscoe."

"And your point is, Mr Tattinger?"

The faintest hint of judicial impatience led to the bouquet in counsels' row being refreshed by a re-arrangement of silk and Tapsell was encouraged by the mild tone of irritation creeping into Tattinger's submissions.

"May I draw your Lordship's attention to the schedule of unused material at item six? This is an entry referring to the police file on the investigation into the death of Vanessa Symonds. My Lord will see that it has been marked 'Clearly Not Disclosable'. Indeed, none of the file, or even a summary of its contents, has been made available for the defence to inspect."

The judicial attention transferred to the other side of counsel's row.

"Mr Tapsell, am I right in saying that the file has been examined by a Senior Crown Prosecutor who has concluded that it neither undermines the prosecution case, nor assists the defence?"

Tapsell elevated himself half-way to the upright position to affirm that that indeed was the case and the judicial scrutiny immediately reverted to his opponent.

"Mr Tattinger, it seems to me that this is fishing, pure and simple. There are no grounds to suggest that there was any cover up. Indeed, even if there were a cover up, how on earth could it assist your client to establish it? The only possible motive for any cover up would be to protect your client from suspicion, would it not?"

"My Lord, that is precisely the point. It is in order to rebut any suggestion by the prosecution that there has been a cover up and that my client was somehow involved in the death of Vanessa Symonds, that we seek to have sight of the file."

The eyes again swivelled to the left. “Mr Tapsell, is it any part of the prosecution case that the defendant was in any way involved in the death of Vanessa Symonds?”

“Absolutely not, my Lord.”

“And you would be prepared to edit the witness statement of Rector Symonds to remove any possibility of the jury being left with that impression?”

Tapsell was grateful for the judicial prompt. “Absolutely my Lord.”

“Thank you, Mr Tapsell. Well that deals with your first point Mr Tattinger. What is the second?”

Tattinger protested. “But my Lord, surely the defence must be entitled to see the file?”

“Move on please, Mr Tattinger.” The judicial displeasure was rising to the surface.

Tattinger stifled a further protest and filed it for later. Tarquin’s keyboard protested from the rear.

“Certainly. At the risk of understating it, there is something of a gap in the evidence. There are no statements from the original officer or officers on the scene and precious little evidence at all about the early stages of the investigation. My Lord will see at page I/36, a statement from Detective Chief Inspector Michael McKendrick of Special Branch, who took over as the investigating officer in early May, shortly after the arrest of my client and some six weeks after the body was discovered.”

“Yes, and he gives a very comprehensive account of the progress and findings of the investigation up until that point, does he not?”

His Lordship’s assistance did not appear to be appreciated. The keyboard was not appeased and nor was Tattinger. Tapsell had to stifle a nervous laugh as a silken rustle was followed by a heady waft of perfume.

“My Lord, there is a black hole at the centre of the prosecution case.”

“Well, that should assist you Mr Tattinger if it swallows the prosecution evidence.”

Tapsell’s efforts to stifle his laugh were failing. There was no admonition from the Bench.

“My Lord, the defence must be entitled to know the following, if I might list them?” The deferential tone in Tattinger’s voice was slipping. “Item seven on the schedule of unused material.” His Lordship’s eyes remained impassive. “Might I trouble your Lordship to look at it?”

"I've read it," His Lordship barked.

"We are told that enquiries were made with the City of London Corporation for any CCTV footage from the vicinity of Smithfield on 24 March 2020. We are told that there is no CCTV relevant to this case. That is not good enough."

"What else do you need to know? There isn't any."

"There must have been some, at some stage, and on what grounds has any footage been judged not to be relevant? My Lord, those who instruct me have surveyed the area and My Lord will have seen the sketch plan annexed to our application. There are working CCTV cameras situated above the gatehouse leading to the church, above the martyrs' monument, and attached to the wall of the public house, a mere twenty metres from the *locus in quo*."

"Oh dear, Mr Tattinger. You know we are discouraged these days from using latin in the courts. Not everyone has benefited from a classical education," said His Lordship (Westminster and Christchurch).

Tattinger raised his voice. "Twenty metres from the *scene of the crime*. It is inconceivable that there was no CCTV footage of the area at the time of the murder. We are not even told when the police made the enquiry. The footage might have been wiped by the time the Corporation was asked for it – in which case vital evidence which could have proved my client's innocence has been lost."

The sphinx remained unmoved. "This is all speculation, Mr Tattinger. It might just as well have proved your client's guilt for all we know. Anyway, that deals with the CCTV." His Lordship made a point of intoning the letters and making a note on his papers. "Next point."

Tattinger paused and took a deep breath. Tarquin cleared his throat and passed a note to his leader.

"My Lord, the Crown relies on text messages. On the face of it they are very incriminating."

His Lordship allowed himself the most discreet of audible chuckles. "Yes, they are, aren't they?"

Tattinger ignored the intervention. "But we only have an analysis of my client's phone. There is no record of whether or not the deceased had a phone which could corroborate the Crown's assertion that these messages were sent and received as they allege. Indeed, there is no evidence at all about the initial search of the deceased's body."

"Well, forgive me Mr Tattinger. Why does the prosecution need Mr Roscoe's phone when they can show the messages were sent to his number by your client? Whether they were received and read by the deceased is neither here nor there. They are relevant to show your client's intent. It is also a rather interesting coincidence that your client's phone was switched off the day before the murder, isn't it? Otherwise you might be having to contend with cell site evidence as well."

Tattinger ignored the last observation. "My Lord may be aware that it is possible – using the latest telecommunications technology – to import manufactured text messages to a phone in order to create the *appearance* that messages have been sent from that device. In other words, without an analysis of the deceased's phone, it is impossible to rule out the possibility that the evidence has been doctored."

Tapsell sat up. That was the first he had heard of it. He looked behind him for some reassurance from the younger generation. Jane nodded her assent.

But Tapsell need not have worried. His Lordship came to his assistance once again. "Mr Tattinger, we really are entering into the realms of fantasy now. Are you suggesting that the police have fabricated this evidence?"

Tattinger wanted to say, "It has been known for the police to fabricate evidence," but thought better of it. Such a revelation would no doubt have come as a profound shock to this judge who had never sullied himself with a criminal practice in the defence of those accused by the police.

"We have no record of *any* search of the person of the deceased. We merely have the surprising assertion from DCI McKendrick, in a statement dated almost two months from the discovery of the body, that no mobile phone was found. We respectfully ask, why on earth is the defence deprived of the search record? Why have we not been provided with one scintilla of evidence from the original investigation?"

His Lordship, with one eye to what the Court of Appeal might say, turned with an apologetic tone to the other side of the court. "I have to say, Mr Tapsell, it is rather unusual not to have a statement from the investigating officer."

Tapsell got to his feet. "My Lord, it is my intention to make an application to withhold certain material on grounds of public interest immunity and I hereby put my Learned Friend on notice of that application."

"Is there any reason why that application cannot be made now?"

"None at all my Lord."

“Very well, I will see you alone in my room Mr Tapsell.” His Lordship rose, the clerk barked, “All rise,” and the assembled audience rose and bowed, as the Learned Judge exited stage right.

By the time Tapsell had been taken around the back to the Judge’s room by the usher, His Lordship was reclining in an armchair with a cup of tea; his wig discarded on the desk. His hair, prematurely grey, was pruned meticulously, like the coiffure of a Roman senator one sees on display in the British Museum.

“Tapsell, take a seat. I anticipated your application. This is one of those cases where the officer has been *seconded to other operations* I suppose?” The Judge emphasised the words ‘other operations’ with a smile and a curious levity in his voice, as if there were some shared secret between them. Tapsell felt as if he had mislaid his invitation to the party somewhere.

“My Lord, we seek to withhold material relating to the initial investigation into the case because the officer is now involved in a sensitive operation, and there is a risk of his identity becoming known through these proceedings. The other operation is entirely separate from this case, and DCI McKendrick, who now has conduct…”

The Judge interrupted. “I’ve read the papers, Tapsell. I’m quite satisfied that the early stages of this investigation are adequately summarised in the statement of McKendrick and that all material arising therefrom may be withheld by the Crown on the grounds of public interest immunity.”

“But my Lord, I’m referring to the schedule of sensitive material.”

“Yes, I know. Seen it. I’ll give my ruling in court for the record. Now, why don’t you have a cup of tea? How are things in the Temple? Holding up under the present unpleasantness I hope?”

And that was it. There was no further mention of the sensitive material, or anything to do with the case for that matter. Tapsell enjoyed the unprecedented generosity of Her Majesty’s Courts’ Service – a cup of Earl Grey and a chocolate digestive – entertained the Judge with a story or two about life at the grubbier end of the Criminal Bar (his self-respect had long since been abandoned), and was then ushered out by His Lordship’s clerk.

He could hardly believe it had been so easy. He had mentally prepared himself for a difficult day and the relief was palpable. At the same time there was something about the whole process which made him a little uneasy. The Judge would not normally have been given access to the sensitive material in advance of an application to withhold it.

As Tapsell came back into court he tried to look impassive. “You look as if you’ve been caught with your hand in the till,” joked Tattinger. “Well, that was quick – application fallen on stony ground? What have you got for me?”

Tapsell laughed nervously. “The judge is going to give a ruling in a moment.”

His Lordship emerged from stage right.

“All rise!”

Mr Justice Guggenheim took his seat and pronounced judgment.

“Having heard prosecuting counsel in chambers and having reviewed all relevant material relating to the preliminary police investigation into this case, I am entirely satisfied that such material is in no way capable of undermining the case for the prosecution, or of assisting the defence. Moreover, I rule that no questions may be asked on behalf of the defendant with a view to probing the police investigation before the involvement of Detective Chief Inspector Michael McKendrick. I am satisfied that the summary provided in his witness statement is both sufficient and accurate and that any questions with the object of going behind it are entirely irrelevant to this case. This ruling will, of course, be kept under review throughout the trial process. Well gentlemen, we will meet again, I believe in March, when this case is to be tried.”

His Lordship began to raise himself from the bench when Tattinger protested. “My Lord, we object in the strongest possible terms to this ruling. In our submission the defendant cannot possibly have a fair trial unless we are able to examine the early stages of this investigation. Will my Lord grant permission to appeal this ruling?”

His Lordship did not bother to resume his seat. “No. This ruling is made as part of the trial process and cannot be reviewed by the High Court, as you well know Mr Tattinger. Your remedy will lie to the Court of Appeal in the event that your client is convicted. 8 March 2021, gentlemen.”

As soon as the judge had disappeared from view, Tapsell turned to O’Brien and McKendrick behind him. “Let’s have a quick conference shall we? Let’s bag the room outside the court before anyone else gets it.”

Tapsell did not relish the prospect of an immediate confrontation with Tattinger and Quinell-Smith. He didn’t quite understand what had happened, and wanted an excuse to make a quick exit. Whilst his opponents were trying to placate their benefactor, in the person of Sir Joseph Fairford, Tapsell ushered his retinue into the conference room just outside Court Six.

After explaining what had happened to Mr and Mrs Roscoe and bidding them farewell until the trial in the spring, Tapsell sat with Jane at one end of the table; O'Brien and McKendrick at the other. O'Brien said nothing. He sat down and took out his notebook. McKendrick looked delighted. "Well done, Mr Tapsell. Whatever you said in there certainly did the trick."

"I didn't say very much at all as it happens. But that effectively puts to bed the whole issue of disclosure for the purposes of this trial. I can hardly believe it was so easy."

"He's a good judge, Guggenheim. He's been in on a couple of our jobs." McKendrick looked thoroughly pleased with himself.

Tapsell took a rather old fashioned view. The role of a good copper was to make sure a case was investigated thoroughly and fairly and then to present the evidence to be properly addressed by the trial process. No officer had a right to have that look of triumph about him before a defendant had been convicted fair and square, especially when there was a bad smell in the air, which there undoubtedly was here.

Tapsell exhausted thirty minutes or so going over matters such as the witnesses who were required for the trial and the timetable. He felt uncomfortable about what had happened and didn't want to bump into Tattinger in the robing room. He would not have liked to have been on the receiving end of that judgment if the roles had been reversed and he believed that Tattinger had a right to feel aggrieved.

After McKendrick and O'Brien had left, Jane reviewed her notes.

"I thought it was going to take longer than that, in the Judge's room, I mean."

"So did I. I don't suppose you've much experience of public interest immunity applications, have you?" She shook her head. "I didn't have to explain anything to the Judge. He seemed to have seen the sensitive material already."

"Isn't that how it usually happens?"

"No. I would usually have to take the Judge through the material I was seeking to withhold and justify why it couldn't be served on the defence. And the Judge would have to be entirely satisfied that the defendant could still have a fair trial, even without the withheld material. He didn't need to hear from me at all. It was as if it had already been explained to him. I just don't get it. Especially in a murder case when I'm effectively seeking to hold back all the material arising in the immediate aftermath of the discovery of the body. And then to get a blanket ruling prohibiting the defence from even probing what had happened. I didn't even have to ask for that."

Jane shrugged. "Remember he was a special adviser to the government on national security before he became a judge and Treasury Counsel before that. This must come pretty easily to him."

Tapsell stood in the robing room, wrestling with his collar. "These bloody things get tighter every time I wear them," he said.

The stud snapped and he cursed.

A familiar voice came from the other side of the mirror. It was Tattinger. Tapsell cursed again under his breath. Tattinger had waited for him. He removed his collar and went around to the other side of the partition. Tattinger was seated in the lounge area, disrobed, nursing a polystyrene cup.

"Jack, how long have we known each other? Must be twenty years."

"Yes, you were Peter Dobson's pupil weren't you? You've come a long way since then. Certainly left me behind."

Tattinger put down the cup.

"Do you know Jack, I was close to giving up in those old Sumping Court days. I didn't think crime was for me – something grubby about it. I was thinking of joining a City law firm. Do you know what changed my mind?"

Tapsell shook his head.

"You did… I remember shadowing you in an armed robbery case. Must have been in '98, '99? You were prosecuting a young lad who said that he was being forced to take part in the robbery because the other members of the gang had threatened his mother with a gun. Do you remember?"

Tapsell sat down. "Yes, as a matter of fact I do – it must be over twenty years."

"That's right. You wanted to disclose material about an ongoing police operation. It wasn't directly relevant to the case but there was intelligence about how similar gangs in the same area were using under-age accomplices to carry out their dirty work by making threats against their families. The police resisted. They didn't want you to disclose it and insisted it would prejudice their ongoing operation. You insisted and said you could not proceed with the case unless the material was disclosed because the defendant couldn't have a fair trial. In the end, you prevailed. The material was served. The jury heard the evidence and the defendant was acquitted. Young lad – what, sixteen, seventeen – would have gone to prison for twenty years if it hadn't been for *you*, and you alone. You made a life-changing difference to another human being through sheer persistence, decency and integrity."

Tapsell laughed. "Maybe I was just being an awkward sod for the sake of it. It wouldn't be the first time. I'll tell you what, though, I certainly never got another brief out of that department."

"Yes, I heard that. But I'll tell you what. It changed the course of my career. That's why I stayed on at the Bar. I saw what a difference one individual can make in a single day to another person's life." Tattinger stood and picked up his briefcase. "I've always looked up to you Jack, until today. What was it that changed you? See you in March."

At around the same time that Rock Tattinger QC left the robing room of Southwark Crown Court, just before lunchtime on that September day, Detective Chief Inspector Peter Bonik, of the City of London Fraud Squad, was sipping his first coffee of the morning, approximately 4,650 miles to the South West. He sat in the Emperor Dining Room of the Seafront Boutique Hotel on the waterfront in George Town, the capital of the British Overseas Territory of Grand Cayman in the Western Caribbean Sea.

Since that day in late April on his roof terrace, when he first learned of the news that he had been taken off the case of Daniel Roscoe, Bonik's fortunes had taken a turn for the better. The following day he had been summoned by the Divisional Superintendent who broke the news that a most shocking discovery had been made in the Cayman Islands, namely that a major money laundering conspiracy was operating out of the territory, that it needed the immediate attention of a reliable officer from City Fraud, and that he, Bonik, had been warmly recommended by his superior officers for the job. He would be seconded to the Royal Cayman Islands Police Service, with the enhanced rank of Chief Inspector and would be given a generous tax free salary in line with his new responsibilities.

Along with the generous tax free salary would come a generous expense account too, and rooms had been arranged for him in one of the best hotels in Grand Cayman, the Seafront Boutique. Bonik, with no ties in London, or anywhere else for that matter, accepted with alacrity. Two days later the Divisional Superintendent further informed him that, so impressed were his superior officers with how he had worked with PC Wendy Graham on the Daniel Roscoe case, they had decided to send her as his assistant with the honorary rank of Detective Sergeant and with an expense account to match.

Five months in the Caribbean had certainly done wonders for Bonik's complexion. Each morning from Monday to Thursday inclusive, after breakfast, he would make his way from the hotel to the police station, a pleasant walk along the waterfront which lasted all of twenty minutes. At the police station he would be greeted by the local constabulary with a deference he found a little embarrassing. He would then sit in his air-conditioned office, and would spend a couple of hours sipping freshly squeezed orange juice until lunchtime. After the hour of eleven he might even allow himself the indulgence of a nip or two of vodka in the orange juice and he would sit and read the London papers, or listen to the radio, or just doze.

Occasionally, but not often enough to be much of a distraction from the London papers, somebody would bring some work to him – the occasional spreadsheet, the odd bank statement, the infrequent file of fishing licences – just to see if anything occurred to him which required his immediate attention, rather than the attention of one of his subordinates.

At around lunchtime, Detective Sergeant Wendy Graham would take over, having made her way from the George Town Splendide, the five-star hotel to be found at the other end of the waterfront. She and Bonik would exchange pleasantries, perhaps share a pot of coffee, and only the very occasional jug of Pimms, and they would tacitly congratulate themselves on the fortunes of being a police officer in the early twenty-first century.

According to the terms of his secondment, Bonik would then knock off for the rest of the day. He would spend the afternoon reclining on the beach, indulging in a little fishing and even sipping the odd cocktail. He had a deep Caribbean hue, had lost weight, and, although the volume of his alcohol intake had declined only marginally, its quality had improved remarkably. In short, exile had been good for Chief Inspector Bonik.

One late September morning, some five months into his exile, Bonik was relaxing in his office having reviewed a particularly demanding fishing licence, and was reading the London Times. The tempo of his life no longer demanded close attention to the news, and so he eschewed online content, and was happy to wait for the hard copy from London. The ten-day time lag appealed to him now. There was something a little incongruous in the intrusion of contemporary news into his Caribbean idyll.

He turned to page five. "Son of TCC chairman, Sir Joseph Fairford, faces trial for murder," said the headline. The article was short and to the point. "The story of Thomas Fairford, son of the industrial magnate, remains a mystery. Having disappeared for almost a year, he turned up last April at a hostel for the homeless in Rochester Row, Victoria, having suffered a mental collapse. Apparently unable to explain his disappearance, or his recent history, he was placed into protective custody in view of the snake flu pandemic which was then at its height. A routine DNA sampling provided evidence to link him with the death of fellow Oxford student, Daniel Roscoe. Roscoe was found dead in Smithfield in late March, some five weeks before Fairford's re-appearance. A profile of DNA taken from Roscoe's coat matched that of Fairford.

"Both men were associates, having dated the same girl at Brasenose College Oxford the previous year. The circumstances of Mr Roscoe's death seem to be equally mysterious. Roscoe's body and the surrounding area were searched, and nothing of significance was found which could be linked to the deceased, not even a mobile phone. Both sides no doubt hope that the mystery will be finally solved. The trial is fixed for March of next year at Southwark Crown Court."

That was all. Bonik waited for Graham to put in an appearance.

"Wendy, I, for one, have never had any complaints about being sent out here and nor I suspect, have you."

She shrugged her shoulders and laughed, gesturing out of the window at the sea view.

"But you must have wondered why?" He indicated the empty in-tray on his desk. "This isn't a full time job, or anything like it and why it requires a DCI and a DS from London is a mystery in itself." He pushed the paper across the desk. "The Roscoe case has reared its head again just when I had almost forgotten about it."

Graham took the paper and casually perused it. Five months of the Caribbean life had somewhat altered her sense of priorities too. She put the paper down nonchalantly and Bonik continued.

"The Fairford boy was up in court a couple of weeks back. The trial's coming up in March of next year. Tell me, has anyone ever approached you to make a witness statement about our involvement in that case?"

"No, nobody has approached me about the case at all. To be honest, I'm not that bothered."

"No but think about it. It's a bit of a coincidence, isn't it? There we were both working on the Roscoe case. An arrest is made back in April and then days later we are both shunted out to the Cayman Islands. I know that neither of us has much experience in homicide. The only reason we were drafted into the Roscoe case in the first place is that nobody else was available because of the snake flu, but we were still the original investigating officers. It has always struck me as a bit odd that we were suddenly removed from all contact with the case."

"What business is it of ours anyway? Lighten up. Look out of the window." She raised her glass to the sea view.

"You see, by the end of it, I was convinced there was a bit of a cover up surrounding the death of that girl. What was her name? Vanessa Symonds. Thames Valley had closed the case as a suicide which Roscoe didn't buy. Something dodgy about the psychiatric report, remember?"

"Zeitmann – dodgy record to do with doctoring reports, and then I could find no trace of where the toxicology report had come from."

"That's it. I always thought that it was to do with this guy, Thomas Fairford. Son of Sir Joseph Fairford, wealthy industrialist and donor to the powerful. I guessed it was a cover up to protect his son who must have been the prime suspect. Fairford goes missing. She starts seeing Roscoe, and then Fairford returns and commits the traditional crime of passion, and her body ends up in the Cherwell. But now Fairford's been charged with the murder of Roscoe, the idea that it was all a cover up to protect him falls apart."

"And if they've put us out in the long grass as part of a cover up, what has that got to do with the death of Vanessa Symonds?"

Bonik sat back and chewed the end of his pen. "Remember Sir John Fawcett? Did I tell you what he told me about Roscoe?"

She shook her head. "I lost track after that. I was too busy packing for the Caribbean."

"Quite. Well apparently Roscoe had been calling Fawcett. Remember Fawcett's contact details were in that notebook I found in the church. Fawcett said that Roscoe had some wild conspiracy theory. Vanessa was some sort of animal rights activist – remember the Rector told us he had fallen out with her about it? Well, according to Fawcett, Roscoe believed that Vanessa Symonds had stumbled upon something to do with that lab in Oxford. You know, the one where all those demos were taking place. He thought that it was being used by the US government for research into biological warfare. Fawcett thought that the snake flu pandemic had sent Roscoe over the edge, and he was behaving irrationally."

Graham pointed to the paper. "According to this report nothing of significance was found which could be linked to Roscoe either on the body or in the vicinity. What about the notebook?"

"Exactly, the notebook! That's what was troubling me. I couldn't make much out of that notebook, but I do remember that there was a reference to snake viruses. Even if Roscoe was a nutcase, the notebook was, on anybody's definition, 'significant'. His blood was all over it. Whatever happened to it? You booked it into exhibits, yes, a few days after the murder?"

"Yes, but I booked it out again just after the arrest of Fairford. I wanted forensics to check for Fairford's prints."

"OK and what happened to it?"

"I don't know, sir. That was just before we were taken off the case."

Chapter Twelve

London did not return to normal, even after the vaccine. It was cleaner, brighter, safer and just a little kinder. Peter Bonik's rooftop musings had proven to be a little optimistic, rather than wholly fanciful. Slowly as the vaccine began to work its magic, as the Christmas lights turned on one by one, people went about their business again without masks, and with the instinct to distance from their fellow man receding into the subconscious.

But they did not return to work in their former numbers. They had learned, so many of them, that the office was largely redundant. If the office was redundant then, for many of them, so was public transport, or even private transport. The reduction in pollution, and the improvement in air quality, was not temporary. It turned out to be symptomatic of a cultural shift; a shift in what people were prepared to tolerate, and a shift in their expectation about what their governments could and must achieve.

And this cultural shift did not stop at pollution, its compass extended to the role of the state, and what the state could and must do about crime, and what it could and must do about homelessness, and about communities. Because people had become aware of their communities and had come to value them as something other than a medium through which they must travel to reach their place of work.

And Tapsell felt unusually optimistic as he emerged from Temple tube station. The air was still fresh and as crisp as a chilled martini that early December evening. The courts were getting back to normal capacity again. He was getting some cash flow for the first time in months and he had a murder to look forward to in the spring. If he made a good fist of that, maybe it would revive his flagging career. Perhaps he had a swansong, a late flowering, to look forward to at the fag end of his career. He laughed at the appalling mixed metaphors, and then he stopped to look at the headline in the Standard – "Climate

Breakthrough at G20 – new treaty to be signed in the spring." Things were certainly looking up.

As he walked into Sumping Court he glanced up at Chambers. Yes, it looked like the Christmas party was in full flow. The windows were steamed up, and there was Blackford leering over Jane like a vampire. He took a deep breath and went in. The air was thick, and slightly fetid. Joe, a bottle of beer in his hand – by the look of him by no means the first – offered him a warm glass of white wine. "Hello sir. Merry Christmas!"

"Merry Christmas, Joe." Tapsell took the view that if he had to drink warm wine it had better be red. He picked up a glass of the budget cabernet sauvignon and set off on a relief mission towards Blackford, who had cornered Jane by the photocopier.

"Jane, how are you?" Tapsell was pleased to see the look of relief on her face at the sight of him.

"Fine, thanks Jack." She bore the rictus grin of someone enduring a tortuous experience for the sake of career prospects.

Blackford was red in the face and not particularly pleased by the interruption. "Jack. How good to see you. Prosecuting murders, eh? Well, well. How old are you now, 55, 56? You'll be taking silk by the time you're 70 at this rate." He was holding his glass unsteadily at an angle of just over 45 degrees and the wine was dripping remorselessly down his shirt front.

Tapsell laughed politely, and directed Jane away from the embarrassment. "Jane, I hear Tim Larkin's doing a case in Highbury Mags tomorrow. Not long before you're on your feet – why not go and see if you can tag along. There he is, over by the drinks table conveniently." She moved off with a wave.

"How much have you had Dom? A skinful by the look of it." He indicated the state of Blackford's shirt.

"Fuck off! Anyway, talking of that murder, I think I ought to let you into a little secret Jack. I was at a reception last week for the new Chief Crown Prosecutor of Greater London. A little birdie told me that the only reason you were instructed in that murder was because of your reputation after Operation Pellew." He punctuated his slurring by stabbing his finger into Tapsell's chest.

Tapsell moved back. "What on earth are you on about? Haven't you had enough?"

"Turns out the CPS were desperate to get somebody who would roll over on disclosure. After Pellew you were known as a brief who wasn't too particular about the unused material." Blackford laughed, his breath stank of red wine and stale tobacco. "They wanted somebody who wouldn't look too closely under the carpet. You got the brief because you're no fucking good!"

Tapsell moved out of range towards the bar and helped himself to another cup of the barely drinkable. He chatted to Jane and Tim Larkin and allowed the alcohol to dull his wits. He left early, a little fuzzy, but not drunk. And when he emerged into Sumping Court the air was even brighter and crisper than it had been before. He breathed deeply and enjoyed the feeling of the accumulated sweat of the party evaporating in the cold night air.

His mind returned anew to what Blackford had said. *Was Dom trying to rile him?* It was the sort of banter he tended to come out with when he was in drink. The problem this time is that what he had said rang true. *Why had the CPS instructed him?* There was clearly something which he was not being told, and which they didn't want made public. The optimism Tapsell had felt earlier that evening evaporated as quickly as the party sweat from his forehead.

It was three months later that Tapsell stood up to face the jury for the first time in the case of The Queen v Thomas Fairford. Five looked at him with expressions of intelligent enquiry. Four looked at him with expressions of indifference, two with expressions of bafflement and the twelfth looked up at the ceiling.

"Members of the jury, in this case I appear on behalf of the Crown to present the case for the prosecution. The defendant, Mr Thomas Fairford, is represented by my Learned Friends, Mr Rock Tattinger of Queen's Counsel, and Mr Tarquin Quinell-Smith." A disrespectful snort of hilarity from the back row of the jury greeted the last announcement. Tarquin shifted in his seat.

"This case is about the death of a young man called Daniel Roscoe. A 22-year-old law student at Oxford University, with his whole life ahead of him, found stabbed to death in Smithfield, in the City of London, on 24 March of last year. The prosecution case is that this man," at which point Tapsell pointed at the dock, "Thomas Fairford wielded the knife, and plunged it into the back of Mr Roscoe with malice aforethought, that is with the specific intention of killing him. Members of the jury, the prosecution say that Thomas Fairford murdered Daniel Roscoe on 24 March 2020."

He now had the attention of all but the young man in the back row, who was at this point more interested in the young, female clerk of the court than the ceiling.

"The prosecution relies upon three strands of evidence." He had decided to deploy the rope analogy. "First, you will hear that the defendant and the deceased were rivals at Oxford for the attentions of a young woman called Vanessa Symonds." Now he had the young man's attention. "Second, you will see text messages sent by Mr Fairford to the deceased, in the days before the murder took place, threatening him with violence and in particular, members of the jury, threatening to kill him. Third, you will hear that traces of genetic material were found on the collar of Mr Roscoe's coat which matched the DNA profile of the defendant; in other words, incontrovertible proof that he had had close physical contact with the deceased in the period leading up to his death."

Several members of the jury were now looking across at the dock, having formed their tentative conclusions and fascinated to see what a real murderer looked like in the flesh. The diminished, emaciated figure which sat there was something of a disappointment.

"Each of these strands of evidence would point to the guilt of Mr Fairford. Here, all three strands of evidence taken together form a rope, a case, of such strength, that you will be driven to the inevitable conclusion that there can be no reasonable doubt that Mr Fairford is guilty of this crime."

A ruffle of silken feathers from the other side of counsels' row perfumed much of the remainder of Tapsell's opening speech as he expounded further upon the strength of the evidence. He sat down with a degree of satisfaction. The attention of the jury had remained intact and Jane muttered a word of encouragement from behind; even His Lordship's expression of boredom had mutated into a look of benign indifference.

Tapsell proceeded to call his first witness.

"Could you tell us your full name please?"

"William Francis Compton." He was a large man and struggled to fit his frame within the witness box.

"Thank you, and is it right that you are currently an undergraduate at Brasenose College, Oxford?"

"Correct."

"I do not think there is any dispute in this case that you knew Daniel Roscoe, is that correct?"

A mutter of objection came from stage right. “Don’t lead!”

His Lordship’s attention swivelled from the witness box to defence counsel. “Are you saying it *is* in dispute, Mr Tattinger?”

Tattinger rose to his feet with palpable irritation. “My Lord, it is not in dispute that this witness knew the deceased. But I would prefer it if my Learned Friend did not lead the witness.”

“Well really Mr Tattinger, if the defence is to take that attitude we shall be here until Christmas and I’m sure the ladies and gentlemen of the jury have better things to do with their time before then.” His Lordship treated the front row of the jury to his most sympathetic smile, as if commiserating with them on having to perform a most distasteful public duty.

Tattinger sat down heavily back into his seat, his frustration palpable. Tapsell felt a twinge of pity. The Judge was sailing pretty close to the line.

“Please continue Mr Compton. You knew Daniel Roscoe.”

“Yes, we met in our first term and became good friends. Drinking buddies, I suppose would be the best description.”

“Thankyou. Could you tell us if you know the defendant, Thomas Fairford?”

Compton looked to the dock. “I do. Tom, that is Mr Fairford, was a postgraduate student at Brasenose.”

“Can you please tell us what you knew, if anything, about the relationship between Mr Fairford and Daniel Roscoe?”

“I cannot say that I knew, er, Mr Fairford at all well, but I was aware that he was seeing a girl in College called Vanessa Symonds. They were boyfriend and girlfriend as far as I could tell, that is before Tom disappeared. I know that Dan was keen on Vanessa. He mentioned her a few times. I remember he was upset – it must be around a year or so before he was killed that he told me about it. He had a date to take her to a ball. I think it was at the Union and Tom took her instead. The reason he was particularly cut up about it is that they waited until he was in sight before walking off together, arm in arm, to the party. He thought it was a deliberate attempt to humiliate him.”

“And what happened after that?”

“Well, shortly after that – it must have been in the Easter vac I suppose – Tom just vanished. No one knew where he had gone. And then of course she was found dead in the Cherwell just before the summer vacation – suspected suicide. I can only assume…”

A cloud of scent preceded the inevitable objection. Tapsell anticipated it. “Thank you, Mr Compton, wait there please. There will be some more questions.”

Tattinger rose to his feet. “Mr Compton, did you ever see my client, Tom Fairford, strike the deceased?”

“No.”

“Did you ever see him in any sort of argument with the deceased?”

“No.”

“Did you, in fact, Mr Compton, ever see my client and Mr Roscoe in the same room together?”

“Er, no, I don’t think so. They didn’t really mix in the same circle.”

“Exactly. You have no evidence that my client bore any ill will to Mr Roscoe whatsoever?”

“There are the text messages.”

“Never mind about the text messages, Mr Compton. I’m asking you about *your* evidence. What you can tell us from *your* experience. I’ll ask you again. To your personal knowledge there is no reason to suspect that Tom Fairford bore any ill will to Mr Roscoe whatsoever, is there?”

“But what about the cover up? Dan didn’t believe Vanessa had killed herself. He thought she had been murdered.”

His Lordship looked up from his notes and directed a malevolent smile at learned counsel for the defence.

Tattinger cleared his throat. He had asked a question too far. “Mr Compton, there is no doubt in this case that Miss Symonds took her own life and the ladies and gentlemen of the jury will hear a formal admission from the prosecution to that effect in due course. Now will you please answer the question?”

“I have no personal knowledge that he bore any ill will towards Dan, no; apart from the Union ball.”

“But that could have been the work of Miss Symonds, could it not? A practical joke, if a little cruel – or indeed even a coincidence – would you agree?”

“I suppose so, if you put it like that, yes.”

“Thank you Mr Compton. That is all my Lord.” Tattinger resumed his seat.

The next witness was John Symonds, Rector of St Bartholomew the Great. He took the oath sanctimoniously, replaced the New Testament and surveyed the court room scene from the witness box, as if he had entered a urinal. His evidence to prosecution counsel was confined to his discovery of the body.

Tattinger then rose to cross-examine. “The day upon which you, er, stumbled upon the body was the day after the imposition of the lockdown, was it not?”

“I believe so, yes.”

“Difficult for us to remember now but in those early days, people took the lockdown seriously. There was nobody about, was there? In fact, from the point at which you entered the Smithfield area from Giltspur Street, until the arrival of the police, some 10–15 minutes later, you saw nobody else? Is that correct?”

“Nobody at all. I was frightened myself to come out of the Rectory – it’s near St Paul’s you know – but there were matters which I had to clear up in the church.”

“And am I right, that you have never seen my client, Mr Fairford?”

“I’ve seen Sir Joseph on television.”

“No, I mean my client in the dock, Mr Thomas Fairford.”

“No, I’ve never seen him but I understand he was seeing my daughter some months before her death.”

“We are not interested in what you have heard, Rector, only in what you can tell us from your own knowledge.”

“But there was a cover up surrounding her death. That is why Mr Roscoe was coming to see me.”

His Lordship once again treated Tattinger to a smile laced with malice. “Another question too far, perhaps Mr Tattinger?”

There was an audible titter from the jury. Tapsell had to cover his mouth, and wondered how his opponent could have got so far on so little talent – with the sort of effortless charm which had always eluded *him*, no doubt.

“My Lord, may I address the court in the absence of the jury?” said Tattinger.

“Certainly. Ladies and gentlemen, as I explained yesterday, there are certain matters of law which do not concern you, and which I have to address in your absence. Please retire to your room, and I will call you back in due course.”

Tattinger paused until the witness had withdrawn, the last of the jurors had disappeared at the back and the usher had closed the door. “My Lord, these references to a cover up are deeply prejudicial to my client and clearly give the impression that he was somehow involved in the death of Miss Symonds.”

“But that is a result of your rather loose questioning, Mr Tattinger. You should keep a tighter rein on your cross-examination. I think it is far better if all of this is out in the open in any event. It seems to me that the rest of the evidence cannot properly be understood without it. Mr Tapsell has already indicated that he will make an admission in due course that the young lady's death was a suicide and that there is no suggestion that your client was involved. Bring the jury and the witness back please."

His Lordship aimed a patronising smile at the witness. "Now, Rector, you said that Mr Roscoe was coming to see you because of the cover up surrounding your daughter's death. What did you mean by that?"

"When the police sent me the report into my daughter's death, I found it hard to believe. They said that she had been depressed. I tried to contact the psychiatrist who had assessed her but he fobbed me off. First he claimed not to remember the case, and then he went sick. In the end I could simply make no contact with him at all. Daniel Roscoe had called me several times before his death. He thought she had been murdered. That must have been why he was coming to see me. You see, he had made a note of the psychiatrist's details in his notebook – name, Harley Street address, telephone number. I think he had some more information for me."

Tapsell heard a shuffling behind him at the mention of a notebook. McKendrick approached him from behind and started hissing in his ear. "Is this relevant, Mr Tapsell? What's this got to do with anything?"

Tattinger picked up the thread. "You mentioned a notebook, Rector. What notebook is this?"

"There was a notebook. Inspector Bonik found it in the church. It was smeared with blood. Daniel had clearly been looking for me in the church. There was a trail of blood you see. It must have been his because the Inspector showed it to me later. That's why I know it contained the details of Dr Zeitmann. I think the notebook belonged to my daughter because it had her initials at the front, and I recognised her handwriting."

Tattinger turned around to consult his learned junior and then continued. "In any event, Rector, at the time of Mr Roscoe's murder, you had never even heard of Thomas Fairford, had you?"

"No, but I hadn't been in contact with my daughter for some time. She was heavily into the animal rights movement, demonstrating outside laboratories and the like. We had clashed over it. You see, Daniel believed that my daughter had been murdered because she had removed some papers from the lab, the Anglo-American Laboratory for Bio-Chemical Research."

Mc Kendrick was becoming agitated and tugged at Tapsell's sleeve. His Lordship glanced across. "Do you object to this line of questioning, Mr Tapsell?"

Tapsell remembered what Blackford had said to him at the chambers party.

They wanted somebody who wouldn't look too closely under the carpet.

"No my Lord."

"Well I do," said the Judge. "I think we have strayed into the realms of pure speculation now, Mr Tattinger. Do you have anything else?"

"Not in front of the jury, my Lord, no."

"Very well, members of the jury. I think that's quite enough for one day. Please remember my warning. Forget about the case over night. No research on the internet. No discussions between yourselves. Let's keep the evidence between the four walls of this court room, and I'll see you tomorrow at 1030 please."

The jury filed out and Tattinger rose to his feet again. "My Lord, the fact that speculation about the death of Vanessa Symonds has been aired in front of the jury is most unfortunate but your Lordship has allowed this to happen."

"And I will direct the jury in due course that it is of no relevance to the issues they have to determine. Anything else Mr Tattinger?"

"Yes, my Lord will recall that there is no evidence in this case from the original investigating officers on the scene. We have now heard mention of an Inspector Bonik."

"I am not going to allow you to explore that. It is entirely irrelevant to this case, and you have had my previous ruling. You have the statement of Chief Inspector McKendrick who deals with the circumstances of the original investigation."

Tarquin pulled on Tattinger's gown from behind and gestured to the right.

"I see that Mr McKendrick is sitting in court. May I ask him to withdraw during the discussion of this issue?"

Tapsell turned and asked McKendrick to go outside. After some resistance, he left.

Tattinger continued. "But my Lord will recall that the evidence of Mr McKendrick is that nothing of significance was found in the vicinity which could be connected to Mr Roscoe, save for an identity card, and in particular there was no mobile phone. We now know that there was a notebook in which Mr Roscoe had made entries."

"How could that possibly assist your case? It is pure speculation. We have no idea what it contained."

"The point is that we simply do not know. Has the notebook been reviewed by those who instruct my Learned Friend? Presumably not because Mr McKendrick makes no mention of it in his statement. Indeed, he asserts that there was nothing of significance which was found. If it contains notes made by Mr Roscoe in the period leading up to his death, not to mention notes made by Vanessa Symonds, it could very well be of material assistance to the defence. Until somebody has looked at it, we simply do not know."

"Of course, you are making a rather large assumption that what the witness says is accurate and true; namely that there was a notebook. That is his evidence. It is not the same as confirmed fact." His Lordship sighed. Now this was out in the open, it couldn't be swept under the carpet. "Mr Tapsell, perhaps you could look into this overnight, and confirm whether or not such a notebook was ever recovered by the police."

"I will, my Lord."

"In that case, I will rise. 1030 tomorrow morning gentlemen."

Tattinger cornered Tapsell before he could leave court. "Jack, this stinks. Did you know anything about this notebook?"

"No, nothing at all. Look, I will get to the bottom of this. Believe it or not, I really haven't changed since you saw me prosecuting that armed robbery all those years ago. I promise you."

"What about Pellew?"

Tapsell was taken aback. He didn't realise the Pellew case had achieved such notoriety. "In Pellew I was kept in the dark. I knew nothing about that telephone evidence until we got to the Court of Appeal, and then I was hung out to dry by the CPS when the shit hit the fan. I'm not going to let that happen again."

Tattinger turned to leave. Tapsell took him by the arm. "Rock, it meant a lot to me what you said about that case, when you were a pupil I mean. We go through our professional lives and so often we don't look back to see what wreckage or treasure we leave in our wake. I'm glad that experience stayed with you. Thanks for reminding me."

Tattinger looked around. "Don't mention it."

McKendrick was waiting outside with O'Brien. Tapsell began to usher them into a conference room when a man wearing a raincoat, with a cadaverous appearance, approached them from the corner. "Excuse me. My name is Donnelly. Can you tell me if I am likely to be called today?"

"Mr Donnelly, the forensics officer?"

"That's correct."

"No, I'm sorry, you won't be called today. I hope that we will be able to take your evidence tomorrow morning, Mr Donnelly. Thanks for waiting." Donnelly showed no reaction and faded into the background as silently as he had emerged.

Tapsell, McKendrick, O'Brien and Jane filed into the conference room.

"Chief Inspector, what is this about a notebook? As I understand it, nothing of significance was ever found either on, or in the vicinity, of Roscoe. Is that right?"

McKendrick was not as composed as usual. He was blinking. "Correct sir. I've been through everything. Nothing was found."

"The problem is that we are now going to find it very difficult to keep a lid on this. The defence are going to want to know about this Inspector that Symonds referred to. The one who found the notebook."

"Symonds is simply wrong about that sir. There was no notebook. There was no nothing."

"What was the Inspector's name? Bonik?"

McKendrick reverted to his impassive mode. "I can neither confirm nor deny sir. You know the background to this. The Judge has ruled in our favour and we're bullet proof."

"You can give me a guarantee that there is no notebook?"

He looked Tapsell in the eye. "Absolutely."

Jane noticed Tapsell looked a little down as they were leaving court. "You look as if you could do with a pint."

"I could certainly do with something. Not the Butcher's Hook though – its full of lawyers. I can't stand them. There's a wine bar next to London Bridge."

It was a dusty old place, quiet enough, with sawdust on the floor, and bistro style wooden tables. Tapsell ordered a bottle of red.

"How are you getting on, Jane. Been on your feet for a couple of months now, haven't you?"

"Yes, I've done a few trials in the mags. Nothing in the Crown Court yet."

"Don't worry. It'll come. Let me know if there's anything I can do to help. I don't hold much sway in Chambers, I'm afraid, but if you ever need any advice, just pick up the phone." He took a large mouthful from his glass, and inspected the bottle. "Not bad this – Loire valley."

"I just thought I'd take a few days out and come and see you in action. Someone told me you're one of the best."

Tapsell looked up from his glass and laughed. "Oh, who's that then?"

"Judge Monkford – I was marshalling for her in Snaresbrook before Christmas."

Tapsell leaned back and reminisced. "Dear old Brenda. Do you know I led her in a fraud – I don't know – probably fifteen years ago now. Big case in Luton. Last year I appeared in front of her prosecuting a shoplifting."

"Well you're in a murder now. Career's on the up. How do you think it's going anyway? You don't look as if you're enjoying it!"

"A few years ago I did a case which fell apart because of disclosure. The CPS sat on some evidence which could have helped the defence. I was criticised by the Court of Appeal for not pressing the police for more information. My career never really recovered. I haven't forgotten it, and I've been a little bit paranoid about disclosure ever since. Well, it looks as if this case is going to be riddled with disclosure problems. I'm pretty convinced the police are sitting on something they shouldn't be. What's Special Branch doing on a case like this anyway? No statement from the investigating officer. We now know his name – someone called Bonik. No mention of the notebook – I can't believe the Rector of St Bartholomew the Great just dreamed that up. I'm beginning to wonder now about the telephone evidence. It is right what Tattinger said then? You can manufacture outgoing messages on a phone?"

Jane nodded. "Yes, and so long as you don't have access to the other phone, there's no way you can tell the difference."

"Mmm. Then of course we have a Judge who seems to be quite happy to go along with all of it. Special adviser to the government on national security – and just made up to the High Court Bench with no previous judicial experience." He drained his glass and picked up the bottle. "Well this time I'm not going to sit on *anything*. Fancy another?"

It was after eight when Tapsell emerged from the tube station. It was drizzling. He put his collar up. A small man in a raincoat jostled through the commuters six feet behind. This man emerged onto the pavement, propped a cheap, pop-up umbrella over his head and followed Tapsell to the right, along the Edgware Road. Tapsell slowed as he passed the steamed up countenance of the kebab shop, eyeing the revolving doner in the window and weighing up the delights of a shish against the more delayed comforts of a curry. He decided on the former. He emerged from the kebab shop five minutes later, grasping a white carrier bag. The pop up umbrella resumed its progress, maintaining a respectful distance of ten feet or so behind him.

Tapsell crossed to the junction with Maida Avenue and entered an off licence on the corner of the road. As he purchased a rather indifferent bottle of red, the small man in the raincoat waited by the window, peering through a small hole in the condensation he had wiped with his sleeve. The rain had stopped by the time Tapsell left the shop. He turned left and walked along the canal. It was pretty, the moisture on the pavement reflecting the lights from the canal boats.

Tapsell opened the gate and walked to the door of the block of mansion flats in which he lived. He was struggling to fit the key into the lock of the street door when he was interrupted by a reedy voice from behind.

"Mr Tapsell? Can I have a word?"

Tapsell turned around. He recognised the pale face from earlier, rendered even more cadaverous by the light from the entrance lobby. It was Donnelly.

"Mr Donnelly, what are you doing here? I shouldn't be speaking to you. You're a witness."

"I am an expert witness. The rules are a little different."

"Hardly. Even so, following me to my home address is most irregular to say the least. What can I do for you?"

Donnelly was one of those people with little instinct for personal space, not through malice but through a complete absence of empathy. Tapsell leaned back to avoid his breath which smelled of coffee and something even more malodorous.

"I saw you leaving the bar in London Bridge. I stayed on at court to look through the exhibits list. It isn't there."

"What isn't there."

"The notebook. I heard you talking to Mr McKendrick about it. I couldn't understand what he was saying. There *was* a notebook you see. Inspector Bonik found it in the church. Instead of drawing it to my attention he handled it." He mouthed the words with some relish, as if describing an act of gross indecency.

"I found the fingerprints of the deceased on the pages of the book, together with a matching profile of his DNA in the samples taken from the blood staining. There's no doubt it was his property."

Tapsell had the weird feeling of being the lead character in a thriller. For no particular reason he found himself looking up and down the road. "Look, you'd better come in. It's started raining again."

He opened the door to his ground floor flat and ushered Donnelly in.

"Live here on your own, do you?"

"Yes, take a seat. I'm going to have a glass of wine. Want one?"

"Just a glass of cold tap water please." Tapsell might have guessed.

When he came back from the kitchen, Donnelly was standing by the window. "Lovely view of the canal."

"Yes, look Mr Donnelly. What you've just told me is very serious. Please sit down. When did you last see this notebook?"

"I saw it when Inspector Bonik's assistant," at this point he flicked his lower lip with his tongue, "a young lady called Wendy, I think it was – gave me the exhibit to examine again, after the arrest of the suspect, Mr Fairford. The tests were negative for Mr Fairford's fingerprints and I replaced it in the exhibits store. Now it seems to have gone missing. It doesn't even appear on the exhibits list. What I thought you might be interested in is that I took a copy of it before I replaced it. You see, I found it fascinating, from a professional – a *scientific* – point of view. Would you like to see it?"

"You made a copy? Yes, of course I would like to see it."

Donnelly removed some folded papers from his inside jacket pocket. It looked like they had been well thumbed.

"It was a standard Oxford University Press, A5 notebook, not new. There were some notes at the front – first few pages and then some jottings at the back but in a different handwriting. I took a photocopy of the pages which had notes on them."

Donnelly handed the papers over. They had been stapled together, and were stained yellow around the edges. Tapsell took them to the side table, unfolded them and turned on the lamp. Donnelly came and stood behind him, to his right, so close that Tapsell could smell his fetid breath and feel it on his neck, but he was more interested in the contents of the notes.

He spoke almost to himself, although conscious of Donnelly's presence. "Yes, 'VS' – Vanessa Symonds – these must be her notes, as the Rector said.

This here," he pointed with his finger, "is this the laboratory in Oxford – it looks like an address in Holywell Road?"

"That's it. The Anglo-American Laboratory for Bio-Chemical Research."

"It looks like she is referring to another document, doesn't it? Does this refer to the index number of a research paper perhaps? The transference of – what's that?"

"The transference of pathogenic viruses from snakes. That's the subject matter of the paper."

Tapsell looked up. "Quite prophetic then." He read on, "'Structure of proteins', 'mammalian carriers', 'zoonoses' is it? I'm a lawyer, Mr Donnelly, I'm afraid this is way over my head."

Tapsell returned to his armchair, still puzzling over the notes. Donnelly perched on the end of the table.

"Mr Tapsell, I'm a chemist by background but I know enough about bio-chemistry to have some understanding of what that is all about. It looks as if she is referring to a paper summarising a research project into how a new virus – apparently originating in snakes – might be transferred to the human population via the medium of another mammal, such as a pig."

"What!" Tapsell recalled the evidence of John Symonds. According to his evidence, Roscoe had told him that he believed Vanessa had been murdered because she had removed a paper from the lab. Hadn't he also said that there had been a cover up involving the psychiatrist. Tapsell turned to the last page. Yes, here were some notes which were clearly in a different handwriting. The Rector was right. There was a note of an address in Harley Street.

He turned back to the notes at the front. "These notes appear to have been dated – April 2019. If that is the date when the notes were made, then she appears to have got her hands on a research paper which was predicting the outbreak of a pandemic some eight or nine months before it happened. Is that right?"

"Correct. But it wasn't just predicting the outbreak of any pandemic. It was predicting the outbreak of *this* pandemic – the snake flu." Donnelly's face looked rather ghoulish in the light from the lamp. He was clearly relishing it.

He got up from the table and pointed a pencil like index finger at a notation in the middle of the page. "Do you see this?" He pointed to a series of letters and numbers on the second page.

"Acl19266int6+red31[susB77]. This is a genetic nomenclature for a virus. She has done her best to replicate the printed version in manuscript. The 'A' is the Greek letter alpha. The underlined sections would be italicised in print – 'cl', 'int' and 'red'. They indicate the mutations in the gene. The square brackets indicate the insertion of a DNA sequence into the virus. Take away the underlining – the italics – and take away the square brackets, and you have the precise genetic name for snake flu."

Tapsell was beginning to wish he had not had the wine. He tried to focus. "But how could somebody predict the precise make-up of the virus before it even existed?"

"They couldn't. This shows that the virus existed as long ago as April of 2019. But it goes further than that. This notation indicates that the disease was manufactured. It is the mutation of a virus, indigenous to reptilian organisms, such as snakes – that's the 19266. At least one part of the DNA sequence has been inserted. That's the square brackets. Mr Tapsell, this is a virus which was created by man and almost certainly in this laboratory in Oxford."

Tapsell rubbed his face, and tried to think. "But your theory depends, doesn't it, on when the note was made. It appears at the end of the second page. It could have been inserted as an addendum to the note at a later stage. Do you know anything about handwriting evidence? If we could prove that Vanessa Symonds wrote these notes, somebody who died in the summer of 2019…"

"Handwriting evidence is not an exact science though. Half the time it's not much more than guess work. If only we had the original notebook we could date the ink. There is reliable technology to do it, to put a date on the notes themselves. If we could show that this note had been made around April of 2019, it would prove that the pandemic was deliberately manufactured in a laboratory."

Tapsell's heart was pounding. "What the fuck have I got myself into?"

"The biggest story of the century. That's what." Donnelly was grinning and Tapsell couldn't wait to get rid of him.

"Look, we shouldn't be talking here like this. We could both get into serious trouble. You're a witness in a murder trial for God's sake, never mind about all this." He brandished the papers in the air. "Leave this with me. Tomorrow morning, we will have to act as if you have just produced it. Heaven knows what's going to happen then."

"This represents quite a breakthrough in bio-chemical research. The combination of a red31 mutation with the insertion of a sus sequence demonstrates some remarkable advances in DNA engineering. It has extraordinary implications for medical science."

Tapsell ushered him to the door. "Donnelly, it appears that this remarkable advance, as you put it, far from leading to a cure for cancer or the elixir of life, has caused the death of over a million people worldwide. I will see you tomorrow. Do not mention this meeting, or the notebook, to anyone. Understood?"

Donnelly nodded. Tapsell shut the door on him and downed the rest of his glass. He felt soiled and took a hot shower. Before going to bed he scanned the photocopy of the notebook onto his phone and sent it to his secure email account.

He spent much of the night awake. First he sat in an armchair, nursing a tumbler of scotch, trying to figure out what to do. He couldn't take the copy to McKendrick. McKendrick had denied the very existence of a notebook. O'Brien had barely opened his mouth and was little more than a cipher for McKendrick.

He could hardly take it to the press. His first duty was to the integrity of the trial process. He couldn't proceed with the trial – how could he call McKendrick to give evidence which he knew was untrue. He would have to take the matter to the judge. Guggenheim's behaviour had been a little surprising during the early stages of the trial, but he had a solid background as a national security adviser to the Crown. He could surely rely on the integrity of the judge.

He spent much of the rest of the night lying on his bed staring at the ceiling, trying periodically to drift into sleep and failing abysmally with the dreaded combination of bed-spin and a pounding heart.

At half past four in the morning, or thereabouts, he gave up, made himself a cup of coffee, showered again, dressed, and decided to walk to court. He left around half past six. He took the scenic route through the Royal Parks and as he wandered along the Serpentine and through Green Park, the black turned to indigo. The early spring sun came up in his face as he crossed Westminster Bridge, daring him to blink and yet the air was still crisp and refreshing. He felt a little more cheerful. He was at the fag end of a pretty undistinguished career. He had nobody to support anymore. He had a little money put by – enough to support himself frugally until the state pension came in – if he lived that long. *What was the worst that could happen?* He wouldn't work again – put out to grass. So what? He was sick of the fucking job anyway.

He sat for a while on the south bank, opposite St Paul's and then at about 8:30 made his way along the embankment to Southwark Crown Court. The queue was short at that time, but as soon as he had cleared security he saw Donnelly waiting for him.

He held up his hand. "I can't talk Mr Donnelly. You are a witness. Please report to the CPS room." He walked on without waiting for an answer.

He sat in the corner of the robing room and took out the document. Donnelly had been absolutely right. If – and it was a substantial 'if' – this document was what it appeared to be, it was the biggest story of the century and would have incalculable geo-political implications. If the snake flu had been deliberately seeded in Wuhan by agents of the US or UK government, the ramifications would be immense – at the very least a complete diplomatic isolation of the two most important powers in the west.

"Morning Jack, feeling better now?" It was Jane. Christ, he had to get her away from this mess.

"Hi Jane. Can I have a word? Let's find a conference room somewhere." He led her to a room just outside the Bar mess. "Jane, I think it's best if you head back to Chambers and tell the clerks you're free for work this week. The quicker you start getting into court in your own right, the better. You don't want the other pupils to get a head start on you."

"But there really isn't any work around until next week. I really wanted to see this case. I haven't done anything wrong have I?"

"Not at all. You've been of invaluable assistance and have given me great moral support. You have a glorious career ahead of you. I've no doubt of that. I'm coming to the end of mine. You'll have to trust me on this one. It's better if you are out of this case. It's going to get messy and it won't do you any good to be associated with it – even as a pupil."

She looked at his face and tried to read him. He placed his hand on hers and nodded. She nodded back almost imperceptibly, smiled, gathered her things and opened the door. She looked back. "Good luck Jack" she said, and gently closed it.

By the time he had returned to the robing room, Quinell-Smith had arrived. His face wore its perpetual broad smile of smug self-satisfaction.

"Got something for us this morning Tapsell?"

"I'm afraid you are going to have to wait just a little longer Tarquin. I'm going in to see the Judge *ex parte* again. You are formally on notice. Let Rock know please."

"More cloak and dagger stuff eh? So there was a notebook. Don't bother putting that poker face on for me Jack. Why else would you be going in to see the judge. I shall wait with bated breath."

Tapsell wanted to tell him to go and fuck himself, but thought better of it.

As Tapsell entered the Judge's room, His Lordship was munching on a biscuit. "Jack, do take a seat. Can I interest you in a chocolate digestive?"

"No thanks Judge. It's about that notebook. You recall Reverend Symonds referred to it yesterday."

"Yes, no doubt the old dear was a bit confused. He didn't look the full ticket to me."

"It turns out that there was a notebook. A copy of it was given to me by Michael Donnelly, the Crown's forensic scientist, last night. He took a copy of it before it mysteriously vanished from the exhibits."

His Lordship's smile evaporated as Tapsell passed him the dog-eared photo-copy. He put his biscuit down and scrutinised the document.

"This is the copy of the notebook. It was found in the church. It has Roscoe's fingerprints and DNA on it. Your Lordship may remember the evidence of the Rector – Roscoe believed Vanessa Symonds had been murdered because she had stolen a paper from the research lab. If you look at the second page, there is a reference to what appears to be the title of the paper – 'The transference of pathogenic viruses in snakes'."

"So what? So what if she had been murdered? What does that have to do with whether Daniel Roscoe was murdered by Thomas Fairford?"

"This." Tapsell pointed to another note a few lines below. "It's the genetic code for the snake flu virus, Serpensvid 19. According to the date at the top, this note was made in April 2019 – eight months before anyone had even heard of the virus."

"What?"

"This is despite the fact that McKendrick…"

Guggenheim held up his right hand to silence him.

"Let's just think about this for a moment, Tapsell. Roscoe's become obsessed about the death of his girlfriend about a year before. He's cherished her notebook ever since. Rightly or wrongly he suspects some sort of police cover up. She'd been involved in the animal rights movement, right? Who's to say that he hasn't simply made a note of this code, or whatever it is, once the virus had been analysed and catalogued by the scientists? He's put two and two together and made six with some madcap idea that the snake flu was being created in this lab that his girlfriend was investigating."

"My Lord, I still think I now have no choice but to disclose this to the defence."

"Why? Tapsell this is pure speculation. They are fishing for any defence they can invent and you seem to be helping them. The jury have to judge this case on the DNA and the text messages. It's obvious Fairford did it."

"My Lord, if Vanessa Symonds was murdered by someone trying to protect the truth about the origin of the snake flu pandemic, then Roscoe could have been a target too. He held the evidence in this notebook."

"But the suggestion that the virus was created in a lab for some joint Anglo-American project is fanciful Tapsell and so is the suggestion that Roscoe was murdered by anyone else. Fairford doesn't even put up a defence. He has nothing to say for himself. This is obviously a note made by Roscoe, or someone else, *after* the event, after the virus had been identified and it had become public knowledge. I give you permission to withhold this document under my previous ruling to do with the early stages of the investigation."

"But I was assured by Chief Inspector McKendrick that there *was* no notebook. How can I call him as a witness of truth to say that nothing was found by the original investigating officers?"

"Call another officer to give the same evidence from the search records and the investigation log. I will allow it in as hearsay."

"But there's something else. The notebook was analysed for the DNA and prints of the defendant. Nothing was found. That has to be disclosable."

"Nonsense. We have no idea whether Fairford had any contact with this notebook or not. The fact that there is no trace of him on it tells us nothing. Tapsell, I am not going to have this trial derailed. I was wondering why you have never taken silk. I can see why now. You do not have the balls for a hard fight. Now go outside and get on with this case." Guggenheim threw the papers back across the desk.

"With all due respect my Lord, you are supposed to be the impartial referee, not my Learned Leader for the prosecution."

Guggenheim stood up, red in the face. Tapsell picked up the papers and left before His Lordship could say anything more.

Tattinger was waiting for him in the courtroom. "So Jack, what about this notebook that we heard so much about yesterday?"

"Notebook?" Tapsell removed the dog-eared photocopy from his inside pocket and placed it on the bench in front of Tattinger. "What notebook?"

Chapter Thirteen

And yet that summer of 2021 was, all in all, a good one for Jack Tapsell. And one early September evening, towards the end of it all, he sat back at the waterfront café on the Via Francesco Caracciolo, inclined his face to receive the late sunshine and watched the light recede on the Bay of Naples. The merest suggestion of the waning of the year tempered the warm sea breeze as he sipped a chilled glass of the Lacryma Christi del Vesuvio. It was almost a year, to the day, that he had first heard of the case of the Queen against Thomas Fairford.

At first it had been bad. McKendrick's anger was almost physical. The CPS immediately dropped the case; Fairford, or what was left of him, discharged into the care of his father. It would have been impossible to have proceeded with the case, given that the integrity of the entire investigation had been undermined. Without a hint of irony, the CPS then proceeded to lodge a complaint about him to the Bar Council and they had threatened to withdraw all work from Chambers if he remained a member.

He had received some support. Some of his older friends and acquaintances in Chambers and a few others who only did defence work, stood by him. Blackford, unsurprisingly, turned upon him without apology, more interested in his own career prospects than any semblance of collegiate loyalty. Most movingly Jane had spoken up for him after she had been given a tenancy in Chambers later that spring. But the weight of opinion was against. He had acted without instructions and disclosed material without authority, which the CPS had deemed to be sensitive. He couldn't deny that. Never mind the merits of the case itself. That didn't matter. It was the principle. He was a security risk and he had to go.

He didn't wait. In advance of the Chambers meeting to decide his future and before any Bar Council disciplinary proceedings were able to get off first base, he resigned from Chambers and surrendered his practising certificate. By the beginning of the summer he was retired and all the accumulated stress of thirty years of practice at the criminal bar began to lift from his shoulders like the dissipation of the clouds on a warm, early summer's morning.

There was the media attention for a while of course. He had never got to the bottom of how the notebook had been leaked to the press. Either Donnelly or Tattinger he supposed. There was a big splash in the papers the Sunday after the case had been dropped. The sources were anonymous but the papers had latched onto the genetic name for snake flu and so it was likely that Donnelly had been speaking out of turn, aided and abetted by Tattinger or, more likely, that slime-ball Quinell-Smith, who had added some juicy titbits from the aborted trial.

"Proof: Snake Flu – a man-made death virus", or variations on the theme, were the headlines in some of the more sensational Sundays; "The Truth About the Fairford Case: Cover Up or Conspiracy Theory" was the more measured response from the broadsheets.

The journalists had focused on the death of Vanessa Symonds. They had got hold of some of her friends and acquaintances in College who had spoken of her activities as an animal rights activist and of her relationship with Thomas Fairford. Try as they might, they had got nowhere with obtaining the story from Fairford himself. His father had obtained a restraining order in the courts, deterring all but the most determined paparazzi who continued to camp outside the family estate in Berkshire without result.

And they had spoken to Vanessa's father too. He appeared to have relished his moment in the spotlight. He recounted what he had been told by Daniel Roscoe: Vanessa had obtained a secret paper that proved the snake flu had been manufactured in the Anglo-American Laboratory in Oxford and that she had then been murdered as part of a cover up. A copy of the police report into her death was published in full. The press had gone after Zeitmann but had found nothing. All trace of his practice had vanished in the course of an investigation by his professional body into allegations of corruption.

And then there was the notebook. Who exactly were Perkins, Chevening, and Giddens? Were they scientists or spies? The 'three stooges' they were called in one paper; in another they were likened to the three witches from Macbeth, with a cartoon depicting them brewing a deadly virus in a steaming cauldron. And how could the genetic identification of snake flu have been known, months before the outbreak of the disease in China, unless the virus had been deliberately manufactured and seeded?

There were questions in the House: questions to the Prime Minister and a plethora of written questions to Her Majesty's Secretary of State for Foreign and Commonwealth Affairs. Eventually the identity of the witches became public. There was no secret about it, so they said. It turned out that Brad Perkins was the Assistant Under Secretary of State at the US Department of Defence, and Giddens was his deputy. Tom Chevening was CIA, the Assistant Commissioner at the Department for China and the Far East. None of them had the slightest knowledge of any paper emerging from the Anglo-American Laboratory and were prepared to go on the record to confirm it. A minor sub-committee of the China Sub-Committee of the United States Senate Foreign Affairs Select Committee, convened a meeting, heard evidence and confirmed their stories.

And questions were asked of Sir John Fawcett. After all, if any conspiracy theory to do with US foreign policy needed any corroboration, then the man to corroborate it would be Sir John Fawcett. But to the disappointment of the papers, he did not. He went on the record to describe his meeting with Daniel Roscoe. Roscoe, he said, was obviously a troubled young man. Distressed by the death of his girlfriend to begin with, he appeared to have been sent over the edge into insanity by the outbreak of the snake flu pandemic and had jumped to the fantastical conclusion that she had made a devastating discovery about the Anglo-American laboratory, and had been murdered in order to silence her.

Fawcett claimed to have humoured the young man before sending him on his way. It was obvious to him that Roscoe had simply jotted down the genetic notation of the snake flu after it had been identified, as part of his wild conspiracy theory, and had made notes of individuals who, his confused mind supposed, might have had a hand in any conspiracy. So the explanation went.

And there were questions for Her Majesty's Secretary of State for Education and Science, and Her Majesty's Secretary of State for Health. Eventually, and with considerable reluctance, and on the most solemn understanding that no precedent was being set in the cause of open government, it was confirmed that indeed there had been work at the laboratory with a view to addressing the risks posed by zoonoses. However, the work done into pathogenic viruses in snakes was just one of hundreds of research projects into such viruses, snakes being merely one of a few hundred species identified as posing a potential risk. To prove the point a choice selection of (heavily redacted) papers were put into the public domain, on the strict understanding that no precedent was being set, etc.

And so eventually interest in the story waned. And when a third-tier royal was photographed *in flagrante* with a second-tier film star in a first-tier hotel in California, the story appeared to die a death as final as that which had been suffered by Daniel Roscoe.

For a while, a few of the less illustrious paparazzi even found their way up the Edgware Road into W2, and, until the second Sunday of the story at least, one or two cameras, from the bottom end of the market, would be trained on the ground floor flat in Maida Avenue where Jack Tapsell had holed up.

He rather liked it at first. Instead of phoning for a takeaway, he would wander up to the Little Venice Tandoori and pick up his curry. Sometimes he would be more adventurous and go for a walk to Paddington station to stock up from the supermarket. A couple of the little reptiles would follow; shouting questions. He would smile benignly, and he hoped a little enigmatically, and otherwise ignore them. Over his morning coffee the next day, he would then scour the morning paper and the internet for the little snapshot of himself. Actually, he looked rather distinguished.

Unfortunately, his career had been so *un*distinguished that they had found very little to put in the column below the snapshots. The best they could manage was "Barrister in snake flu case refuses to comment." He was a little disappointed that they had not described him as "Fat Cat Barrister refuses to comment" – the appellation usually attributed to lawyers in the tabloid press. They had uncovered an article or two about the Pellew case, and in one or two articles he was apparently "Accident Prone Barrister", or even "Formerly Disgraced Barrister". Frankly, he couldn't give a damn. He had retired.

And by the time the third Sunday had come around, and the third-tier Royal had fallen to the fourth tier, and the second-tier film star had risen to the first, Tapsell was anonymous once more. There was still the occasional story in the papers but only in the context of the aftermath of the pandemic. And so you would have "impetus from international snake flu cooperation drives global initiative for climate pact". And then at the end of the story, "Suggestions that the virus originated in an Anglo-American research laboratory are now dismissed as a hoax."

Or, "G20 leaders push for worldwide cease-fire and global peace conference in the wake of the pandemic." And then, "the leadership of the Chinese Communist Party have officially dismissed rumours that the pandemic was deliberately seeded by the west as a conspiracy theory propagated by the animal rights lobby."

And so the clouds of life at the criminal bar dissipated for Jack Tapsell. He eased himself into retirement by putting his feet up. As April turned to May, he transitioned from the red to the rosé, from Beethoven to Mozart; and as May turned to June, from the rosé to the white, from Mozart to Handel.

And so his spirits lifted. He calculated that he had enough money to get by. The *chateaux* on the labels had to transition as well, to the likes of the 'economies', and the 'values', and the 'best of own brands'. The eating out had to be replaced by a little bit of home cooking from time to time. But, all in all, he was grateful for the case of The Queen against Thomas Fairford – after all, it had rescued him.

His brief moment in the spotlight bore further fruit. His daughter, Lucy, came to stay for a weekend in late June. She was just starting out as a junior doctor in a West Yorkshire hospital, and he did not get to see her as often as he would have liked. She had gravitated to the north with her mother, after the divorce.

On the Saturday evening he took her to the little restaurant over the canal, where he had once taken her for lunch when she was a little girl.

"How's Mum?" he asked, knowing that the enquiry would please her; a fleeting glimpse of parental unity, like a passing ghost.

"Not so well since she broke up with Paul."

Tapsell chuckled. "Am I supposed to feel sorry for her?"

"Dad, she's not well. She's not eating properly and she's losing weight. I've told her to see a doctor but you know what's she's like."

"Stubborn, like you." He caught the look on her face. She wasn't amused. "I'm sorry," he said, and held her hand.

She brightened once more. "Anyway. You're footloose and fancy free again, in more ways than one. What are you going to do with yourself?"

"Not much. Take it easy. There's more to life than work. You come to realise that as you grow older. I might try to write a novel. I've got some material now you know."

She smiled and looked out of the window. There was a view all the way along the canal to Warwick Avenue. "I love this place. The light on the water. I remember at Christmas the fairy lights all the way along. We came here one Christmas Eve, do you remember?"

"Yes, you must have been about seven. We went to Suffolk that year for Christmas. That's when your grandad was still alive."

"We had some good times. You should come and stay over in the summer, Dad. I think Mum would like to see you. She's still fond of you, you know."

He sighed. "Sometimes it's best to let the past go. The only thing that your mother and I have in common now is you. We will both always love you, no matter what. We always have. But you're right. We did have some good times. Do you remember that holiday we had in Naples?" She smiled. "You must have been, what, 12, 13? That's the last time I remember us being really happy together, your mum and I. I've got loads of photos – we can look at them again later, if you like."

They did. And that August he and Lucy spent two weeks together. The first week they hired a car and explored the Amalfi Coast again, revisiting the places they remembered and more. Then they took a small apartment in the centre of Naples, in San Guiseppe. They explored the old town, and took the funicular up to Montecalvario. On two consecutive days they took a train to the archaeological sites at Pompeii and Herculaneum.

It was a bitter-sweet time for him. He was revisiting some of the happiest times he had known and yet he knew that those memories could never be re-created. They were a mere shadow of what had been. Yet, he was happier than he had ever been since that last visit to Naples, almost ten years before. The cares of the criminal law had evaporated and he had not spent such a time with Lucy since her childhood.

Shortly after that first holiday to Naples his marriage had broken up. Lucy's mother went off with a mutual friend and six months later they moved to the north. In retrospect, it was clear that his career had gone up in smoke along with his marriage – the divorce followed in tandem with the debacle which was Operation Pellew.

"*You got the brief because you're no fucking good.*"

The words of Dominic Blackford returned to torment him just once in Naples. Lucy had asked him about the Fairford case and he gave her a fairly honest account. He knew now that what Blackford had said must have been true. The CPS had instructed him because they supposed he wasn't too bothered about making full disclosure to the defence. How ironic. It was precisely because of Pellew that he was determined not to make the same mistake again. But why had they been so desperate to cover up the notebook if it were nothing but the product of Roscoe's fevered imagination?

That night, the last night before Lucy's flight back to Leeds, they shared a bottle of prosecco together on the balcony of their apartment. As they observed the Neapolitan street life below, about as far removed from the stuffy rooms of Sumping Court as it was possible to imagine, he resolved to banish all thoughts of the Fairford case to history, and concentrate only on the future.

Lucy had a memory of a pizzeria which, she said, had over-shadowed every pizza experience since. They found it, after a while, on the Piazza del Gesu Nuovo. They had a huge margherita, with a little dried oregano sprinkled on the top, some anchovies for him carefully arranged on one side, crisp as it should be at the edge, soft as it could be in the middle. They grazed happily with a bottle of Aglianico and talked of past times. After a while, Lucy – always with a tendency to the maudlin after a couple of glasses – spoke of the divorce.

"Dad, did you and Mum ever really love one another?"

"I think we did, yes. Almost twenty-five years. It's a long time to be married."

He looked out into the Piazza, his mind elsewhere. She took his hand. "Dad?"

"I've never told you this but I was engaged before I met your mother, at Oxford – a young PPE student called Becky. She met someone else, fell in love with him and out of love with me and that was the end of it. I was heartbroken for a time. Then I met your mother, in the summer of 1990. She exorcised the pain but she never replaced Becky. I pretended to myself for a while that she had but it wasn't true. Yes, we loved each other, your mother and I, but, I suppose if truth be told, towards the end we stayed together for you."

The next day they parted at the airport, feeling closer than they had in years, and determined to see much more of each other. He had booked a hotel in Chiaia for a few days to take stock, on his own. And so, on that early September evening, having finished the last of the prawn linguine, with the final drops of the Lachrymi, he strolled along the Riviera di Chiaia, almost at peace with himself once more.

Chapter Fourteen

19 May 2016. Moscow. Rain. Mikhail Nikolaevich Verenikov squeezed his rather corpulent body through the obscure tradesman's doorway, at the back of the Kremlin Arsenal, onto Zhitniskaya Street. He looked left and right, and left again. There was no sign of his driver. Good. Then he looked up, and opened his umbrella. In order to avoid the Kremlin, he turned left, left again and then along to Mokhoyava Street to the river. Turning from time to time to make sure he was not being followed, he headed west along the north bank of the Moskva until he came to the Krymsky Bridge.

By now the rain had soaked him and he was glad to turn his face from the driving westerly wind in order to cross the river. He walked across the bridge, and continued south along Krymsky Val Street, the rain continuing to assault him from the right. He was glad to see the familiar gateway leading into Gorky Park. He took shelter under its arch and looked at his watch. 1252 – he was early.

He shook his raincoat, swivelled his umbrella and tried to squeeze himself, along with a family of tourists, into the corner of the portal offering shelter from the driving rain. Then, at one minute to one, the car drew up, a brown Lada X-Ray, dented to the offside, registration MSK 45 GROM, exactly as described. In the back was a fat man, wearing a black leather jacket. The window was wound down. Verenikov approached and spoke the words.

"With a helper…"

The fat man replied, "… a thousand things are possible. I'm Balsov, get in!" He opened the rear passenger door and Verenikov climbed inside.

The air was rank with sweat and cigarette smoke. Balsov leaned across him and closed the window against the pelting rain. Verenikov undid his collar.

"Where are we headed?"

"Not far."

"Thank the Lord for that."

The driver turned to Balsov who nodded. The car continued along Krymsky Val street and then swung around the Garden ring road at such a pace that Verenikov grabbed the door handle to avoid a collision with the black leather jacket. Then they re-crossed the river and headed east along the Entuziastov Soseo.

"Slow down, will you!"

The fat man removed the fag end from his mouth. "There cannot be any risk of being followed."

"I was careful. There was no one. In any case, there's a speed limit along here. We'll attract the attention of every traffic cop in the neighbourhood."

Balsov leaned forward to the driver. "OK Viktor. Take it easy."

The car slowed to around 60 kilometres per hour. Verenikov noticed that Balsov had an old scar leading from his left ear to the corner of his mouth. His complexion was red and the scar stood out white. Balsov leaned to his left, and whispered into Verenikov's ear. His breath reeked of rough vodka and cheap cigarettes.

"Calm down, Mikhail Nikolaevich. We are nearly there."

"Thanks and its *Secretary* Verenikov to you, if that's quite alright."

The fat man sneered and then pointed to the entrance of an industrial estate, barking an order to the man in front. The Lada took a sharp turn to the right, causing Verenikov to lurch left and stopped abruptly on a dirt track in front of, what appeared to be, a disused warehouse. Balsov got out and spoke rapidly on his phone. Then he came around and opened the rear passenger door. Verenikov got out. It was still raining.

"This way." Balsov indicated an entrance into a red brick building which was in a state of disrepair.

The door was off. The rain had come through the roof and the floor was slippery with a thin film of mud. They went up a flight of steps to a narrow corridor lit with bright strip lighting. It was dry, and lined with parquet flooring. Verenikov lowered his umbrella. Balsov turned to the right. At the end of another passage was a door – it looked freshly painted – with a doormat in front of it.

Balsov pointed at the mat. "He likes people to wipe their feet." Then he knocked three times on the door, and a voice from within bade them enter.

Verenikov entered, and squinted. The light was dim compared to the corridor. There were no windows. The room was large – maybe twenty metres long by fifteen wide. It was lit by a lamp in the corner, and a spotlight above. At the far end was a large desk. A man stood behind it.

"Did you wipe your feet?" Verenikov nodded. "I don't want to be rude but the carpet is Persian and this building – although in an ideal location for our purposes – is not in the finest state of repair, as you will have noticed. Please."

The man gestured to two armchairs, arranged around a marble-topped table. Verenikov approached. The man – around forty-five years old with a mop of black hair – extended his hand. "Mikhail Nikolaevich, if I may, I think we have met." His ample frame was squeezed into an expensive, but ill-fitting, silk suit. He spoke with an accent from the Urals. The voice was familiar enough.

Verenikov took his hand. "Yes, I remember you from my days in London. The gold frauds – you were working from inside the department then, yes? At least that is what I understood."

Brazhensky laughed, a smoker's laugh. "Yes, still inside the tent pissing out, at that stage. Nowadays we like to be a little more, how shall we say, semi-detached."

Verenikov sat in one of the armchairs; Brazhensky in the other. Balsov stood at a distance, his hands held behind his back. Brazhensky gestured to him. "Perhaps a little refreshment." Balsov went to a kitchen area at the opposite corner of the room.

Brazhensky lowered his voice. "I'm afraid you will have to forgive our friend. Some of us get a little rusty at the social graces on the outside but, as you will see, we can still import a little bit of civilisation into our cubby hole."

Balsov returned with a silver tray, placing it on the marble topped table. A chilled bottle of Oval Swarowski Crystal vodka, straight from the freezer by the look of the frost, stood proudly in the middle with two crystal glasses. A ceramic pot, with two mother-of-pearl spoons, was at the side – grey fish eggs sparkled through the glass lid.

Verenikok decided he could afford to show his ignorance in this company. "I thought caviar was meant to be black."

"I prefer the Savruga. It has a higher brine content than the Beluga – it suits my rather unrefined palate."

"I see. My public sector salary doesn't allow me to taste the difference."

Brazhensky laughed, displaying a row of tobacco stained teeth. He reached forward and took the vodka, opened the bottle and poured two generous shots. "Your very good health, my friend." He tipped his head back, emptied the glass, and immediately took a spoonful of caviar, massaging the eggs between his tongue and the roof of his mouth, and making appreciative noises, not dissimilar to those of a truffle pig.

Verenikov downed his glass too. It was excellent. "I will stick to the vodka thanks and perhaps some coffee, if I may? I got a little chilled in the rain."

Brazhensky signalled to Balsov, and refilled the glasses. "Now, how can we help the Department for International Relations Mr Secretary?"

Verenikov downed the vodka, gasping with pleasure as the liquid numbed his throat and then warmed his insides. "That is good. I haven't seen it recently, not that I could afford it of course."

"It isn't readily available in the shops. I get it on the black market, as you can imagine. Now, to business."

"Mother Russia once again requires the assistance of the Director in the management of a delicate issue of international relations, Brazhensky. Now, the Presidium is working on the assumption that the foreign policy of the governments of the United States and the United Kingdom is set for the next five, and quite possibly, eight years at least."

"Is he? That's quite an assumption."

"The Presidium is an 'it', not a 'he'. You will have to remember that, Brazhensky, if you want to benefit from any more contracts from my department."

Brazhensky let out another belly laugh, helped himself to some more of the Savruga and re-filled the glasses.

Verenikov continued. "In London, the Cameron government was surprisingly re-elected last year with a majority for the British Conservative party. They no longer have to rely on their coalition partners. They are free to pursue unchecked their policy of *rapprochement* with China – commercial, diplomatic and even military. We calculate that Britain, following the renegotiation of the terms of its membership with the European Union, will have an increasingly powerful influence over the whole of European foreign policy."

"Isn't he – excuse me – isn't *it*, the Presidium, making assumptions about a certain referendum that is taking place next month?"

"Brexit? Haven't you seen the latest polls? The campaign to remain has a clear lead with little over four weeks before the vote. In any case, there is no way that the British government is going to allow Brexit to happen. The vote is a cosmetic exercise to appease the nationalists. Cameron promised the referendum in the election but he never expected to win a majority. He could afford to promise what he liked, knowing he could blame his coalition partners for not delivering it. The referendum will only be allowed to deliver one result. No government would permit such an act of national self-mutilation. It won't happen. Unless you have any inside knowledge of course."

Brazhensky snorted, and scratched his nose. "Of course not. But you may be underestimating the commitment of the British government to democracy, or at least overestimating their competence in rigging votes."

Verenikov ignored the intervention. "Equally certain is continuity of US foreign policy. Hilary Clinton will be Obama in a skirt, or should I say a trouser suit."

"Again, a little presumptuous about a certain election in November, wouldn't you say?"

"Have you seen the latest revelations about Trump? His campaign is dead in the water."

Brazhensky downed his third glass, scratched his nose again and laughed. "I have to say it is quite remarkable how decentralised the operations of the Presidium have become in recent years."

"The Presidium, as you know, has to be shielded from certain operations. What was it the late Dr Kissinger used to say? 'Plausible deniability' I think the phrase was. Another favourite phrase of the good doctor was 'triangulation'. It is just as true now as it was in the seventies. The West, China and Mother Russia. The balance of power hinges on how each constituent part reacts with the other two. In short, the Presidium is concerned that the interests of China and the West are becoming increasingly aligned, to the detriment of Russian power."

Brazhensky chuckled and held up the bottle. Verenikov raised his hand. "That's enough for one lunch time thanks."

Brazhensky beckoned to Balsov who presented a small tray holding a pot of coffee and a jug of cream. "And the Presidium would like the assistance of the illegals in this process of… triangulation?"

"You are as perceptive as ever, Brazhensky. That is exactly what the Presidium would like." Verenikov was conscious of Balsov's presence behind his right shoulder. "Shouldn't we be alone?"

"Balsov is my trusted lieutenant, Mikhail Nikolaevich. There is nothing you confide to me that I would not be willing to share with him in any event. As you subcontract to me, we subcontract to others. Balsov is in charge of sourcing the subcontractors, if you follow my meaning. Now, what does the Presidium have in mind?"

"Something which is going to lead to a severe and public breach between the West and China to such an extent that the geo-political structure is re-triangulated for years, or even decades, to come. We will leave it to you and your subcontractors to work out the details but what the Presidium has in mind is an event, or initiative, perceived as the work of the West, which is severely damaging to the People's Republic of China, and which will not only lead to a breach in relations between the West and China, but which will also severely damage relations between the US and the UK on the one hand and the European Union and the non-aligned world on the other. Think you can manage it?"

"How destructive do you want it to be? Are we talking Exxon Valdez or Chernobyl?"

"One of the Presidium's stipulations is that there must be no damage to the environment. You will remember the historic links between the Presidium and the city of Gomel in Belorussia. The effects of that unpleasantness back in '85, although little publicised outside of Gomel, were, I have heard, quite devastating."

"No damage to the environment," said Brazhensky. "Well that rules out a number of options Balsov." He looked to his side-kick and Balsov frowned. "Indeed it does your Honour."

"We also do not want to see any permanent damage to China's economy," Verenikov added. "No damage to infrastructure and no irreversible reduction in the growth of China's Gross Domestic Product. We hope increasingly to benefit from China's long-term growth in prosperity going forward."

"And this initiative, is it supposed to be at the instigation of the British or the American government?"

"Oh. We envision that it will be very much a joint Anglo-American project."

Brazhensky re-filled his glass. "And deaths?"

"As you well know, the Presidium is supremely relaxed about deaths."

Balsov chuckled behind him as Verenikov raised his glass. Brazhensky downed his in one. "*Nostrovia*, my friend."

Chapter Fifteen

It was well into the November, following his semi-voluntary retirement, that some of Jack Tapsell's past came back to haunt him. It was a call initially from his old senior clerk in Chambers, late one Friday afternoon.

"Morning, sir. It's George." There was a pause. "Clerk, sir, 2 Sumping Court." The *faux* deference was still familiar.

"George. I recognise your voice. I haven't gone senile quite yet. I just didn't expect to hear from Chambers again. I do hope you've not called to offer me a bail application in Norwich."

George laughed. "No, sir. How's it going now you've hung up your wig?"

"Brilliant thanks. Never been better."

"It's just that we've had a call for you. We didn't want to give out your number without your say so, not with all that unpleasantness with the papers back in the spring. A fellow called Robert Whittaker, says he's an old friend of yours. Wants you to call him back as a matter of some urgency, so he said."

Tapsell was silent. It was a name he had not heard spoken for over 30 years.

"Robert Whittaker, sir, do you want his number?"

"Is that Professor Whittaker – Pembroke College, Oxford?"

"Don't know about the Oxford sir but now you mention it he did say something about being a professor."

"I'll take his number, thanks."

The name resurrected so many memories of his days at Oxford, some real, and some now half-imagined, some the product of dreams and others of nightmares. So many memories that he needed time, once again, to process them before he could possibly call Bob Whittaker.

He relived those memories for a few hours before going to bed. At first it was the unalloyed pain which he relived. At a distance of thirty years, resurrected without warning, it was still as potent as a punch in the stomach. It had been the unbearable feeling of knowing that she loved another and had never really loved him. Then the memories of the cancelled plans, and hopes and dreams, followed by the pointless speculation of what might have been. The years of the pure unadulterated joy, in his imagination at least, which had been denied him.

And then, as he took solace in some wine to medicate his pain, his thoughts became more nuanced, as they had over the years. He remembered that he would never have had Lucy, and that the unconditional love he felt for her, and the unconditional love he received from her, was something which was priceless, and could not have been traded for anything.

And then he remembered that segment of joy he had known with Becky, those precious eighteen months and he was grateful for it. But he did not know that he could bear to see her again, nor even her husband of thirty years. He sensed there would be an unbearable atmosphere of pity on one side, and a profound regret and sense of loss on the other. The meeting would not revive the joy of those eighteen months, rather it would summon all the demons of the intervening thirty years, and every sinew of self-respect and self-preservation in his body was instinctively straining to avoid it at all costs.

And so he spent a restless night in which these emotions and remembrances ebbed and flowed uneasily, in and out of his dreams. He awoke at that hour dreaded by depressives, insomniacs and all those without peace of mind, the dead of night. That hour when even the early risers have not yet risen, and the revellers have lapsed into unconsciousness; namely 0320 in the morning.

At first he awoke and remembered nothing. Then his stomach lurched when he remembered the call from Chambers. Then at the back of his mind he was conscious of something else. There it was again. It was the doorbell.

Cautiously he looked through the peep-hole and saw a young man in black leathers, carrying a crash helmet and a brown paper package. He called through the door. "Hello?"

"Good morning," came the reply, in a distinctly non-threatening voice. "Delivery for Mr Jack Tapsell."

"Delivery. From whom. It's a bit early, isn't it?"

"Special delivery, sir. Avoids the rush hour traffic."

Tapsell checked the security chain was in place before cautiously opening the door and signing for the package through the gap. It was a padded envelope, addressed to Jack Tapsell Esq, 15 Newbury Mansions, 7 Maida Avenue, London W2. He felt it, shook it, sniffed it and then opened it. It was covered in bubble wrap. It was a notebook. Blue, hardback, pages a little dog-eared and yellowed, brown stains on the front and on the sides.

He opened it. And even nine months after he had handed over the copy to Rock Tattinger, he recognised it at once. The text no longer in black printer ink, reproduced on a sub-standard police photocopier, but in the original manuscript. Presumably in the hand of Vanessa Symonds. There were her initials at the top of the page 'VS'. The words of the girl he had only read about and heard about, the Oxford post-graduate, now dead, staring up at him from the page. The pages were a little sullied with brown smudges. He now understood that to be the blood of Daniel Roscoe. They were a little disfigured too with water stains. He supposed that to be the rain, mixed possibly with the tears of Daniel Roscoe, shed – who could say when?

And there was the name of Sir John Fawcett, along with those of Perkins, Chevening, and Giddens. And there was the note of the title of the paper. He could make it out now. 'The transference of pathogenic viruses in snakes'. He recalled the story given by Fawcett at the height of the media storm back in March. Roscoe was hysterical to start with over the death of his girlfriend, and after the outbreak of the snake flu pandemic, his fevered imagination had created a wild conspiracy theory involving the CIA and the Pentagon.

And there too was the genetic notation. It meant nothing to Tapsell, for whom science had always been a bit of a blind spot, but, according to Donnelly, this was the genetic shorthand for snake flu. According to Fawcett, this too had been noted by Roscoe, as part of his wild imaginings, but crucially only after the virus had been identified and its coding released into the public domain.

But wait. There was something not quite right about that. It hadn't been possible to distinguish one bit of handwriting from another on the photocopy, especially with the staining and the smudging. But here on the original one could see the ink which had been used. It was the sort of distinctive ink which a student may have used to mark-up lecture notes for the purpose of revision. In particular, it was the sort of ink which – and Tapsell was in some respects a little unreconstructed – a girl might have used. It was a shade of pink; a distinctive shade of pink and it was common to all of these notes on the first few pages. It was obvious to Tapsell, at least, that all of the notes made at the beginning of the notebook had been made by Vanessa Symonds.

He turned to the back. Yes, there were the notes, clearly in a different hand, which must have been made by Roscoe later. There was the note of the Rector's contact details and of Emile Zeitmann's practice address. The handwriting was not particularly distinct. But it was the ink which was important, because these notes appeared to have been made with a blue ball-point pen.

And then he recalled what Donnelly had said; ink can be scientifically dated. A forensic examination of this notebook could prove that the note of the genetic notation for the snake flu had been made (in that distinctive pink ink) in April 2019 and that the virus had been identified from a research paper produced in the Anglo-American Laboratory in Oxford, months before the pandemic had even broken out. Tapsell realised that in his hand he held potentially one of the biggest news stories of modern times. The interference in his mind between the contact from Bob Whittaker, and the receipt of the notebook, cancelled each other out. He went back to bed and drifted into a kind of sleep.

He was woken by another bell but this time it was the telephone. It was Whittaker.

"Jack, I hope you don't mind my calling so early." It was 0915. "When you didn't call back yesterday, I managed to persuade your clerk to give me your home number. I didn't think you would mind."

The voice was almost the same, the timbre a little deeper perhaps.

"Bob. It must be thirty years. What can I do for you?"

"Did you receive it?"

"What are you talking about?"

"Jack, we both know what I'm talking about. The notebook. Did you receive it?"

For a moment Tapsell thought he was still dreaming. "You sent the notebook? How? Why?"

"Look, why don't you come to dinner tonight. Come up to Oxford. We can have dinner in Hall. There are things I need to talk to you about. It can't be done over the phone."

"Well, yes. I suppose so. I'm baffled."

"I can't go into specifics over the phone but you know I have been drifting in and out of – shall we say – public service for years. At present I'm on sabbatical, back at Pembroke working on a public policy project for the Home Office. I need to talk to you about the notebook. I sent it to capture your attention."

"You certainly did that." There was a pause. He forced himself to say it. "Will Becky be there? You know I haven't seen her since…"

The pause was longer. Whittaker cleared his throat and sighed.

"Jack, I assumed that you knew. Thinking about it now I suppose there's no reason why you should. Jack, I'm so sorry. Rebecca died, over two years ago now. Cancer."

Tapsell took a late afternoon train from Paddington. He found an empty carriage. He wanted to stare out of the window and think. He had always hated being looked at by strangers, at the best of times, now he couldn't bear it.

He tried to rationalise his feelings. Most of the memories seemed to have burned themselves out overnight, at least for the time being. He was surprised at how he felt and a little guilty. The fact that she was no longer in the world came to him as a kind of relief. The thing which he had lost, and never really come to terms with, was no more and, in a sense, it was no longer a loss, merely an idea.

He would no longer wander the streets and the shops, frequent the museums and the concert halls, without having the apprehension, somewhere in the back of his mind – the largely subconscious, but no less attritional thought – that he might bump into her and have to arrange his face and deal with all the hurt which had festered inside him for thirty years.

When he alighted at Oxford station he felt, unabated, a feeling of coming home. This was the city he knew better than any other place, save for London. It was the repository of his youth. It contained just about everything in his past between the callow expectancy of his late childhood on the one hand, and the onset of disappointment, failure and remorse on the other. It contained the memories of all of his mature consciousness, before it had become scarred, jaded and all but petrified.

Twice, since he had come down in 1987, Tapsell had returned to the city of his dreams. Once for a gaudy ten years later. That had been a mistake. The wounds were too raw and they were opened up afresh. Then, over ten years after that, to take Lucy for her Oxbridge entrance interview. That was tolerable. He was present but vicariously, through his daughter.

But even then, the memories were visceral and there were places which he had had consciously to avoid. The Turf Tavern where they had met. Somerville, and all its environs; Becky's college and the scene of many meetings, some contrived and some planned. Botley Park where he had proposed and Port

Meadow where she had accepted him twenty minutes later. And even his own College, Pembroke, he had had to approach from the rear when he had taken Lucy to see it, along Saint Ebbes Street and into Beef Lane. That final evening in Pembroke Square was one he could not bear to relive.

But now, over thirty years since his graduation, she was no longer in the penumbra of his life. She was dead. He found that her memory had lost its potency. He walked straight up St Aldates, into Pembroke Square, and with a sharp intake of breath, into the College. Apart from the fact that everyone looked a great deal younger, it had not changed.

Whittaker had been appointed to an academic post at Pembroke after taking a DPhil in public administration. He had risen to the full rank of professor a matter of a few years later. Now he occupied some of the most desirable rooms in College, just by the chapel. Tapsell ascended the sixteenth-century wooden staircase, in one of the oldest parts of College, reserved for the Senior Fellows.

He paused. The butterflies in his belly were going berserk. With a deep breath, he knocked at the door.

"Come in. It's open."

The voice was almost unchanged, the self-assured accent and intonation with which he had never been able to compete. The door opened and there he was, Bob Whittaker. His voice was the same, but his appearance had altered. He had aged more than the thirty years which had passed. His hair had thinned and turned grey, and not just at the temples. His face, once handsome and urbane, had sunk. The light in his eyes had dimmed. The muscles in his mouth, once animated with a love of life, had turned down at the edges, and gone limp. His shoulders arched. His once athletic body atrophied – all, Tapsell told himself, by grief. There was no doubt that Whitaker had loved her too.

"Jack, it's good to see you. Truly it is. You've aged well." He *had* aged better, that was true at least.

Whittaker gestured to a leather armchair by the window. It was an old, typical, college-style sitting room lined with books. There was a large bay window looking out onto the front of the chapel and the main quadrangle. A couple of aged leather armchairs and a sofa were arranged around a desk in the middle of the room.

"May I offer you an aperitif? We've got thirty minutes until the Master's sherry reception."

"I never did get to experience High Table cuisine. Is it really so different?"

"Oh yes, if the students got a taste of what we're served at High Table, there would be a revolution, I can tell you."

Jack looked across at the well-stocked drinks table in the corner. He could do with a drink to calm his nerves, just a little.

"I'll have a gin and tonic please, if you have it. Do you live here? It looks very comfortable?"

"Yes, it is. I still do a little teaching but it's mainly research these days. The department allows me to spend a good deal of my time here and I can still service the department remotely. There's a bedroom, and a little kitchen through there. Of course, I spend a lot more time here now than I used to; since Rebecca..."

His voice tailed away and he turned his back to prepare the drinks. "I'm sorry you didn't know Jack. I just presumed, but I suppose I had no right to."

"I've had no contact with Becky since that night over thirty years ago, the last time I set eyes on you too Bob. In the early years she used to send a Christmas card, from you both of course, but I never responded. I wish I had. Then I met my wife. We were married and I moved on." He lied.

"You have a daughter?"

"Yes. She's a junior doctor now in Yorkshire."

"Children are such a comfort, aren't they? Forgive me, I heard that you divorced. After Rebecca died, I think it was the boys that saved me. I don't know what I would have done without them."

Whittaker took the armchair opposite him. There was a pause. When Tapsell looked up, Whittaker was looking directly at him but there was something vacant about his eyes, as if he were looking at something beyond.

"Why am I here Bob?"

He took a sip of his whisky. "I suppose I wanted to tell you face to face how much I loved her. I know that you did too – deeply – but I wanted you to know that when you gave her up, it was to somebody who loved her profoundly too. Nothing was wasted, Jack. Do you see?"

"Perhaps, but I don't recall giving her up."

"We both know that she would never have left you if you had really pleaded with her to stay. She had made a commitment to you. She had so much respect for you. She cared for you so much. Do you know that she mentioned you, almost right at the end? She never forgot you."

Tapsell got up and turned to the window. The lights of the College were blurred by the moisture in his eyes.

"The truth is, Jack, you knew that she loved me, and, deep down, that she didn't love you. You made it possible for us to be together, for us to have all those happy years together, for us to have the children. It is all down to you. I wanted you to know that. She would never have left you without your blessing."

Two students, arm in arm, laughing and kissing intermittently by the library steps, blurred by the moisture in his eyes.

"You're right Bob. Children are such a comfort."

Tapsell waited until he could be sure he was in control again and sat back down in the armchair.

"But that isn't the reason you called me, is it? When I spoke to you on the phone, it was I who asked you about Becky. You assumed I knew about her death. You called me about the notebook. How on earth are you mixed up with the Thomas Fairford case?"

Whittaker stood up and buttoned his jacket. "Let's go to dinner now. We'll have plenty of time to talk later."

Dinner was indeed very different from how he remembered it as an undergraduate. There was a very civilised sherry party, with canapés, in a splendid reception room, attended by most of the fellows and dons of the College. The party then proceeded into Hall. It had been extensively refurbished since the late 1980s but it looked as magnificent as he remembered it, with the medieval hammer beam roof, and stained glass windows, and the walls lined with portraits of the founders, benefactors and former Masters of College.

At the near end, as they entered, was High Table on a raised platform. Along the length of the hall, perpendicular to the platform, were three long tables at which the students sat, all of whom stood as the High Table party entered.

The Master said grace. "*Quidquid nobis apositum est, aut quidquid aponetur, Benedicat Deus haec Sua dona in usum nostrum, necnon nosmet ipsos in servitium Suum, per lesum Christum, Dominum nostrum. Amen.*"

This had been translated on the embossed menu placed on the table in front of Tapsell. "Whatever has been or may be set before us, may God bless these gifts of His in our use and ourselves also in His service, through Jesus Christ our Lord." Tapsell, a reluctant atheist for over thirty years, joined in with the "Amen", and tried in that moment to believe it.

After grace, they sat down to more earthly matters, namely a Mousse d'Asperges, served with a well-chilled Alsace Gewurztraminer 1983, followed by Cotelettes d'Agneau Dubarry, with a Chateau Cos D'Estournel 1976. Tapsell knew these things because they were also printed on the menu.

He was seated next to Whittaker, and itching to know the connection between him and the notebook but there was little opportunity to talk freely. Whittaker had the Master to his left and was engaged for most of the evening with him. To Tapsell's right was a history don called Penelope and opposite him a classics professor and his ancient wife. As the Couronne de Framboises was placed in front of him and the sommelier filled his glass with a Lanson 1976, he noticed the old lady looking at him, apparently expecting some attention.

He couldn't think of anything sensible to say. "The food is quite splendid. Do you dine like this every day?"

She tittered into her champagne flute. "Oh no, my dear. Whatever must you think of us – only on High Table days – Wednesdays and Saturdays."

After dinner they took coffee and then made their early excuses to the Master. They returned to Whittaker's rooms shortly after half past ten.

Whittaker went behind his desk, took a cigar from a cedar wood box and lit it. He held up the box; Tapsell lifted his hand in refusal, and returned to the armchair.

"What are you going to do with it Jack? The notebook."

"I don't know. I only received it this morning."

"Did you bring it with you?"

"No, I have a habit of losing things on trains – usually umbrellas, but not exclusively."

"That's wise. The notebook is pretty hot property, as I think you know."

"I still don't understand how you got it and why you sent it to me."

Whittaker sat on the edge of the sofa. "It's true what I said this morning. I did send it to you to get your attention. I needed to talk to you about it. When you didn't call me back yesterday afternoon, I sent it by special delivery."

"Why take the risk?"

"Because I don't know what to do with it either, and I reckon you're a better man than I."

Whittaker moved to the drinks tray. "Do you still appreciate a good single malt?"

"Of course."

He held up a bottle. "The Macallan, 1979 Gran Reserva. Let's enjoy a dram of this and I'll tell you what I know."

He poured generous measures into two heavy crystal tumblers, handed one to Tapsell and sat in the armchair. He took a good draft from his glass, revolved the liquid around his mouth and swallowed it in several instalments. Then he sat back, took a long pull on his cigar and exhaled the smoke through pursed lips.

"What is it, Jack? Thirty-three, no thirty-four years now since we both came down from Oxford. I always had you down as the academic type; never envisaged you as a high-flying advocate."

"You weren't far wrong there."

"Well, anyway, I was always destined for the civil service. I was sponsored as an under-graduate by the First Class Civil Service fast track scheme, and went straight into the Treasury. You were never into university politics much from what I remember?"

"I went along to the occasional debate at the Union. It all seemed a little childish to me; the rivalry, the back-stabbing – playground politics."

"In a way. I was Chairman of the Labour Club. I never made it to Union President – Trinity term 1986. I lost to John Fawcett – remember him? He put out a smear story the week before the election that I had been cooking the books as the Union Treasurer."

"I didn't know him then, but his name has become more familiar to me since, as you well know. Is that the connection?"

"In a sense. I'm going to confide in you Jack. If you ever repeat what I'm going to tell you, I will simply deny it. Nobody will believe you. You are a retired barrister, with – forgive me – a slightly sullied reputation and with a motive to discredit me, albeit over thirty years old. In any event, I know you to be a man of honour and I tell you this in confidence.

"I was recruited back in 84–85 by Soviet intelligence." Tapsell choked on his drink. "Yes. Everyone remembers Burgess and MacLean in the fifties, but there was a second wave of recruitment after Afghanistan and the deterioration in Soviet – American relations in the early eighties. If you were destined for a high profile career in the civil service and you were involved in leftist politics in those days, then you were ripe for recruitment."

Tapsell wiped the whisky from his chin and put down his glass. "Are you telling me you became a Soviet agent?"

“Things are rarely as black and white as that Jack. You should know that as a criminal lawyer. Spies are not divided neatly into national camps. It would be more accurate to describe them as operating along a spectrum. I have always considered my loyalty to be primarily to the United Kingdom but I had links to the Soviet state in its final years, before *glasnost* and *perestroika* rightly finished it off. The Cold War was being fully waged by both sides in those days; Gorbachev or no Gorbachev.

“There was of course a brief hiatus in the early nineties. But make no mistake, the same people who were in control before Yeltsin, are in control again now. The alphabet soup has been stirred around a little – KGB, FSB – but the agenda is precisely the same; the extension of the power of the Russian state through what it sees as its sphere of influence – from Central Europe to the Far East.”

“What did you do it for, money?”

“No, I never received payment, directly that is. Although I suspect my advancement up the Whitehall ladder was, shall we say, assisted by certain contacts. Fawcett – the back-stabber in chief – he too was recruited at the same time as I. Our old Union rivalry never quite went away, but we’ve had a working relationship ever since. He has been in the pocket of Moscow for thirty years; even when he was working for the Clinton campaign in ’92, he was reporting to rogue Russian agencies. Since the late 1990s, he’s actively been working for the Russian state.”

“OK, you’ve certainly succeeded in getting my attention. Now, what does any of this have to do with me and more to the point, the notebook?”

“I followed the Fairford case with interest Jack, and the aftermath, and forgive me, not just out of an interest in your career development. You see, Serpensvid 19 did not originate in the Anglo-American Laboratory. Fawcett was telling the truth about that, at least. It originated – or at least it was designed – in a laboratory in Vladivostok by scientists in the pay of a faction in the Russian government. Fancy a top up?”

Tapsell pinched the bridge of his nose and closed his eyes. “Yes, I feel as if I’m about to wake up and find out this is all a dream, so I might as well make the most of it.”

Whittaker refreshed the glasses and then took some time re-lighting his cigar. He looked thoughtful, as if he were weighing carefully what to say next.

"There are elements in the Russian government which became increasingly alarmed about the shift in the policy of the West towards China under the Obama and Cameron administrations. In 2016 they concluded that this trend would accelerate. Cameron had won a surprise victory in the 2015 general election and Hilary Clinton looked a dead cert for the 2016 presidential election. They assumed that Cameron had the Brexit referendum in the bag, as indeed we all did."

"Was that down to the Russians too?"

"I honestly don't know Jack. My position on the spectrum was somewhat closer to London than that occupied by John Fawcett. In any case, you would be amazed at how disintegrated the Russian machinery of government is. Half the time the departments of state are conspiring against each other. Much of their dirty tricks stuff is contracted out to semi-autonomous organisations.

"It was one such organisation which was commissioned to instigate a severe breach in relations between the West and China. Their brief was to cause an incident which would cause no permanent damage to the Chinese economy or its infrastructure. They came up with the idea of a biological attack. The virus itself was engineered in Russia and seeded into China via a Russian sponsored terrorist cell in Japan. But here's where the story links in to the Fairford case. You see an elaborate paper trail was created to point the finger conclusively at the American and British governments."

Tapsell felt like his head was exploding. "But if they wanted to point the finger at the American and British governments, why would they go to such lengths to cover up the stolen paper from the laboratory and the notebook? Wouldn't they want it to be discovered?"

"The paper trail was specifically designed to be discovered by the World Health Organisation. They calculated that, in the aftermath of the pandemic, the WHO would commission a formal investigation into the origins of Serpensvid 19. The paper trail was far more sophisticated than the research paper taken by your Vanessa Symonds. It would to all intents and purposes have provided conclusive proof that the US and UK governments were responsible for the engineering of the virus and its seeding in the wet market of Wuhan. The research paper was just one link in the chain. They were concerned that if the story were broken prematurely by animal rights activists it would undermine the credibility of the whole plot; the authorities would be able to explain away the evidence. And that is precisely what happened, as you know."

"And the Fairford case? The girl, Daniel Roscoe?"

"Johnny Fawcett. He is the main UK point of contact for the faction of the Russian state which was responsible for commissioning the operation. It was he who found out about the security breach at the laboratory and the loss of the paperwork. How he came to know about it is not entirely clear to me, but he certainly had links with the animal rights movement. But what I do have, on impeccable authority, is that it was Fawcett who authorised the murder of Vanessa Symonds, and later, Daniel Roscoe. They could not risk the premature leaking of the biggest story since 9/11."

"What about Thomas Fairford?"

"I'm afraid that he was, as they saw it, a necessary casualty of war. They needed somebody as the patsy to take the blame for Roscoe's death and possibly hers too, if required. He was held for months; tortured, drugged, effectively rendered a vegetable. They knew he was a natural suspect. He was known to have been dating Ms Symonds, and was a potential rival to Roscoe. There was a ready-made motive which formed the basis of a case. All that was needed was a little enhancement with some DNA on the corpse and a bit of work on Fairford's phone."

"The text messages?"

"Exactly. The messages were manufactured and his phone reformatted to create a digital trail. It would appear, even under close forensic analysis of the handset and the sim card, that the threatening texts had been sent from Fairford's phone to the number registered to Daniel Roscoe. Roscoe's handset, of course, had been destroyed."

Tapsell stood up. "But what about me, Whittaker? Why was I brought into it? Was that anything to do with you?"

"No, Jack. I've observed this business from a distance. Your involvement had nothing to do with me. In fact, it had nothing to do with Fawcett either. Well before you had been briefed in the case, the British and American intelligence communities had become aware of the security breach at the lab. Their investigations revealed a Russian infiltration, not just of the facility itself, but of the whole of B Section; the division of British counter-intelligence concerned with biological and chemical national security. They became desperate to limit the potential political fallout. That is why every effort was made to cover up any connection between Roscoe's death and the laboratory, and in particular, the existence of the notebook."

"So what are you telling me? There was a conspiracy involving the police, the Crown Prosecution Service, and the judiciary, in an attempt to pervert the course of justice?"

"You have to understand that most of the individuals involved would have had no knowledge of the details. They believed they were acting in the interests of national security and were following orders which had been issued from far above."

"How far?"

"Far enough."

"So now I can rest easy in the knowledge that our great English criminal justice system is not controlled by Washington or Moscow, instead its thoroughly rotten and corrupted from the inside. Is that it?"

"Jack, don't be naïve. There is no absolute good, or absolute evil. It isn't just spies that operate on a spectrum, so does justice. There is no such *thing* as perfect justice. Everything is ultimately a trade-off. In the Fairford case, the untainted due process of Her Majesty's courts had to be compromised for the sake of the security and integrity of Her Majesty's state. In any case, neither the judge nor the Crown Prosecution Service, or even the police for that matter, would have had any knowledge of the true reason that Roscoe died. Are you familiar with the concept of a 'D notice'?"

"Yes, a notice put out to the press by the government not to report something in the interests of national security. It happened during the Second World War, and for some time afterwards, as I understand it, but that went out years ago, didn't it?"

"Yes, along with the integrity of much of the British press industry. I'm using it as an analogy. Imagine a notice put out by the security services, not to the press but to other organs of the state – do not look behind this curtain, or under that carpet, in the interests of national security."

"I see. There's another one of my naïve illusions gone. It looks like I retired at the right time. But what about me? Why was I involved?"

"I think you know that Jack. Because of Operation Pellew. However unfairly, you had the reputation of somebody who would not look behind the curtain. As it turns out, in that respect, instructing you for the prosecution was clearly a big mistake."

"How did you get the notebook, anyway, if they're trying to cover it up?"

"The notebook, after it had vanished from the possession of the police, came into the possession of the Russian illegals. Remember, it's a spectrum Jack. And the Russians no longer have any interest in covering it up. Do you still read the papers in your retirement? The World Health Organisation, with the approval of the United Nations Assembly, decided last month to grant what amounts to a blanket amnesty to any state, organisation or individual who may have been culpable in the propagation of Serpensvid 19. In the interests of the global peace initiative, and proposed climate pact, they decided not to launch any investigation into the origins of the virus – not to look under the carpet, you might say.

"As you can imagine, this was not a development which was welcome news to those in Moscow who had invested so much time and effort in the Serpensvid plot, and so they decided to accomplish their aim by the more traditional method of leaking information. In this case in the form of the notebook with its dateable and distinctive pink ink. Although I suspect that they did not anticipate that it would fall into my hands. I have contacts, as it were, on both sides of the, er, curtain."

Tapsell proffered his glass. "Any chance of a top up?"

Whitaker took the bottle from the drinks table and refilled the tumbler. Then he sat back on the edge of the table and regarded Tapsell, the cigar in his left hand, the faintest trace of a smile at the corners of his mouth, waiting for a response.

"This is all fascinating stuff Bob. You should write a treatise on international relations. It'd be a bestseller. But why on earth have you sent the notebook to me? What do you expect me to do with it? Do you suppose that I'm inclined to act as some sort of proxy agent for the Russian government?"

"No and to ensure that you do not unwittingly do so, I have included another morsel of information at the back of the notebook. It's a link and a password to a secure website, which cannot be discovered via a public web-browser. It contains everything the press and the authorities need to know about Fawcett and his activities, including the Serpensvid 19 conspiracy. If you decide to release the notebook, it will not incriminate the UK and US governments, it will incriminate, and blow apart, the axis between the Russian illegals and the Moscow sponsored cell in Whitehall. In particular, I suspect that it will see Fawcett in prison for most of the rest of his natural life."

Tapsell reached into the inside pocket of his jacket and removed the notebook.

"Ah, so you did bring it with you after all."

Tapsell turned to the back. There on the second to last page was a third hand which had not appeared on the photocopied version. It was written in thick black ink. 'The truth about Serpensvid 19: 370-579-min7-docs.gov.uk. [Password: RWd250320].'

"Of course I brought it with me. I didn't know if I could trust you. Besides which, the safe in my flat is broken. But why don't you simply leak this to the press yourself?"

"I can't. It would lead to too many questions. You're the ideal man for the job – you leaked the photocopy in the first place. Besides which, I've been so compromised over the years I no longer know right from wrong. I do not know if releasing this information is the right thing to do. Who could predict the consequences? But you are the most honourable man I've ever met, Jack. I owe you for all of the best things which have happened in my life – Rebecca and my sons. I could think of no one I would rather trust with the decision."

"And this website, is it all the result of some personal feud you've had with John Fawcett over student politics?"

"No. It goes deeper than that. Look at the password again: RWd250320. It stands for Rebecca Whittaker, died 25 March 2020. You see Jack, Rebecca didn't die of cancer two years ago. She died of Serpensvid 19 last year."

That night sleep did not come easily to Jack Tapsell. Before leaving London he had booked a room at the Randolph, unsure that he would be able to sleep in College. He rose early and took breakfast in the hotel. The papers were all about the imminent G20 meeting. "Christmas Cease-fire Top of the Agenda in Washington. Climate Pact Expected to Follow." Maybe some good had come out of this wretched plague after all.

Then he took a walk along St Aldates to the High and he thought of Becky. Everywhere he looked there were memories of her. He had been fooling himself. The memories were just as raw. He felt for the notebook in the inside pocket of his coat. *Why shouldn't he leak it to the press?* He could send it by secure delivery to that investigative reporter at the Standard.

You got the brief because you're no fucking good.

And then he walked along to Magdalen Bridge. This is where he had stood and waited for Lucy, six years before, during her Oxbridge entrance interview. He remembered how proud he had felt when she obtained her scholarship to read medicine at Magdalen. And he realised that all of his hopes for the future rested with her and with people like her.

Who could predict the consequences?

Then he took the notebook from his pocket, let it fall into the Cherwell, and watched as the waters swallowed it up.